INTO THE STORM

THE FORCE OF NATURE SERIES

AMBER LYNN NATUSCH

Into The Storm - Force Of Nature Book Two

ISBN-13: 9780997076578

Published by Amber Lynn Natusch
Cover by Regina Wamba, at Mae I Design
Ebook Formatting by Pure Textuality PR
Editing by Kristy Bronner

http://amberlynnnatusch.com

ALSO BY AMBER LYNN NATUSCH

The *CAGED* Series

CAGED

HAUNTED

FRAMED

SCARRED

FRACTURED

TARNISHED

STRAYED

CONCEALED

BETRAYED

The *UNBORN* Series

UNBORN

UNSEEN

UNSPOKEN

The *BLUE-EYED BOMB* Series

LIVE WIRE

KILLSWITCH

DEAD ZONE

WARHEAD

The *FORCE OF NATURE* Series

FROM THE ASHES

INTO THE STORM

BEYOND THE SHADOWS

BENEATH THE DUST

The *ZODIAC CURSE:*

***HAREM OF SHADOWS* Series**

EVE OF ETERNAL NIGHT

Contemporary Romance

UNDERTOW

More Including Release Dates

http://amberlynnnatusch.com

www.facebook.com/AmberLynnNatusch

http://www.subscribepage.com/AmberLynnNatusch

To Jena,
The organizer of my chaos.
I couldn't do this without you.

ACKNOWLEDGMENTS

I like to keep these short and sweet.

To my team, Jena Gregoire, Shannon Morton, Kristen Bronner, Courtney DeLollis, Kristy Massaro, you guys give me the feedback and encouragement I need to keep going. For this, I thank you.

To my author peeps, Madeline Sheehan, Amy Bartol, Christine Crawford, Leia Stone, and my whole FanX crew, thanks for keeping me sane when I start to spiral (as we all do) during this process.

To my family, thank you for sharing me with the crazy voices in my head...not that you really had a choice. It seems those bastards are here to stay.

PROLOGUE

He had the nerve to look unfazed when I stormed into his office. His eyes drifted up to me and then back down to the paper he held in his hands. A silent dismissal. Little did he know, I had no intention of being sent away like a child—a nuisance. I was there to have a little chat with him.

And he was damn well going to listen.

"Why did you do it?" I asked, stepping farther into the room.

"I haven't the time to answer your poorly directed questions at the moment, Piper. Unless you're more clueless than even I thought, you know there is a war going on in this city."

"One you no doubt had a hand in."

That comment didn't go over well. He placed the paper down on his desk and pinned murderous eyes on me. My instinct was to run, but I held fast against his glare. I wouldn't be scared off.

"Explain yourself well while you have the chance, girl, because it will be the last one you're given."

I let my eyes drift away from the predator ready to fly over the top of his desk and strangle me and stared at the wood fire burning to my right. The flames flickered and danced and sparked, spitting embers and ash that fell slowly to the floor like grey snow.

When I looked back, the vampire king was only inches away, his wrath wound tightly around him like a second skin. His hand shot forth to grab me, but it met fire instead. Fire that came when I called to it.

That murderous expression bled to one of fear and regret.

"You know what I am, don't you?"

His features tensed.

"What do you want, Fire Bender?"

I leaned forward, an evil smile overtaking my countenance; one that mimicked the same expression I'd seen him wear more times than I could remember. He'd caused me so much pain—pain I was still trying to dig my way out from underneath. It wasn't the time to answer his question. No—it was time to warn him of my intentions.

"To bring you to your knees."

With a gust of wind and swirling fire, I picked him up off the floor. His screams—loud and tormented at first—were eventually swallowed by the twister's howls and the crackle of flame. I laughed aloud, the sound of it slightly unhinged even to my own ears. I was drunk with power and bloodlust and the desire to destroy things in a way that should have scared me, but it didn't. Instead, I reveled in it. Gone was the weak little Piper who needed the protection of others. Dead was the girl who had been used and cast aside. That shell of a Magical being had been shed, leaving behind a force of nature in her wake.

And her fury would know no mercy.

1

I tiptoed down the butler's staircase, attempting to be stealthy in a mansion full of vampires and werewolves with superhuman hearing and an ornery grizzly bear. Even if the odds were against me, I was desperate for a moment alone, so I sought refuge in the one place I'd always been able to find it: the kitchen. But the moment I arrived, reality pulled the rug out from under me.

Knox's pack crowded the room, which suddenly seemed much smaller than before.

It was only our second day at the mansion after arriving from Alaska, where I'd met Knox and his pack of werewolves, so my mind hadn't fully adapted to our new living arrangements. Grizz, my furry sidekick, had taken up residence next to my bed and growled at anyone that tried to make him leave. Knox and his boys were crammed into the mansion wherever there was room, most of them sharing rooms with at least three other wolves, if not more. They didn't seem to mind, though. They just rolled with it.

Just like they'd rolled with their home in Alaska burning to the ground and their move to New York City.

I hovered in the doorway for a moment, watching the wolves as they moved around one another as if they were extensions of Knox—each a part of the whole. One being. There was something so peaceful about being near them, getting caught up in their energy. Except for their first day in NYC. That had been a total shitshow of testosterone and rage and a whole slew of other emotions I couldn't even begin to label, let alone understand.

It made me miss the days when things were (slightly) simpler. When there wasn't a war among the breeds, or the Alaskan pack in the mansion, or the awkwardness looming between my mate, Merc, and me because he had tried to kill me once. Though it may not have been his fault, I was having a hard time reconciling that truth with what I'd been through. He'd nearly beaten me to death that night.

There would be no forgetting that. Ever.

"Hey Piper!" My name jarred me from my thoughts. When my focus returned to the scene before me, I saw Foust, Knox's second in command, looking at me with concern. His eyes—ever shrewd—were assessing me, looking for something to report on, but not in a bad way.

"I didn't know you guys would be up already," I replied with a smile.

"Yeah, we went out early to check out the property. It's huge; never would have guessed that."

"The beauty of glamour, my friend. Only way to hide wilderness in the middle of the city."

"That's some damn impressive magic," he said, smiling wide enough that his teeth showed through his beard. In truth, that thing was starting to look a little unruly. I needed to get him some trimmers ASAP.

"You have no idea..." I winked up at him as I started into the room, headed for the fridge and what was left of its contents. In a house full of vampires, food was scarce because they didn't need it. Though Jase and Dean, the two enforcers that had taken me under their wings when I'd moved into the mansion, had tried their best to prep for our arrival, they'd had no idea what they were in for. They hadn't been human in centuries.

And they'd grossly underestimated how much a pack of werewolves could eat.

"I saved you some," a voice called out through the din. I turned to find a ginger-haired werewolf holding out a plate of food to me that he'd probably fought hard to keep. Jagger was thoughtful if nothing else.

I heard a scoff from the far side of the room and found Brunton standing there, tall and brooding as always, his rugged features homed in on Jagger.

"Fucking kiss-ass."

Jagger smiled at the jab.

"Love you too, B."

Before they could continue what promised to be a verbal war, I took Jagger's offering and kissed him on the cheek.

"You're the best, Jags. Did you get some too?"

His cheeks warmed to a rosy hue and he averted his gaze.

"I, uh... I ate while we were outside."

"Oh," I replied. "Nothing like a little wild game for breakfast. I guess you can take the wolf out of the woods, but some things just stick, huh?"

He shrugged.

"What can I say, I like my meat rare."

"Or still breathing."

Another shrug.

I didn't bother to reply, choosing to take my plate (and my clever comeback) down the hall to the dining room. The likelihood of it being empty was slim to none, but I didn't want a pack of hungry wolves watching me eat. The way they paced around as if they were waiting for a piece to drop was unnerving.

It was early enough in the morning that the sun was just starting to think about rising. Most of the enforcers—the vampire king's special warriors—had likely returned, but a few of the stragglers would soon be filing through the door before the rays of the sun could touch them. I'd seen what that could do to a vampire. It was not a pleasant way to go.

As I rounded the corner to the dining room, I saw Merc's brothers, Jase and Dean, approaching. They were covered in blood, their dark hair matted with it and other bits I tried not to analyze. I felt my body go numb. Then the sharp sound of my plate breaking into pieces on the floor echoed through the hallway.

"What happened?" I asked, rushing toward them.

"We're fine, Piper," Jase said, holding up his hands to ward off my panic. As if he could.

"Blood's not ours," Dean added, looking down at the front of his soaked tee.

"But we need to talk to you." Jase's eyes fell past me to where I could only assume a wall of werewolves stood, ready to pounce at the first sign of my distress. Though I was glad they had my back, Jase and Dean did too, and I didn't want a fight breaking out between them. It was literally my worst-case scenario—unless a fight broke out between Merc and Knox.

I shuddered at the thought.

"What's going on?" I asked, shaking my head in an attempt to clear it.

"Not here," Jase replied, looking at the pack again.

I looked over my shoulder to find Foust and Jagger in front of the others, their expressions stern.

"I'll be right back."

I navigated my way through the porcelain minefield I'd created and followed the brothers down the hall and up the stairs of the main foyer until we reached the second floor and, eventually, Jase's room. Dean led the way in, with me behind him. Jase eased the door shut behind him and locked it for good measure. Whatever they were about to tell me, it sure as hell wasn't good.

"Piper, I need you to be calm," Jase said, doing his best to instill the emotion that he knew I lacked as he spoke.

"You're scaring me, Jase."

"I know, and I'm sorry. It's just—there's no good way to say this."

"Then just say it!"

"I will once you promise not to—"

"Merc is missing," Dean blurted out, taking my hand in his. "We can't reach him. He didn't check in where we were supposed to meet up, and he's not here now."

"Are you sure? Did you check everywhere? The infirmary?" I bolted for the door, wondering if Merc was in the basement, wounded. Because the alternative was too unappealing to consider: that he was stuck somewhere out in NYC with the rising sun and his impending doom.

"Everyone has searched the premises. He's not here."

"Did you track his phone?"

Jase eyed Dean, and they had one of their silent internal conversations; the kind that only they and their brother could share.

"Kat did."

Silence.

"And?"

"And it was in a dumpster somewhere in Times Square."

I collapsed onto the edge of the bed, staring off at nothing as reality threatened to consume me.

"Could he have dumped his phone for some reason?" Jase's expression tightened before he shook his head. "You think someone's taken him?" He nodded. "Who? Who could overpower him, Jase? He's lethal even without his mind-screwing abilities. It's hardly like someone could walk up to him, slip a black bag over his head, and throw him into the back of a van."

"We know, P. That's why we're as lost as you are."

"Why were you guys separated? Why weren't you with him tonight?"

"Because he got a call and said he'd meet up with us later at the park. When he didn't, we waited as long as we could until we had to come back home."

"Who called him?" I asked as all the blood in my face emptied. "Who did he go to see?"

A pounding on Jase's door followed by a bevy of colorful swears from a female announced Kat's arrival to the would-be search party. Jase unlocked the door and let her in. The feisty auburn-haired werewolf was at my side in a second.

"They told you already?" she asked. I nodded. She turned to stare down Jase and Dean, her glower telling them exactly how she felt about that. "Thanks for waiting, assholes."

"The phone!" I shouted, grabbing Kat by the shoulders. "Did you see who Merc last spoke to tonight?" She hesitated for a second, which did nothing for my anxiety. Kat didn't hesitate. Kat was a bulldozer of truth, whether you liked it or not. "Kat..."

"The phone was trashed, but we were able to hack into

his account and look up the number of the person who called him."

More hesitation.

"Who was it?" Jase asked, stepping toward us.

Kat took a breath, her eyes desperate as she looked at me before turning to Jase to answer his question. But her pause did little to prepare us for what she was about to say.

"The king."

2

'Oh shit' alarms were going off in my mind like crazy.

The king, last I'd heard, didn't know about Merc's little mental break or that he'd tried to kill me, so why he would do something to one of his top enforcers was beyond me. But he was the king of the vampires for a reason. I didn't put anything past him.

While I tried to gather my wits, a knock on the door cut through the room. Kat walked over and let in another of the enforcers. Her mate, Jensen, kissed her softly before making his way into the room. The other three filled him in on the situation, and they began to argue about what to do next—and how. The vampires' options were limited, given the status of the sun, but mine weren't. And Kat's weren't either.

"I'll go," I said, barely loud enough to be heard over their argument, even with their superhuman hearing. The four of them turned slowly to look at me as though I'd lost my mind.

"Piper... you've been through a lot. You need to rest. You

can't just go chasing after Merc, especially not if the king is involved," Kat said.

"I'm going and that's final. The only question is whether or not you're coming with me."

"She's not," Jensen said quickly. "Last time you two went out alone, bad shit happened."

Kat didn't even bother arguing; she basically ignored his comment entirely. Instead, she looked at me like I was a halfwit for even suggesting she wouldn't follow my lead.

"Of course I'm fucking going."

"Kat—"

"She's going to go with or without me, Jensen, and that's not how we roll in this friendship. You know that."

His tight expression said he did know that, and he hated it.

"You're flying blind, Kat," he said, trying a softer tone with her. "You can't ask me to like that. To be on board."

"I don't like it either," Jase added.

Kat and I looked at Dean, who merely shrugged in response.

"What can I say? We're males. We don't like our girls risking themselves, especially when we aren't there."

Kat groaned in the most put-upon way.

"Well you three can commiserate all about it while we're out finding Merc."

"Exactly!" I agreed. "You three stay here and let us know if you hear from him somehow."

"Piper—"

I cut Jase off.

"We've got this, Jase. Have you forgotten that I made the ground swallow an entire army of warlocks whole? I can handle whoever has Merc."

Jase opened his mouth to answer, then snapped it closed

and shot a nasty look over at Dean. I could only imagine what he'd said to earn that level of anger from his brother, but my guess was that it had something to do with me being right. That I had been the one to end the battle with Kingston, the asshole warlock with a hard-on for killing me, and his crew of lackeys. With one rage-fueled command from me, the Earth had opened up and inhaled them, never to be seen again. With power like that on my side, they really didn't need to worry about us.

Providing I could figure out how to call that level of power again without it consuming me like it almost had.

Not waiting for another argument, Kat stormed over to the door, ready to go on a manhunt, and I followed her. She threw it open to find a sea of werewolves eavesdropping on our conversation. Knox, their alpha, stood in front of them all, staring at me with a mix of emotions in his piercing blue eyes.

The pack had allied itself with me, which, in a roundabout way, had allied it with the vampire enforcers. Apparently that made Merc their problem too, if only in their own minds.

"You weren't planning on leaving without us, were you, Piper?" Knox asked, his pale blue eyes flaring.

Ummmm...

"No?"

His eyes narrowed.

"No answering a question with a question, lady."

"Okay, fine. I wasn't planning on leaving without you on purpose. I was just too focused on the leaving part to remember that I had an army of werewolves who might want to help at my disposal."

A wry smile overtook his expression.

"Truth."

I really hated his lie-detecting ability. It was such a roadblock sometimes.

"Great. So I'm going to go now..."

"And we're coming with you."

"Fantastic," Kat said, with an eye roll so dramatic I could practically hear it.

"Take us to the dumpster you found the phone in," Knox ordered. "We'll go from there."

"Really, Sherlock? That's your plan? You're going to sniff him out?" She tapped the side of her nose for effect and leaned in closer to him. "I can smell things too, remember? And there was no scent trail to be found.

Knox took a step toward her, his shaggy blond hair falling in his face as he did.

"And maybe your sense of smell has been dulled by the pollution in this city. Now take me to the fucking dumpster."

Kat, unfazed by Knox's demand, shot me a dubious look.

"If Merc hadn't tried to kill you, Piper, I'd be so on his team right about now."

"I'm sure he'll be glad to hear that when we find him," I said, pushing past Knox to step into the hallway. The pack parted to let me through, and I continued down the hall to the grand staircase that led to the front door. Knox was at my side by the time I reached the keypad to unlock the security door. I hesitated there for a moment, my fingers lingering over the buttons. The last time I'd touched them, I had been fleeing from the man I was about to go searching for. What a difference a few weeks on the run had made.

How jarring the truth behind that night really was.

With a shake of my head and the press of Knox's hand on the small of my back, I punched in the code and proceeded through the holding room—the room that kept the vampires from accidentally frying themselves by going out too soon and prevented sabotage from someone opening the door to let the sunlight into the exterior door on the far side of the room. Both doors couldn't be opened at the same time, a necessary fail-safe for a mansion full of vamps.

The light of the sun felt amazing on my face, but my enjoyment of it was short lived. There would be no enjoying anything until we found Merc.

"What's the plan?" Kat asked, striding toward Knox and me.

"We'll follow you to where you found the phone, park, and go on foot from there."

"He could be anywhere, Knox. Who says he's still in the city?"

"We start there," he said, his tone stern. "Once we know what we're working with, we'll decide our next move."

My lips pressed into a thin line and I nodded.

"Great," Kat said, heading for her magically refurbished sports car—the one that had been pulled from the depths of the East River after one of Kingston's warlocks had send us over the edge of the Brooklyn Bridge. "Piper, get in. Knox... try to keep up."

She jumped into the front seat and cast me a look that said 'don't make me tell you twice'. I sighed and walked to the passenger's side, leaving Knox and the pack to the fleet of vehicles parked in the driveway. To his credit, he didn't argue about my choice of riding companions. He knew I still needed space.

That didn't make me feel any better about it, though.

Before I was even in my seat, Kat fired up her baby and threw it in reverse. She backed up too fast, spitting up random rocks as she did. By the look of irritation on Knox's face, one must have hit him. Or maybe he was pissed at me. I chose to believe the former.

As Kat peeled out of the driveway, jerking the car onto the road, I thought about all that Knox had sacrificed for me —how much the whole pack had. I knew some of them were less than thrilled about being in NYC, and who could blame them? The second I'd arrived near their home in Alaska, everything had gone to shit, ending with their home —their refuge—burning to the ground. Even though Knox had said they'd had a choice in the whole matter of moving, I knew they hadn't. That was not how packs worked. It was a dictatorship, not a democracy. I prayed that his lack of consideration for them wouldn't come back to bite us all in the ass.

I needed to do something for them other than constantly put them in danger.

"Earth to Piper," Kat said, waving her hand in my face while we idled at a red light. "Are you falling apart on me already? Because I haven't had enough sleep to do the hand-holding bullshit thing today."

"I'm good. I was just thinking."

"Yeah, I got that much. Care to share what you were thinking about?"

Not really.

"I was thinking about the pack. How they've been dragged into this mess all because of Knox. I'm worried that's going to cause problems."

She laughed at my reply, which surprised me. I turned to find her shaking her head, smiling at the traffic in front of her.

"You really don't get it, do you?"

"Apparently not."

"It doesn't matter what they want."

"I'm aware of how a pack works, Kat."

"No. You're not." Her laughter choked off in an instant. "They defer to Knox in all things. They're wired to. Whether they think they want to be here or not, they do—because he does. Even that Brunton asshole." She squeezed the wheel a bit tighter at the mention of his name. "I still owe him for his cheap shots."

"And you have my blessing once we deal with this missing mate situation."

"Finding Merc is the least of your worries," she muttered to herself.

"Excuse me? It seems like a pretty fucking big deal, Kat."

"And it is, but not nearly as big a deal as you having to sort out your one-too-many-mates situation that'll be waiting for you once we bring him home."

"If," I said softly, fear creeping into my mind. "If we bring him home."

Kat looked over at me and exhaled hard, the frustration in her eyes giving way to sympathy.

"We will find him, Piper, but I'm telling you, this mess you're in… it's not going to go away quietly."

"I know that."

"I'm just not sure you do. Vampires bond for life. For eternity. They take that whole 'til death do us part' shit seriously. And with Merc's instability, I'm just not sure how all this is going to end."

"You think he'd hurt me."

She turned away to look at the road, her tense jaw cutting harsh lines through her profile.

"I think it won't end well. That's all."

"I guess we'll find out once we get him back."

"Yeah. We sure as fuck will."

❧

IT TOOK the boys a while to find parking, but eventually we all ended up in a group in the alley where Kat had found Merc's phone. The dumpster had been emptied, leaving only a trash bag or two that had been tossed in that morning. Knox and the boys scoured the surrounding areas, but nobody came up with Merc's scent.

Kat, though disappointed for obvious reasons, looked mighty pleased about Knox's failure.

"Guess that nose of yours isn't so superior, is it, big guy?"

A low warning growl was his only reply.

"Whoever dropped the phone here did not have the vampire in the vehicle."

"So what do we do?" I asked, the edge of worry in my voice plain.

Knox pinned serious eyes on me.

"I don't know."

Kat reached out and put her hands on my shoulders, forcing me to look at her.

"Piper, you're his mate. Try to use your whatever-the-fuck-it-is magic you have and focus on him. Call to him. Ask your magic for help. If anybody can hunt him down, it's you." She gave my shoulders a squeeze. "You can do this, Piper. You have to..."

She's right, Piper. Get your shit together...

"Okay," I said, closing my eyes. "You're right. I can do this."

She kept her hands on me, which seemed to ground me in the middle of the concrete jungle, connecting me to nature in a way. With a deep breath, I silently called out to whomever was listening for help. Help to find Merc.

Help to find my other half.

A swirl of wind kicked up, tossing my long black hair around my face wildly. When I opened my eyes, I could actually see the air dancing before me, its pattern mesmerizing. Then I heard it rush past me, heading down the block before it stopped, kicking up dust at the corner as if waiting for me to follow.

"Will you show me?" I asked it, not caring how crazy I looked.

With a wild gust, it blew around the corner. We all ran after it, following it like the beacon it was. Our ticket to find Merc.

We must have looked ridiculous, running through the city like the most poorly dressed running club imaginable, but I doubt any of us cared. Minutes and miles ticked by before we wound our way into Chinatown. There, the mini-twister came to a sudden stop, and the dust it had collected dropped to the ground slowly until not even a breeze stirred where it had once been. It had led us to a hole-in-the-wall restaurant. The sign wasn't even in English, and the glass was frosted opaque. We couldn't see who was inside, but my heart tightened with every beat. That glass wouldn't let light in.

Maybe Merc was okay.

Kat eyed up the door, taking a step back as though she were about to kick it in. I caught her arm and shook my head, looking around at all the humans rushing about on the sidewalk. We couldn't make a spectacle of ourselves in plain sight. And we sure as hell didn't need the cops showing up.

Before she could even argue with me about it, Knox spoke. His words made her whole body tense.

"Excuse me?" she said, turning to pin narrowed eyes on the alpha.

"We're leaving. Now."

While Kat looked like she was ready to throw down, I was confused as hell.

"What? Leaving... why?"

"We're not going in there like this. We need the enforcers."

Kat scoffed.

"Fucking coward."

Knox growled at her for the second time that morning.

"Do you know what this is? What's inside?"

Kat made a dramatic show of looking up at the menu taped to the exterior door, then back at him.

"A noodle shop, so I'm guessing noodles."

Her deadpan reply was not appreciated. She soon found herself pinned against that menu, Knox's face crammed into hers.

"This noodle shop is a front for the fey." Her eyes went a bit wide before she steeled her expression, showing no fear. "So unless you have some insight as to who is in there and how many, I'm not setting foot in that building. Not until we have more backup."

"How do you know this?" I asked, unable to ignore the niggling sensation at the back of my mind. The one telling me that something was wrong. Very, very wrong.

"Yeah, Knox. How does an alpha from Alaska know something like that?"

"That's a question for later. For now, you need to call your boys and let them know we have a bigger problem on our hands than we thought. The king doesn't have Merc. The goddamn fey do."

"But we have an entire pack, Knox. And I have my powers. Surely there aren't enough of them in there to stop us."

His head turned slowly to look over his shoulder at me. His eyes held a combination of anger and hatred and fear that my mind could not comprehend. I'd never seen anything like it there before.

"Because, Piper. It's not what's inside the building that worries me. It's where the building *leads* that does."

"I don't understand."

"When we walk through those doors, we aren't walking into a restaurant. We're walking into Faerie."

"Holy shit..."

"Exactly, which is why we need all the help we can get. Preferably from someone who's been there and back and lived to tell the tale."

"I'm calling Jase," Kat said, pulling out her phone. We all stood there, clogging up the sidewalk while we waited for Jase to answer. "Hey! It's me. We've got a problem. A big one... yeah, we know where he is. Sort of." I could hear Jase on the other line, but I couldn't make out what he was saying. The wolves didn't seem to share that challenge, which irritated the shit out of me. "We're in Chinatown. We're going to head back in a minute. Listen, I think you should call the king... yeah, I get that, but listen... " This time I could hear Jase shouting on the other end. "Would you shut up for a minute? Jesus. Just call him. See if you can find out why he called Merc. We'll be back in a bit."

Kat hung up, clearly exasperated, and tucked her phone away.

"He's making the call."

"Good," Knox replied. "Let's get back so we can regroup. If we have to do what I think we're going to have to do, we need a plan." His serious eyes fell on me. "A damn good one."

3

Jase, Dean, Jensen, and a slew of others were waiting in the foyer when we arrived. We'd barely made it through the door when Jase said something that stopped us all cold.

"The king didn't call Merc."

Silence.

"What do you mean he didn't call him? That was the number on the phone," Kat argued.

"I know that, but when I spoke to the king, he assured me that he didn't reach out to Merc last night. He has no idea why it looks as if he did."

"Maybe because he's a lying bastard," Kat muttered under her breath.

"Easy, Kat," Jensen said under his breath, taking a step closer to her.

"Or maybe the fey wanted it to look like the king called. To point us in the wrong direction," Knox said, breaking his silence.

Jase and Dean turned to look at him with confusion in their expressions.

"Why would you say that?" Jase asked.

"Because we tracked him to a certain place in Chinatown," Knox replied, his tone leading them to the conclusion he clearly hoped they'd grasp. When neither said anything, he let out an annoyed sigh and spelled it out for them. "To a portal to Faerie."

"There's a portal to Faerie in Chinatown?" Dean asked, true surprise tainting his words.

"How can you not know that?" Knox countered. "You're a fucking enforcer and you don't know where the faeries return home?"

"I think the better question is, how do *you* know?" Jase asked, stepping toward Knox.

"That's what I wanted to know," Kat added.

Knox, realizing he wasn't going to be able to wriggle out of the conversation he clearly wished to put off, told Jase and Kat (and me, for that matter) what they wanted to know.

"Because NYC is my home. *Was* my home."

I could feel the weight of apprehension in those words as he spoke them. Knox obviously hadn't wanted to share that part of his past with me—or anyone else, for that matter. The fact that he'd given himself up the second he'd identified the place Merc had been taken told me just how much of a sacrifice he'd been willing to make. And I knew why he'd done it.

It was all for me.

"Knox," I said softly, resting my hand on his arm.

"I would have told you eventually," he replied, his voice no louder than my own. "This isn't how I wanted you to find out."

I forced a smile up at him, and he returned the favor.

"So you're saying that we have to bust into fey territory

—one of the only supernatural factions that the vampires are *not* currently embattled with—to get my brother back?" Dean asked.

"No. I'm saying we need to make a trip to Faerie if you want to go get him."

Dean's eyebrows shot up toward his hairline.

"Faerie? As in the land of the twisted? Where nothing is as it seems?"

"That would be the one, yes."

"Fuckin' A..."

"How can we find him there?" Jase asked. "From all I've heard, the lands are vast and treacherous, and loaded with things that could keep you there for an eternity."

"Well it'd be nice if we actually knew where he was, but since he can't exactly call us up and tell us that, we're going to need a plan B."

Knox's words slammed into my mind like a freight train. No, Merc couldn't call us; that much was true. But he could come to me in my sleep. He'd done it before we were bonded and several times after that, when I was on the run from him. Even though my memories of those dreams were mixed, to say the least, I hoped that it was still an option when he was in another world.

"I need to go lie down," I said, feigning exhaustion. I figured it was believable enough, given how stressed I was with the new turn of events. I hoped it would keep me from having to tell everyone in the foyer about how Merc could reach me.

Jase caught my eye as I turned to walk away, and I jerked my head toward the stairs, telling him to follow me up.

"I'll come with you," he said, taking my arm.

"I'll take her," Knox called out, rushing to my side.

"No," I replied with a bit too much enthusiasm. "You're the one that knows about this portal. You stay and fill everyone in. I'll be back down in a bit. I just need a break for a second. I need to process all of this."

His mouth pressed into a thin line of uncertainty but he nodded, shooting Jase a death glare before returning to the others. Once Jase and I were up the stairs and in my room, I blurted out the plan.

"Merc can come to me in my sleep," I shouted, slamming my hand over my mouth to quiet myself. "Maybe if I can knock myself out somehow, I can reach him—find out what the hell is going on."

"You and I need to have a conversation about this another time, but for now, you need booze and drugs. Lots of them."

"I don't need to be in a coma, Jase. Just out enough for him to get past whatever it is in my mind that shuts him out. I need to be functional when we go after him tonight."

He looked as if he wanted to argue, but thought better of it. He'd seen what I'd done to Kingston. I could hold my own with the fey if I needed to.

Even if I had no clue how to control the power I was capable of wielding.

It was a risk I was willing to take, for Merc's sake.

"I'll go see what Doc has that might work. You and meds don't mix quite right, as I remember. I'm going to have Kat fix you a drink like the one you had at the bar with us that night. That should do the trick."

"Good idea. And worst-case scenario, just punch me or something."

"Piper, I'm not going to hit you. Not even for Merc."

"Fine. Kat will if I ask her to."

He shook his head, letting loose an unstable laugh.

"I wish Merc could hear this conversation. He'd love you even more for it."

Jase walked out of my room, closing the door behind him and leaving me alone with my spiraling thoughts. Thoughts that grew more and more morbid the longer Merc was gone. Needing to squash them before they consumed me, I flopped back onto my bed and focused on my breathing. I knew I couldn't sleep if I didn't calm down, drugs or not.

Maybe Kat really was going to have to hit me.

A couple of minutes later, the sexiest female werewolf alive walked in with a jug of liquor.

"Do I need to stage an intervention right now? Because I gotta tell you, this isn't really the best time to party."

"Gimme that!" I said, launching myself off the bed to snatch the massive drink from her. To my dismay, she yanked it out of my reach.

"Not so fast. Tell me what's going on. You can't hold your liquor for shit. You'll be out cold in no time if you drink a quarter of this."

"That's the point," I replied, reaching for the jug. When I realized she could play keep-away with me for hours, I let out an exasperated sigh and told her the truth. "Merc can come to me in my sleep. I'm trying to make it so he can now."

Her brow furrowed.

"How do you know this?"

"Because he's done it before. Multiple times."

She looked pensive for a moment before her eyes shot wide open.

"That morning—before the call with the king! That's why you were so hard to wake up."

"Yep."

"You dirty dog..."

"Kat. Booze. Now."

"Right! Sorry."

She handed me the container and smiled wickedly at me.

"Tell that crazy bastard I said hi."

Then she sashayed out of the room in true Kat fashion, closing the door behind her. I looked down at the sloshing amber liquid and took a deep breath.

"I hope this works." I placed the jug to my lips and started to chug back as much as I could without vomiting it all back up. I gasped when I finally came up for air and decided it might be best to sit down before I hurt myself. Another few gulps of Kat's concoction and I knew it wouldn't be long before I was out cold. Whatever top shelf/Benadryl blend she'd made for me was already starting to do the trick.

I placed the jug down on the floor and lay back against the silky comforter. The coffered ceiling started to spin like a fan, and I braced my arms against the bed, hoping I could make it stop, but I couldn't. It hardly mattered though; five minutes later, I was dead to the world.

I AWOKE IN A STRANGE PLACE. It was dark and cold and empty, which was exactly how it made me feel. Light shed on the middle of the vast space, though I couldn't see where it was coming from. What I could see was what it illuminated. Standing in the middle of the warm yellow light was the massive vampire I'd bonded with, his dark eyes trained on me.

His expression was grim.

"Are you okay?" I asked as I rushed toward him. My arms wound around his waist as I crashed into him. Though reluctant, he eventually embraced me. "Where are we?"

"Everywhere and nowhere," he replied as though that were explanation enough. "And I am fine." He gently pried me off of him so he could look down at me. "But you shouldn't be here. It isn't safe."

"This is a dream, Merc. How could it not be safe?" My throat tightened a bit at his lack of reply. "Listen, I don't know how long we have, but I need to ask you some things. We found the restaurant in Chinatown; we know they brought you there. We're coming to get you."

"No!" he roared. My body tensed, PTSD from my near-death experience at his hands rushing to the surface. Realizing what he'd done, he let me go and took a step away. "I'm sorry for that, but you must understand. It's not safe. You can't come here."

"We're not leaving you in Faerie, Merc. I don't care what you say or how things were left between us, there's no way that I, or your brothers, or anyone else is going to leave you there."

"Let Jase and Dean come."

"Oh, they will—probably Jensen and Kat, too—but none of them seems to know the first thing about where we're headed. Only Knox has a clue."

"I'm certain he is less than keen on bringing me back." He did nothing to hide the contempt he felt from his voice.

"Actually he's downstairs right now organizing your rescue. He and his wolves."

He took a deep breath, letting it out slowly as though he were trying to cleanse himself of whatever prejudice he had toward the alpha.

"Tell him I'm in the quarry, near the far river."

"Quarry. Far river. Got it."

"And tell him that I think she is watching. That this is a test."

"A test? Test of what?"

"Power? Strength? Loyalty? It is hard to say, but the queen of the fey does nothing without reason. She and the vampire king are kindred spirits in that regard."

"Is this about the war?"

His dark eyes narrowed to slits.

"In a fashion, yes. I believe so."

"Is there anything else? Anything else I need to know—that I need to tell them?"

With a tentative hand, he reached for my face, tucking a stray hair behind my ear. His finger lingered on my jaw for a moment or two before disappearing.

"Tell Knox that less is more. And that if the ground shifts, he needs to get out any way possible. As for you..." He took a step closer. "You need to know that I would do anything in my power to keep you safe. *Anything*, Piper. Do you understand me?"

"I... no, I don't. What do you mean?"

"Stay out of Faerie," he warned, the image of him starting to fade away. I called after him repeatedly, but they went unanswered. Moments later I was back in my room, my face warm and wet. I first assumed that I'd been crying, but when I turned onto my side, I was met with the wet muzzle of a particular grizzly bear. One with deep concern in his warm brown eyes.

"I'm okay, buddy," I said, reaching over to pat him. When I moved to sit up, a shooting pain rocketed through my head, and I crashed back down to the bed. Whatever Kat had put in that drink packed one hell of a punch. Grizz grunted at me, snorting his displeasure. I looked over at him as his gaze drifted to where I'd put down the jug of booze, then back to me again. "No, I wasn't day drinking for fun, thank you very much. We're trying to find Merc. Somebody took him, buddy. We've got to get him back." Grizz's expression remained unchanged. "I know you don't like him, but I can't just leave him where he is. It's not safe; he said so himself."

With a deep breath, I tried—successfully this time—to get up. I made my way toward my bedroom door on unsteady feet. As I reached for the handle, the bear jumped in front of me, pinning disapproving eyes on mine.

"I need to go tell the others where he is, Grizz."

A snort. A stomp.

"Are you really going to pick this fight with me? Now?"

I reached around him and turned the knob, only to have a massive paw reach up and kick the door shut.

"Listen, buddy, I don't have time for this. I love you, and I know you're just trying to protect me, but you can't this time." He shot me a look that said 'try me', then put his paw up on the door to keep it shut. "Don't make me call Knox up here to deal with you. You wanted to be part of the pack, remember? Your idea, not mine. And that means that he's in charge, not you." With a huff, his paw slid down the door, scratching the shit out of it along the way. "I'm sorry to play that card, big guy, but you forced my hand."

I opened the door and slipped past the grizzly bear, who barely budged. Once I was out, he followed me down the hall, right on my heels. The bear was far from subtle. He wanted me to know how pissed he was about what I was going to do; and that was before he even heard the plan. He'd go apeshit when that happened.

The foyer was clear when I started down the stairs, but I could hear voices drifting toward us from the dining room, so I made my way there. I walked into a rather heated discussion about who and how and when we were going to go after Merc. I ignored the tension and continued past everyone until I reached Knox's side.

"How was your rest?" Kat asked with a wink and a smile.

"I know where Merc is," I said, ignoring Kat's shenanigans. I wasn't excited about potentially having to explain to Knox how I knew what I was about to share with him. And if I did, I knew he wouldn't be too thrilled either.

"He's in Faerie," Knox said, looking at me as though I were coming unraveled. Then he sniffed the air and caught wind of what I'd been up to. A frown tugged at his lips.

"Yes, I was drinking and yeah, I know Merc is in Faerie, but that's not what I meant. I mean I know where he is in Faerie. He's in the quarry by the far river." Knox's eyes went wide and he shot up from his chair to look at me more closely. I have sworn I heard him sniff at me again, but at that point, I'd closed my eyes to prepare for the onslaught of questions headed my way, so I couldn't be sure.

"You smell of him," Knox said. His words were barely more than a growl.

I ignored his observation and continued.

"I think bringing a small army with us is a bad idea. I think less is more."

"Okay," Jase said from across the table. "Anything else?"

I sighed, unable to figure out a way to spin Merc's last warning in a way that wouldn't sound like I'd been told it directly. But I couldn't so I just blurted it out, hoping for the best.

"Yeah. He said if the ground shifts, we need to get out ASAP."

"He said?" Knox asked, leaning closer toward me.

"Yes. He said."

"Truth..." He pulled away, shock in his blue eyes.

"It's a long story. Maybe I'll share it with you when you share with me exactly why you knew that building was a front for the fey. But for now, we worry about the matter at hand."

"Did he say anything else? Anything pertinent to this rescue mission.""

Yes.

"Not really."

Knox's expression turned harsh.

"Lie."

"Fine. Yes, he said that I shouldn't go. That I needed to stay away because it wasn't safe."

"He's right about that. Nothing about Faerie is safe."

"But I'm going anyway."

"Piper—".

"Not up for discussion," I said, cutting Knox off at the knees.

"If Merc specifically told you not to go, then you should listen."

"So now you want to consider his opinion on things?" I countered, doing nothing to water down my acerbic tone.

"He and I agree when it comes to your safety."

"Oh good. Some common ground between you."

I felt Grizz snort behind me and I turned to see that he was agreeing with the wolf.

"Et tu, Grizz? Really?" He made an awkward gesture that looked oddly like a shrug, then sat back on his haunches. I quickly turned my attention back to Knox. "I'm going and that's final. You don't like it, too bad."

"Piper," Jase said carefully as though he didn't want to incur my wrath. "Was that everything?"

"No. He said to be careful because he thinks the queen is watching—like this is a test of some sort."

"Or a trap," Dean added, leaning back into his folded hands.

"That too, I guess."

"But why? Why would the queen move against us? And like this?"

"Dude, there's a war going on," his brother said.

"Right, but the fey and vampires have made no moves against one another."

"Or they just did," I said, leaning my hip against the massive wooden table.

"Maybe they know how valuable Merc is," Knox suggested. But there was something more to his statement—a sense of knowing that I just couldn't shake. I stared up at his profile, hoping to find something in his expression that would give him away, but it never faltered. It remained stern and commanding.

"Kingston did, so that's a possibility. Who knows who else he told," Jase said.

"Or who Sylvia told," I added, her name sliding off my tongue like something thick and acrid. She'd been the one to tell Kingston about Merc's mind-invasion abilities. I didn't trust that he was the only one she'd shared that info with.

"Fucking bitch," Dean muttered under his breath. "You should have killed her, Jase."

"I was too busy rushing back to save your ass," he replied.

"From your half-cocked brother," Knox added, not improving the mood in the room.

"Who was being controlled by Kingston at the time," I said in the missing vampire's defense. "'We're just going in circles here. We need a plan. We need to be ready by nightfall."

That comment seemed to snap the boys back to the matter at hand.

"I need to go see someone first," Knox said, looking down at me. "Someone who can help."

"I don't want anyone knowing about Merc being gone," I replied.

"I won't disclose the why, but I think this particular person might be able to give us something that will give us an edge."

"Like what?" Dean asked, leaning forward in his seat.

"Like a cloaking spell."

"That would be pretty fucking handy."

"And just how are you going to get one?" Jase asked, looking doubtful.

"I told you—I know someone." Knox's tone was clear. He had zero intention of telling them who he was going to see. I wondered if he planned on keeping me in the dark as well. "I should go if I'm going to get what we need before dark. It might take a while to track her down." Her? "I need to talk to you first, Piper."

"Yeah. Sure."

I turned to leave the room, my mind trying to puzzle out just who Knox knew that could provide such a powerful spell. My silence must have spoken volumes because he rested his hand on the small of my back as I punched in the code to the front entrance—an effort to calm me. Unfortunately, it didn't work. I was a bundle of nerves, fraying by the second.

I felt the magic crackling in my veins.

By the time we stepped outside, I was ready to explode. I managed to take a deep breath and mumble something about peace on my exhale. A moment later, a gentle breeze wrapped itself around me, easing my chest as it danced along my skin. Then it disappeared as quickly as it came, leaving me a much more calm and rational being than it had found me.

"What do you need to talk to me about?" I asked, continuing to take deep even breaths. He hesitated for a second, breaking eye contact with me. I knew that wasn't a good sign. I needed my little breeze to come back as my respirations increased.

"The person I'm going to find—the witch—she's dangerous."

"Okay..."

"Very dangerous."

I swallowed hard.

"But you think she can help."

He raked his fingers through his hair before turning away from me and exhaling hard.

"If she's feeling charitable, yes."

"And if she's not?"

"If she's not, shit just got a lot more complicated."

"Because we won't have a cloaking spell?"

He barked out a laugh.

"Yeah. That too."

I held my tongue for a moment to ensure I didn't say something I didn't mean. By the time I released it, my mind had taken over again, shoving my heart aside.

"Knox...you said this used to be your home. You clearly still know people here—have ties to the city. Why did you leave?"

"I want to tell you that. I really do, but now isn't the time."

"Okay, then tell me who exactly you're going to see."

He exhaled loudly.

"The name she goes by is Sherry. She keeps a pretty low profile for the level of her ability."

"And you know her because...?".

"That's complicated. And not what you're thinking," he replied. "But know that the only reason I'm going to her is to help you—to get Merc back for *you*."

I couldn't help but shake my head. It was so hard to understand his motivation to bring back the one being that posed him the biggest threat.

"And I appreciate that more than I can tell you, Knox, so don't take this wrong, but why? Why would you do so much for him?"

"Oh no," he said, turning back to me in a flash. "I'm not doing it for him. I'm doing it for you alone. I can feel your fear, Piper. It's tearing me up to know how much you're hurting with this unknown hanging over you. If bringing him back will end that, then I'll do it. We all will. The boys feel it almost as much as I do. I told you we're all connected. I wasn't bullshitting you just to get in your pants."

His expression softened a bit after throwing in that last line, a smile tugging at the corner of his mouth. With the sun highlighting his golden hair and mischief in his eyes, he looked like he had the day we first met. The day I'd questioned whether he'd be my ticket back to NYC or my safe haven away from those that hunted me. I smiled at the memory, earning the same from him in return.

"That really would've been a good strategy."

"I know, right?" he replied with a laugh. "But I could feel your pain back then too, so I thought I'd try honesty instead." I swallowed hard. "The getting in your pants thing later was just a bonus."

"Liar," I said, using his favorite line against him. "You did it because you don't believe in double standards."

He walked toward me with a rugged grace that suited both who and what he was. I couldn't deny the reaction it caused within me. It was all I could do to look away from him and steal a breath before he was standing in front of me, his hands resting on my hips.

"For you, Piper, I'd be willing to make an exception," he said, his voice low and husky and full of something I tried to ignore. He leaned in close to me, his lips hovering near my temple. But as quickly as he'd approached, he pulled away. His brow furrowed as he scrutinized my expression. "Something's bothering you," he said, quietly demanding my attention. "Something other than Merc's abduction."

"I'm just stressed," I replied, forcing a smile.

He frowned in response.

"You're slipping, Piper. So sad, since you'd gotten so good at evading my questions."

"Hence the stressed comment. It's messing me up."

"But it's more than that. I just can't quite put my finger on it. Foust said the same thing yesterday. Jagger too."

"Great. The whole pack probably thinks I'm PMS-ing or something."

Knox smiled.

"Oh no. They know when that happens." My eyes widened with surprise. Knox simply shrugged. "What can I say? We sense things."

"That's so unnerving, you know that, right?"

The smile widened.

"There's a lot about me that's unnerving once you get to know me."

"That's not especially comforting," I said with a frown.

"And yet it's true." His jovial demeanor faded slowly, leaving a raw and vulnerable expression in its wake. "I don't want to lie to you, Piper. Ever. But if I follow through on that promise, the reality you face is that you might not love everything you come to know. And you might not love when and how you come to know it. Can you handle that?"

I looked at him in earnest, doing my best to squelch my growing doubt. His question was a fair one, and I wasn't certain of the answer. I didn't want to lie to him, not that that was even an option. I wanted honesty between us. It was the only way to move forward in any capacity. My life was confusing enough already; I didn't need a web of lies and deceit to complicate it further.

But that didn't mean one wasn't headed my way.

"I don't know if I can handle it or not," I replied, "but I'll do my best to."

He studied me carefully.

"Truth."

"So tell me something, does this little caveat have to do with Sherry? Am I not going to like what I learn about her? Or is it something else?"

"I hadn't really prepared a list for you," he said, moving closer to me. "I hadn't really planned to talk to you about this tonight, given the circumstances. I'd hoped to do something that didn't involve talking at all..."

He leaned in close to me again and my heart slammed against my ribs.

"Knox—"

"I know. Piper. Those plans clearly changed the second we learned about Merc. I may not like the guy, but I'm not a big enough asshole to try something with that going on. It's just that when you're near, it's so hard to resist your call."

"My call?"

"You know what I mean."

He took my hand in his and looked down at them, studying them before returning his eyes to mine.

"Tell me you don't feel this," he said softly. "Tell me you don't feel what I feel right now."

"I can't tell you that," I whispered as I ripped my gaze from his, crumbling under the weight of it.

"I need you to understand something, Piper. I won't force you to choose between us. But I still need you to know that my choice has been made, and I won't back down from Merc or anyone else. And I'm sure as hell not leaving."

"I don't want you to."

The second those words left my mouth, I scrambled to shut them back in, but it was too late. The truth was out; the damage was done. I looked up into his eyes and saw the fire of a man on a mission burning deep within them.

And I'd been the one to spark the flame.

"But right now I have to go," he said, pulling me into his chest. He hugged me lightly before kissing my forehead. "I'll text you if I get what I'm looking for."

"Okay. And thank you. For everything."

"Don't thank me yet. The last time I saw Sherry, we didn't part on the best of terms."

While I tried to think of something to say in response, he made his way over to a parked SUV and jumped in. I watched as he drove away, my heart in my throat for more reasons than I cared to entertain. Instead, I focused on his safe return and the cloaking spell we needed. That was much easier than dissecting my conflicting emotions.

Once he was gone, I made my way back inside to wait with the others and worry about both of the men in my life. I didn't want anything to happen to them: either of them. To know that their fates were now somewhat intertwined didn't sit well. I felt helpless knowing that one might die trying to keep me safe and the other could die trying to help me. I needed to know more about exactly who this Sherry witch was.

And whether or not she could be trusted.

4

"Sherry?" Kat repeated, her voice heavy with incredulity. "As in Uptown Sherry, the witch that's about as unscrupulous as that fuckwad Kingston?" I shrugged, not really knowing the answer to her question. She scoffed, shaking her head as she stormed toward me. "If that's who Knox is hoping will help us, then he'd better have a damn big bank account or a dick the size of Texas to get her to do what he wants."

"He said that the witch he was going to was pretty low key."

"Yeah, maybe she was when he lived here. But now? Now that bitch is as brazen as can be. If he thinks going to her is going to be on the down low, he's sorely mistaken. All of NYC is about to be put on blast that Knox is back."

There was something in her expression when she said that—an irritation that I didn't fully understand.

"Why would New York care about the return of an alpha werewolf? They have other things to deal with at the moment. Like a war."

She started to reply then stopped herself, biting her lip. In all the time I'd known Kat, she hadn't ever been one to self-censor. The fact that she'd done just that was cause for alarm.

"You know something..."

"I know lots of somethings."

"If it's about Knox, you need to tell me."

"Wrong. It's because this has to do with Knox that I'm not telling you."

"You think he's hiding something else. Something more than just his story about living in New York before he went to Alaska." She merely nodded in response. "Tell me this, Kat, and I need you to be as blunt as you've always been when you answer." Her eyes narrowed as she stared me down.

"Deal."

"Do you trust Knox?"

Silence.

"I trust that he cares about you. That's it."

"I have no idea how to take that, Kat."

"Take it for what it is: my healthy dose of skepticism over your new boy toy."

"He's not my boy toy."

"He's not your mate either, so what would you call it?"

I considered her question and opted to use Knox's answer regarding Sherry.

"Complicated."

"Yeah, well, you'd better un-complicate that shit ASAP because Merc and Knox are going to last about two days around each other if you don't. Those two aren't the kind of kids who share their toys, Piper. They're the kind that fight over them until the toy's in pieces on the floor." She leaned closer to me, the hard set of her features highlighted by the broken light from the chandelier above. "To be clear, you're the toy in this analogy."

"Yeah, I got that, thanks."

"Just making sure you're seeing this situation for what it is."

"A mess?"

"No, a total clusterfuck. Only you could manage to be mated to the most notorious vampire in existence and have a piece on the side."

"I think you're grossly oversimplifying things, Kat."

"Maybe, maybe not. Doesn't change the outcome."

I wanted to argue that point, but I didn't feel like losing.

"I have a plan," I told her, trying to sound confident when I wasn't at all. "I'm not going to be with either of them until this is all sorted. Merc is still punishing himself for what happened, so it's hardly like he expects me to move back in with him."

"And Knox?"

"Knox knew that I was mated to Merc back in Alaska. He doesn't seem to care, but he's not pushing things either."

"He's crazy if he thinks whatever he feels for you will overcome the blood bond."

"Maybe..."

"Maybe? What the fuck does that mean?"

"I... I don't know how to explain it. I know what you're saying about the blood bond—I do—but there's something connecting Knox and me. Something deep and elemental. When I'm with him, I feel rooted in the source of my magic, just like if I'm standing outside in the woods or a storm or the sun. It's like having a piece of that with me wherever I go. I can't just ignore it. Believe me, I tried for as long as I could."

She shook her head.

"You're toeing a dangerous line, Piper."

"Well the good news is I have you to tell me all about it... and to hopefully have my back if everything goes to shit."

"I tell you what; I'll have your back if you can get your side piece to give me five minutes in a locked room with Brunton."

"Done."

"Consider your backside covered, then."

THE WAIT for Knox to return was brutal.

Everyone was on edge. Jase and Dean tried their best to be normal, but the stress of knowing where Merc was and where we were about to go was clearly weighing on them. The pack was equally riled up from not knowing where Knox was or if something had happened. I tried to tell them I'd know if it had, but they didn't seem sold. Foust did his best to rally the crew in Knox's absence, but it was plain that their leader was gone. It was a grim look at the future they would have if he never returned.

Grizz refused to leave my side, which became awkward when I decided to lie down on the couch in the game room. It wasn't designed to hold the weight of a fifteen hundred pound male grizzly. The legs broke out from under the sofa, and it crashed to the ground. Grizz had the nerve to shoot me a dirty look as if I'd done it, and I burst into laughter. Tense or not, the moment was hilarious.

"I think we need to put you on a diet," I said between gasps for air. His snort in response was duly noted. "I'm only kidding, big guy. You're not fat, just fluffy." He made a sound that was a mix of a cry and a whine, then hopped off the broken couch to curl up in front of me on the floor. "Aw, don't pout. We'll get someone to reinforce it for you so we can cuddle, okay?"

"Piper!" Foust yelled from the hallway outside the room. "He's back."

"Thank God," I replied, jumping up to run and meet Knox when he entered.

But my thanks had been premature. One look at Knox when he staggered through the door told me things hadn't gone nearly as well as he'd hoped.

"Knox!" I shouted, racing down the stairs. "Holy shit, what happened?"

"Let's just say plan B is looking pretty damn good right about now."

"We need to go outside," I said, taking his arm and looping it over my shoulders. Foust took the other side, and the two of us walked him through the security room and back outside, where we lay him on the ground. I put my hands over his chest and whispered on the wind for help. Without hesitation, it came. Knox's wounds started to glow a bright white before disappearing altogether. Unlike the time before, it was controlled and painless. I wondered if I was finally getting the hang of my powers. Or hoped, at least.

"Thanks," Knox said, smiling up at me from his position on the ground.

"Yeah. No problem. Now, care to share what the hell happened?"

"Sherry wasn't in a charitable mood."

"I gathered that. So now what?"

Knox smiled at me, pulling something out of his jeans pocket.

"You didn't think I'd come home completely empty-handed, did you?" He held up a shiny piece of smooth silver metal that reflected the sun as he shook it around in his palm. "I might not have gotten a cloaking spell, but I did manage to snag a parting gift—well I guess it's not really a gift if I stole it, but..."

"What is it?" I asked, reaching for it.

"It's white tungsten."

"Okay..."

"It fucks with fey magic."

"I thought that was iron."

"Iron will—in this realm. White tungsten, on the other hand, works like a charm in Faerie, pun totally intended." He pushed up onto his feet to stand in front of Foust and me. "It won't keep us invisible, but it'll mess with any booby traps or magical pitfalls or sentinels. That might just be enough to get us to the far river and back alive."

I sighed heavily, looking over at Foust, then back at Knox.

"Guess there's only one way to find out."

"At nightfall, it's game on."

5

Once the sun had set, the select group of travelers amassed outside the house. Knox chose Brunton and Foust to come, leaving Jagger behind and in charge. Jase, Dean, and Jensen made up the enforcer contingent. Kat and I rounded out the group, though there was still contention about me going at all. Arguments or not, I was.

All eight of us were headed to Faerie.

We rode into Chinatown in two separate vehicles and parked them close enough to access them when necessary, but not so close as to be easily spotted should the fey be watching over their little storefront portal to the homeland. Jase, Knox, Kat, Jensen, and I rode together, the silence in the car slowly making me insane. For all our 'preparations', we still had no real plan. Knox would guide us to the quarry where Merc had said he was being held. The rest of the crew was essentially there in case something went awry, which, according to Knox, was highly likely in Faerie.

Jase pulled into a spot on the street and parked the car. None of us moved to get out right away. Not until Jase gave the nod. As far as he was concerned, this was his mission; at least on our side of the portal. I knew it was making him nuts to not be in control of his brother's rescue. Though he hid it well, it was wearing on him. The fine lines of worry etched into his brow told me as much.

"All right," he finally said. "Let's go."

I jumped out of the back seat onto the sidewalk, followed by Kat and Jensen. The group from the other vehicle walked up to join us, and we all made our way to the building in question. The one that appeared to be open for business.

"What the fuck?" Dean said, stopping short when he saw the bustling restaurant full of humans. He turned his attention to Knox. "Does this look like a fucking fey portal to you?"

Knox scowled.

"I didn't say that it wasn't a restaurant too, did I?" With no explanation, he started down an adjacent alley toward the back of the brick building. "This part might get a bit hairy. Stick together and follow my lead. If shit goes sideways, kill first and ask questions later."

"Finally! A plan I can get on board with," Kat said from behind me. I turned to look at her and she flashed me a wicked grin. That girl was a loose cannon for sure.

"There's a stairway to the right just inside the back door. That's where we're headed. At the bottom is a gate that, with any luck, won't be shut."

"And if it is?" I asked.

"Then things get harder still."

Nobody bothered to reply. Our mission was becoming bleaker by the second.

There was no ambush awaiting us at the back of the building, unless the hooker giving some poor schmuck a blowjob was actually a fey spy ready to jump off her knees at any moment and take us all. Thankfully that wasn't the case. Knox opened the screen door that led to the kitchen area. I could see the stairs he'd described past his silhouette.

It was go time.

The ruckus in the kitchen provided excellent cover. None of the humans working there seemed to take any notice of us. Whether that was coincidence or by design, I didn't know and didn't care. Knox led the way to the basement, with Jase and Foust close behind him. I went next, with everyone else following me.

The light grew sparse as we descended the stairs. By the time I neared the bottom, it was almost pitch black. I could hear the murmurings of Knox and Jase below, then the clanging sound of metal being shaken echoing up the staircase. Not a good sign.

"Is it locked?" I asked. The curse Jase let loose confirmed my suspicion. "Is there any way to muscle through it?"

"No," Knox replied. I took out my phone to illuminate the cramped space. The expression on Knox's face did not inspire confidence. It looked like our rescue was dead on arrival.

"Is it magical? The gate?"

"Yes. Fey magic."

"Well," I said, squeezing between Knox and Jase. "Maybe you should let me have a crack at it." The two backed up to give me space, not that I needed it. I wasn't about to perform an interpretive dance to coax it open. I was going to do what I always did and ask for help. I'd either get it or I wouldn't.

I wrapped my hands around the bars and immediately felt the magic course through me. I sucked in a breath, surprised by its intensity. Knox's hand was on my back in an instant.

"Are you okay?"

"Yep. No problem. This sucker just has a lot of juice."

I took a calming breath and closed my eyes, trying to push past the feel of the foreign magic and connect with my own. With Knox touching me, it was much easier to do, especially when surrounded by a concrete block foundation.

"Help me open this," I whispered, hoping my plea would be heard.

I felt the metal warming under my fingers, the temperature becoming more and more uncomfortable until it was almost unbearable. The stench of burning flesh filled my nostrils, and I had to work hard to fight back the well of tears and memories flooding my eyes and mind. I wouldn't let go at any cost. I was our only way in.

I heard my name being called out. I felt hands trying to pry me off. But I wouldn't relent. I had to save Merc. I had to get us into that basement.

As I felt the magic starting to override my control, a sharp stinging sensation bloomed across my cheek just as the screech of metal on metal reverberated off the walls around us. The gate let loose, knocking me back into Knox and the others. Breathing hard, cheek and hands throbbing, I stood up to find the gate in front of me ajar.

And an apologetic Kat standing in front of it.

"You looked like you were about to lose your shit like last time, so I had to try and stop you since Merc isn't here."

I rubbed my face.

"Thanks for that."

"Glad to help." She threw in a wink for good measure. "Who knew a slap was all you needed?"

I didn't bother to tell her that I didn't think that was a great game plan. I was nowhere near as far gone to the magic as I'd been in Alaska when I'd tried to heal Knox; the time she was referring to. Only Merc had brought me out of that downward spiral. If we didn't get him back, I wouldn't have him to rely on ever again.

I heard the gate swing open and turned to find Jase standing in the opening.

"You did it," he said softly.

"Fuck yeah, she did," Dean added.

"We don't have time to marvel at Piper's awesomeness right now, even though it really is something to see," Knox said, pushing past me into the abyss beyond the gate. "We need to keep moving."

Caught up in the middle of the group, I shuffled along in the darkness, hoping we wouldn't run into too many more obstacles. I pulled my phone back out to shed some light on our surroundings, but all I found was a tight tunnel of rock and concrete that seemed to lead far beyond the confines of the building's basement. It felt like it would never end.

I don't know how long it took us to reach the end, but Knox called us all to a halt at some point along the way. I looked around to see where the portal was but didn't find anything. It just looked like more of the same to me. But there was a buzzing—a current of magic—that I couldn't ignore coming from somewhere nearby.

"It should be right around here," Knox said, running his hands along the stone wall. The others started to do the same, each searching for something they'd never seen before. I, however, walked on guided feet to just beyond where Knox searched. I knew exactly where the portal was. I could all but see it, its call so strong.

"It's here," I said, pointing to a spot on the wall that looked identical to the rest of it. "Can't you feel it?"

I could sense the eyes of the others on me, staring in the

darkness, but I didn't care. I knew I was right. I'd have bet my life on it.

"Show me," Knox said, coming to stand beside me. I showed him where, and he ran his hand along the wall, smiling back at me. "Not bad for a girl who didn't know how to control her powers."

"Guess I'm just a natural."

He laughed under his breath before saying something in a language I didn't know. The second he finished, a blinding flash of light shot from the spot where his hand was pressed, and the portal opened. A lush forest awaited us on the other side—or at least that's how it looked. I had been told not to believe anything I saw or heard in Faerie. I was taking that warning to heart.

Knox reached into his pocket and pulled out the white tungsten, clutching it in his hand.

"Let's hope this baby works."

Without another word, he stepped into Faerie.

6

We stepped into what looked like a fairytale. A forest so lush and green and beautiful that it took my breath away. It felt amazing standing on the moss-covered ground, the thrum of magic coursing through my body. The others didn't seem to be affected the same way I was. They rushed past me on high alert.

"Stay close," Kat said, taking me by my arm.

I followed behind her and Jensen, caught up somewhere in the middle of our group as we walked through the densely wooded area. Knox seemed sure that he was headed in the right direction, so no one questioned his actions. It did, however, make me question why he was so confident—why he was so familiar with where he was going.

"How long will it take?" I whisper-shouted up to Knox.

"Time moves differently here. I'm hoping that the tungsten will keep that from affecting us too greatly, but I don't know for certain. It could take minutes or hours or days, though it will feel all the same to us."

I let his words settle on my mind. If I'd understood him correctly, we basically had no idea how long we were going to be in Faerie, or when it would be on Earth when we returned. Not a great situation for the vampires with us.

We sped along, careful not to make any more noise than necessary. The woods were quiet in return. Eerily quiet. It made the hairs on the back on my neck stand on end.

"Up here," Knox said, sounding somewhat surprised. "That's the far river."

"Seems awfully near to me," Kat muttered under her breath.

Knox looked over his shoulder at her.

"Welcome to Faerie."

When the trees finally thinned, giving way to the river's edge, I sighed with relief. Beyond it I could see a cliff—part of what I assumed was the quarry. Merc was near.

"So I assume we're not swimming across," Jase said. "Given your inability to do so."

"No," Knox replied. He looked around, searching for something. "There. We cross there." I followed his gaze over to where a massive tree had fallen, its trunk straddling the river at a narrow part.

It wasn't long before we were all lined up single-file to make our way across the fallen tree. Knox went first, with the boys right behind him. Jensen insisted I go between him and Kat, so I stepped up onto the rough bark behind him and took a deep breath. I had a feeling that falling into the river would equal bad things, so my singular focus was on getting across without taking a dip along the way.

Thankfully I managed that without any complications.

Once we were all across, we moved as a unit to cross the rocky outcropping. With every yard closer to the edge of the quarry, I felt my heart race. 'What ifs' were racing through my mind like crazy. What if I'd misinterpreted what Merc had told me? What if we were walking right into the hands of the queen? What if something terrible was waiting for us on the other side of that ledge?

What if the queen had moved Merc before we'd even set foot in Faerie?

By the time my toes touched the sharp edge of the rock, I wasn't breathing. Together we all stood along the steep ledge, looking down into the quarry below. It felt more like a gorge of sorts, long and deep and narrow. And dark. Very, very dark. I couldn't see the bottom of it, let alone whether Merc was down there or not.

It looked damn near bottomless.

"Help me see him," I whispered, closing my eyes to focus. I expected a flood of light to fill the area, but it didn't. Nothing happened. Not a goddamn thing. "Shit. It's not working. My magic doesn't work here." I felt panic creeping up within me. I didn't want to be powerless to help Merc—or anyone else, for that matter, including myself.

"Piper?" I heard the faint voice drift up toward me from the black abyss below.

"Merc!" I shouted, slapping my hand over my mouth. We'd been so quiet up until then. I hoped I hadn't just blown it. "We have to go down there."

"We'll go," Dean said, looking at Jase. They had a silent conversation between them before nodding at one another. "You wait here, Piper."

I wanted to argue, but I realized I'd be no help to them at all. Without my magic, I was all but human in another realm. I'd be cannon fodder for sure if something other than Merc was waiting for us down there.

"You'll have to climb," Knox told them. "And if there's any trouble down—"

"We'll tell you to get everyone the fuck out of here."

Knox's mouth pressed to a thin line and he nodded.

"Get in and out of there as fast as you can."

"Will do," Dean said with a wink. He closed his eyes for a minute, concentration furrowing his brow. For a moment I couldn't figure out what he was doing. Then it dawned on me; he wanted to see if he could ghost down there. "Looks like we really are climbing," he said to his brother. "Race ya."

In a flash he was over the edge and clambering down the steep, craggy wall. Jase wasn't far behind. The rest of us stared over the edge as they disappeared into the emptiness below and held our breath. I looked over to Knox, who was rubbing the tungsten in his hand.

"Will they be protected by that?" I asked quietly, looking at the smooth metal.

"No," was his only reply.

Though it was likely a matter of minutes, it seemed like an hour before we heard voices echo up to us. They'd found him. He was okay. They were coming up. I let out a sigh of relief. Our mission had been successful.

At least that was what I initially thought.

But something had happened down in that cavern, something that triggered a reaction in the realm we didn't fully understand. The one we'd underestimated. Sounds from the previously silent forest began to fill the sky, coming to us from across the river. The wolves were the first to turn and look; Jensen and I followed suit only seconds after. While the brothers traversed their way up from the depths, the rest of us stood stock-still, waiting for an enemy we couldn't see, but knew was approaching nonetheless.

"Knox?" I called, moving closer to him. "What is it?"

He exhaled hard.

"Sentinels. Lots of them." He stepped to the front of the group, Brunton flanking him on his right. Jensen stepped forward to guard his left. Kat looked torn between wanting to stand beside her mate and needing to stay behind and have my back—just like she'd promised. I hated that I needed her to.

The unseen enemy approached, the noise of their growing numbers setting us all on high alert. If it came to a battle between them and us, I knew we were in trouble. There were just too few of us in a land that set its own rules. Not exactly a fair fight.

The crunch of rock behind us alerted us to the brothers' successful escape from the quarry, but there was little time to celebrate. Just as they crested the ledge, the sentinels emerged from the cover of the forest, forming a long line on the other side of the river. I'd never seen the fey in their true form; it was a sight to behold. They were a wall of perfect beings, their beauty staggering. My breath caught in my throat as I looked upon that army of immortals and wondered how we were ever going to return. Armed with bows and blades and looks that would make a human weep, it didn't look good for us.

"Piper," Merc said from behind me, his lips at my ear. "I told you not to come."

"And you should know I don't listen very well," I replied, staring down the sentinels on the other bank. "Are you okay?"

"I am fine," he replied.

Knox growled.

"Lie."

I turned to look at Merc and realized that he didn't look well at all. His pale skin had a grey tinge to it, and his eyes looked dull and lifeless. With his dark hair tied back, his features looked sharp and his face gaunt. Whatever the fey queen had used to keep him down there had lasting effects.

I could practically see the haze of magic emanating from him, and he looked exhausted, like something had drained him of his strength. Strength he was about to need to fight our way out of Faerie.

"We need to get close enough to fight them," Knox said, frustration in his voice. He knew their weapons would keep us from doing that. What he may or may not have known was whether our party could withstand the same amount of damage in Faerie as we could on Earth. Judging by the look on his face, I guessed the answer was no. "Are you up for that?"

Merc didn't answer at first. Instead, he stared down at me as though he'd find the answer somewhere in my eyes.

"I feel better now."

I had no time to dissect his reply and all its potential implications. The fey interrupted me before I could.

"Invaders!" a voice called out from across the river. It was neither male nor female. "You declare war on the queen with your presence here."

"Hey asshole, we're all at war anyway. Or did your fairy ass not know that because you're busy hiding out here in the bushes?" Dean asked, officially throwing the gauntlet.

"You cannot take what is ours."

"We've come to take back what's *ours*," Jase replied, stepping up beside Knox. "And if you were wise, you'd let us leave without a fight."

The fey all smiled the same smile. A dark, all-knowing smile that look photoshopped onto their otherwise unanimated faces.

"If you'd been wise, vampire, you wouldn't have come. But here you are, and here you shall perish."

"What's the plan, boys?" Kat asked under her breath, her eyes glued to the eerily still fey.

"If I could just use my magic somehow," I said, frustrated with my lack of abilities. "I could create a diversion or something."

Merc turned me to look at him, confusion and disbelief in his eyes as they bore holes through me.

"You cannot use your powers here?"

"No. I tried."

He paused for a moment.

"That cannot be..."

Before I could reply, an arrow whizzed past my ear, narrowly missing me only because Merc snatched me out of its path at the last second.

Ready or not, the fey were coming.

With little shelter other than the quarry behind us, we were sitting ducks. Our group scattered like mice when the arrows started flying at us, everyone dodging them as they ran. Merc and Knox, both unwilling to leave me behind, ushered me along the ledge of the cavern, aiming for some rocky outcroppings not too far from where we were. I knew I was slowing them down, and apparently Knox agreed; I soon found myself thrown over his shoulder, bouncing uncomfortably as we evaded the feys' first line of attack. I knew it wouldn't be long before the arrows stopped coming and the fey themselves did. With broadswords as long as I was tall, I didn't think that was an improvement.

Just as we neared the cover of the rocks, I looked up to see a fey jump the width of the river and land right next to Merc, his sword drawn back to strike. I screamed to warn Merc and Knox, but it wasn't soon enough. Just as Knox put me down to fight off the attacker, I saw the fey, with a brutal cut of his sword, bury his weapon deep into Merc's leg, nearly knocking it out from under him—or cutting it off entirely. I just couldn't tell. What I did know was that Knox nearly tore the fey's head from his body with a swipe of his clawed hand. Unable to stop his backward momentum with his damaged leg, Merc fell into me, and I soon found myself looking down into the craggy abyss; then I was falling into it. Merc's grip on me tightened, but the jolt of him catching the ledge with his other hand knocked me loose. I slid forward until all he had a hold of was my foot. A foot that was slipping from my shoe.

"Knox!" I screamed, trying my best not to panic and failing miserably. Without my magic, there would be no surviving that fall. No wind to slow or break my descent.

I looked up at the ledge to find Knox covered in dark blood. One hand still clutched the white tungsten. He threw it aside and bent down to grab Merc's hand and haul him up. With some effort, he dragged us both to safety. Foust and Dean came to his aid, doing their best to hold off the onslaught of fey attacking, but their numbers were just too great for us. There was no way out.

There was no way we could win.

Once I was standing on solid ground again, shielded by a wall of vampires and wolves, I tried to call to my magic. I'd felt it so strongly around me when we'd arrived. I knew it was there, ready to be used. I just had to figure out how.

Then the tungsten lying on the ground near my feet caught my attention. I bent down and picked it up. The second I did, I felt ill, and without thinking, I threw it back down. I watched as it took a bad bounce and rolled toward the edge of the quarry, falling over with one final flip. It disappeared in an instant.

"NO!" I gasped, wondering if I'd sealed our death warrants for sure. "I dropped the tungsten!"

I heard Knox swear under his breath as he dodged the sword aimed at his head. Merc stole the weapon from

Knox's attacker and buried it in the fey's abdomen, yanking it out with a twist.

"What did you just say?" he asked, as though he wasn't embroiled in battle.

"The white tungsten—I just dropped it."

"Piper, call your magic," he said, wincing as another blow landed on his damaged leg. The one he could barely stand on any longer.

"But—"

"Call it now!"

Confused but determined, I closed my eyes and focused on the magic I'd felt when we'd arrived. I tried my best to draw it to me, the swell of my chest growing as I breathed it in like the sweetest scent. Then I blew it out all at once. With my exhale came gale force winds, the likes of which I'd never felt in my life. They ripped past us, nearly knocking us over, but we remained standing. The fey, however, struggled against them.

"Drive them back!" I shouted over the roaring winds. The fey lost ground, their feet scraping against the rock until they lost their footing and landed in the river. Some were blown so strongly that they flew over the top of it, crashing into the trunks of the trees awaiting them on the other side. One by one, they fell victim to my attack.

The shock in their eyes was plain as they stared me down.

"We have to get out of here," Knox yelled to me. "You need to keep pushing them back so we can retreat." I nodded, then looked at Merc, who stood balanced on his one good leg. I dropped to my knees and wrapped my hand around the mangled wound.

"Heal him," I said, hoping that my winds wouldn't stop because I was trying to fix him. Unfortunately, they did just that. It felt like only seconds, but those seconds were all the fey needed to rally and attack again. From far off to my right, where the others had scattered to avoid the initial attack of arrows, I heard a scream that chilled me to the bone. Half female cry, half howl of a wolf, I knew it was Kat.

And I knew something had gone terribly wrong.

7

"Kill them!" I shouted, directing my anger and frustration at our beautiful attackers. Seconds later they all shot up into the air, as if pulled by an invisible cord, and dangled there. That invisible cord appeared to be tied around their necks, choking them to death. I looked on as a darkness grew inside me—a shadow on my soul that begged for pain and vengeance and retribution for the affronts the fey had brought upon us. I liked the numbness that came with it.

I liked watching them die.

It was then that I felt a hand on my arm, pulling at me. Distant voices started to become more clear, words recognizable. A face was in mine, his mouth moving as his dark eyes tried to reach me. He shook me hard, trying to disrupt the joy I felt in that moment. Then, unexpectedly, he bit my neck, drawing away the darkness I was so enjoying. With it came a fear so great it nearly knocked me over. The fey fell from the air, dead, and I shook uncontrollably, terrified by what had just happened.

"Piper," Merc said, his face in front of mine again. "Piper, it's time to stop."

I nodded weakly, unable to move any more than that.

My eyes drifted over to Knox and Dean, who were staring at me with wide eyes. Eyes full of fear and wonder.

"I... I..."

"We have to go now," Merc said gently, taking my arm. I started to walk, forcing my limbs to obey me. With every step, I came back to myself, but I would soon learn that my return was too late.

As we neared the river crossing, I could see Jase hovering over something with Brunton at his side. My heart clenched, remembering the sound I'd heard just before I'd magically strung the fey up to die. Kat had made that sound.

And Kat was nowhere to be seen.

With a different brand of fear coursing through me, I ran toward them, praying Kat was okay—that I hadn't missed my chance to save her. Losing Kat wasn't an option. She'd said she'd always have my back.

I couldn't live with knowing she'd died because I hadn't had hers.

"Kat!" I called out, running like her life depended on it. "Kat!"

That same cry broke out in response to my call, and every hair on my body stood on end. It hadn't been an outburst of pain I'd heard. It had been a call of mourning.

"No," I whispered as I poured on speed. Seconds later I pushed through Jase and Brunton to find Jensen lying on the ground motionless with Kat on top of him.

"Heal him," I said before my knees even hit the ground. Before I even laid my hands on him. Nothing in the air stirred at my request. No light shone down upon us. When I placed my hand upon his cold flesh, I knew why. I hadn't failed Kat by not having her back. I'd failed her by not saving her mate.

Jensen was dead.

"We have to go," Knox said as he and Merc approached. "There will be more."

"And I'll kill them too," I replied, my anger slowly awakening that shadow on my soul.

"Not if the queen comes," Merc said. His sober tone gave me pause.

I placed my hand on Kat's back.

"We have to go, Kat."

"I'm not leaving him," she growled.

"I'm so sorry, Kat."

She looked up at me, tears in her eyes as they begged me to fix what I could not, and I felt my heart break.

Knox and Merc were arguing quietly behind me when Jase shouted "incoming!" Our reprieve from the fey was over. We had to get out of there or risk losing someone else.

I stood up, staring down a different-looking enemy dressed in ethereal clothing of vibrant colors with ornate embellishments. These were not soldiers that had come for us. They were royalty.

"Distract them," I said under my breath as I stared at the female who stood in front of the others. The one glaring at me.

Vines began shooting out from the ground in the forest where they stood, creating an intricate cage around them. If we were going to make a break for it, that was our moment.

"Now!" Knox shouted, darting toward the river crossing. Merc dragged me along with him while I looked over my shoulder at Kat, who lay unmoving on her fallen mate. Then I saw Brunton scoop her up and throw her over his shoulder. She kicked and clawed and fought him along the way, but he didn't flinch. He took her abuse as he carefully walked across the log.

Jase then picked up Jensen's body and carried him over.

He would not leave the enforcer behind.

The ground shook with our pounding footsteps, thunder in the sky above us enriching the sound. A storm was brewing, and it wasn't my doing. Whoever had come to take us out was powerful indeed, and I wondered if I possessed the ability to hold off whatever obstacles they threw our way.

The first bolt of lightning landed so close to Knox that he flew twenty feet in the air before crashing to the ground. I managed to shout "catch him" just before he struck the ground, a swirl of wind winding around him to set him down on his feet. He looked back at me with a sly smile, then took off running, leading us out of the woods and back to the portal. Without the tungsten, I prayed that Faerie wouldn't move our escape or do something else to botch our exit. That was exactly what we didn't need.

After a few attempts to stop the lightning from crashing around us, I managed to come up with a command that wrapped us in a bubble of safety. The lightning would dissipate when it struck the invisible barrier, leaving us alive. Or almost all of us.

"Up here!" Knox called out, pointing to where we'd entered the forest. It looked like a normal tree, but I'd accepted that not everything in Faerie was as it seemed and trusted that Knox knew where he was going.

He stopped in front of it, pushing his hand against the trunk to test it. To my utmost delight, his arm disappeared through it.

"Move!" he shouted, his voice commanding. And we were all too happy to obey. One by one we filed through the portal back into the stone tunnel underneath the city. Once the last person was through, I hovered in front of the innocuous wall. “Piper! We have to go.”

“Just a second,” I said, staring at the wall. “Help me keep them in there.” My words were a whisper, but the call to my magic didn’t need to be loud. It heard me easily. The ground beneath my feet began to rumble as shards of metal—iron—shot out in front of the wall where the portal was, forming the perfect cage for the fey.

I turned to run after the others, but it was hard to find my footing as the ground still reverberated below. A stone from the ceiling of the tunnel dropped before me, nearly crushing my head, and I looked back to find hands sticking out of the portal, pointed at me.

“RUN!” I screamed at the others, picking up my pace. Knox reached back and grabbed my hand. He practically dragged me through the collapsing corridor, staying just in front of the imploding rocks. By the time we hit the staircase up to the kitchen, I feared we wouldn’t make it. My legs had been pummeled by debris, the stones attempting to swallow me whole. But once we started our ascent, everything stopped. No more earth shaking. No more impending doom.

None of us stopped until we reached the back alley. There we paused just long enough to take stock of everyone’s injuries.

Brunton must have put Kat down at some point during our escape because I looked over to find her eyeing him up from across the group. Kat didn’t do emotions well—never had. The only one she knew how to use was anger. And by the look on her face, she was about to channel all of it at Brunton.

Without preamble, she lunged at him, landing a haymaker on his right temple. And she didn’t stop there.

Her fists flew at an inhuman pace, pummeling the wolf that had just saved her.

"Kat!" I yelled, as Knox pulled her off Brunton—off his werewolf who hadn't fought back.

"We need to get out of here," Knox said, tossing Kat toward me. "We don't have time for this."

Dean must have ghosted to get one of the SUVs because, before I realized he was gone, he pulled up into the alley and flashed his lights at us. He left it running and jumped out, looking to the sky and its fading darkness. He gave me a wan smile before disappearing into thin air. Seconds later Jase did the same. Merc, however, looked at me with pain in his eyes, like he couldn't bring himself to leave me alone—like he didn't want to chance something happening on our way home. I gave him a nod that said he should go, and he did the same in return, telling me he agreed. Then he too ghosted off into what remained of the night.

The rest of us filed into the single vehicle and took off for home. Knox and Foust sat up front, Brunton and me behind them. Kat sat in the very back where Jensen's body had been gently laid out. I could hear her sniffles as we drove home in silence.

So much had happened that night that didn't make sense. Too much had gone down to wrap my head around. From start to finish, the whole ordeal had been a whirlwind of crazy stuck in fast-forward, ending with Jensen's death and me being targeted by the fey. It was like my childhood all over again.

Death and fear and running.

I rested my head back against the seat and wondered if those three things would haunt me for the rest of my life—however long that proved to be. Would it all stop once the war was over? Would it cease once I found a mentor who could teach me how to tap into that deeper, scarier magic I possessed that had brought Kingston to his knees? Or would it persist indefinitely no matter what I did?

Those questions ruled my thoughts as I drifted off to sleep.

Sadly I found no answers there.

8

The sun was close to rising by the time we arrived at the mansion. The pack awaited our arrival on the front lawn while the enforcers stayed in, knowing that it was a matter of minutes before the sun would be too high for them to survive. They apparently didn't want to be additional casualties that night.

Knox was bombarded the second he stepped out of the SUV. Brunton joined him to brief the others on our journey to Faerie. Though they were wrapped up in their conversation, they stopped speaking the second Kat hopped out of the back of the vehicle and picked up the lifeless form of her mate. In a show of solidarity, they all stood and silently paid their respects to the widow. She walked by them like they didn't exist—all but Brunton. She managed to shoot him a death glare before entering the mansion, disappearing behind the security door.

There was a general look of relief when I stepped out of the SUV. Jagger ran over and scooped me up, hugging me tightly until he saw Kat rush by, following Jensen's body. He swallowed hard at the sight, knowing what it meant.

"It's good to see you too, Jagger."

"We were so worried, Piper. You were gone a long time."

"Yeah, Knox said timed moved funny there. How long were we gone, anyway? We left right at sundown."

"Two days."

I tripped on my words as his reply registered.

"What? Two DAYS?" My mind couldn't wrap around that fact no matter how hard it tried. "I need to go inside," I said, my voice distant and low. "I need to let Grizz know I'm okay." I walked away without further explanation, leaving the pack outside to have their private conversation.

I passed Foust as he emerged from the mansion, his sober expression telling me everything I needed to know about the tone inside. Not that I was surprised. The loss of an enforcer was rare.

Kat was nowhere to be found when I walked in, but there were enforcers everywhere, their somber expressions evidence that they'd learned of Jensen's death. He was beloved among them and highly respected. It was a loss larger than they were prepared to take.

While they all welcomed Merc, I sneaked up the stairs to find Kat. I knew the enforcers would need to prepare Jensen's body for the death ritual, and I was worried she would fight them on that. Watching the corpse of your mate burn never did sit well with her.

"Kat?" I called from outside her bedroom. I knocked on the door before turning the knob and pushing it open. Inside I found Kat lying next to Jensen's body, her arms and legs wrapped around him so tightly I wondered if she thought she could keep his spirit from leaving. It seemed a bad time to remind her that it had left a long, long time ago. "Kat? Can I come in?"

"You're already in. Don't let me stop you." Though her

deadpan reaction smacked of the old Kat, her tone lacked the punch she'd normally have delivered it with. She was a shell of the werewolf I knew, and it scared me.

"Kat... I'm so sorry."

"I know you are. Everyone is. It's written all over your faces."

"Can I do something for you?"

She pinned deadly serious eyes on me.

"You can bring him back. I want you to bring him back to me."

"I tried to, Kat. It didn't work."

"Try again."

The finality in her tone was frightening.

"Kat—"

"No, Piper. The girl I saw in Alaska could. She split the goddamn world in half to bury that asshole Kingston. Bringing Jensen back would be peanuts in comparison."

"I'm not a necromancer, Kat."

"Try again, Piper. For me. For Jensen... you know he loved you."

Her voice tightened around her words, making my already broken heart shatter a little more. She needed to know that everything that could be done for him had been. I would have wanted the same in her shoes. I owed her that much.

"It works better if I'm outside," I whispered. "With the sun..."

"He'll go up in flames the second we set foot outside! Not exactly what I'm going for."

My lips pressed to a thin line and I nodded. I could do this for my friend. I could give her what she needed in that moment to help her accept Jensen's fate. I walked over to the bed and eased myself onto the edge. Kat let go of her dead mate and backed away so that I could do whatever it was she thought I could do. The hope in her eyes was painful to see, so I looked away, avoiding both her and Jensen.

With a deep breath, I placed my hands on his chest and closed my eyes.

"Help me heal him," I said, my voice shaky with nerves and grief and the fear that what I was attempting to do might actually work. "Help me bring him back."

I felt a slight draft come from behind me, then nothing. Jensen didn't move. My eyes drifted up to Kat, who stared down at her mate like she could will him to wake up, and the tears I'd been holding back rolled down my cheeks.

"I can't do it, Kat. I can't bring him back. I'm so sorry."

"Get out," she whispered. When I didn't move, she repeated her command so loudly that it made me jump. "I said get out!"

In a second I was up off the bed, practically running for the door.

I slammed it behind me and leaned against the wall, cupping my hand over my face to hold back the sobs that threatened to escape. I stayed there for a moment, unsure of what to do, then I ran down the hall and down the stairs, headed for the front door. I had to get out of there. I had to find peace the only way I knew how.

The brothers tried to intercept me along the way, but I brushed them off, slamming the security code into the keypad and tearing open the door. I heard Merc call after me, and my hackles went up. It reminded me too much of the night I'd escaped him. Only this night, someone did die.

I seemed to startle the pack when I staggered out of the exterior door and took off at a dead sprint for the woods. I knew they were following, but I didn't care. I barreled through the bushes, the sharp bite of the twigs on my skin punishing me. When I finally stopped, I was at the bridge I'd found myself on once before; the one I'd nearly jumped off. Though I had no intention of doing that again, the desperation that had coursed through my veins that night was present yet again.

Instead of standing on the railing, I sat down along the edge and let my legs dangle high above the gorge. I felt the bridge shift as someone approached, the hollow sound of his uncertain footsteps echoing all around me. The weathered slats creaked and groaned in protest as he sat down beside me.

"I'm sorry for your loss, Piper. Truly." I couldn't reply without crying, so I just nodded in response. "Kat's going to be all right. I know it doesn't seem like it right now, but she will. It'll take some time, but she will. That's the thing about wolves—we're undyingly loyal to our mates, but sometimes they die and that's just how it is. We move on eventually. We find love again."

I looked over at him, unsure if he was telling me this for Kat's sake or my own. If it was his way of telling me that he'd be okay without me.

"She made me try to bring him back again," I whispered. "I failed, of course, and she got so angry with me. I don't think..." I cut myself off, the tightening of my throat making it hard to talk. I swallowed hard against it, trying to beat back my emotions long enough to actually speak. "I don't think she'll ever forgive me."

"It's not your fault, Piper."

"I know that. I know that he volunteered to go, but he only did that because he knew Kat would have gone without him. He was doing it for her."

"And he died for her," Knox said, slapping me with another reality I wasn't sure I wanted to hear. "I saw him go down. He dove in front of a blade for Kat. She would have been cloven in half if he hadn't." He sighed hard, taking my hand in his and squeezing it gently. "Jensen sacrificed himself because he loved her. I know that's of little consolation right now, but she'll see that one day."

"Kat never wanted a white knight," I replied softly. "She wanted an equal. She thought she'd found that in Jensen."

"A mate's need to protect is strong, Piper. I'm sure even Merc would agree with that."

I knew he would, but I didn't bother saying that out loud.

"You don't know her like I do. She doesn't do emotions well. I'm afraid this is going to break her."

"It won't. I promise you."

"Her whole life is falling apart around her, Knox, in ways you don't even know. She's not a vampire. She won't be allowed to stay here. Jensen was her only tie to this place. Maybe not tomorrow or the day after that, but eventually she's going to be turned away from the mansion. She'll be out on her own, and I think we both know how well that bodes for an unmated female. Even one like Kat."

Knox's expression softened as he looked at me. He released my hand and reached to cup my face as he stared into my eyes.

"Nothing bad will happen to Kat, Piper. I'll make sure of that."

"But how?" I asked, sniffling as I spoke. "You can't guarantee something like that!"

His brow quirked at me and he smiled.

"She can't be kicked out if she's a member of my pack, can she? The enforcers swore that they would keep us for as long as we needed to stay. If she's with me, she's not going anywhere."

"Are you serious? You'd do that for her?"

"After what she did in Alaska with Kingston, I'd do that and more."

My excitement fell when I realized that Kat might not find the idea so favorable.

"I don't think she'll go for it, Knox."

"Not at first, she won't. She's tough and prideful. She won't think she needs anyone, but she does." His hand fell away from my face. "We all do."

I tried to ignore the pain in his voice when he said those final words, but I failed. It was just too thick to deny.

"I should probably head back. The boys are going to need to prepare Jensen for the ritual, and Kat is not going to take that well. Whether she hates me or not, she needs me right now, and I don't want her getting hurt because her grief has overridden her ability to think clearly."

Knox stood up, the bridge shaking beneath me as his weight shifted, and reached his hand out to me. I took it, enjoying the feeling our connection always gave me—the grounding sensation it provided me with.

As we entered the woods, I found a particularly angry grizzly bear headed our way with an apologetic-looking Foust following behind him.

"I think he had to see you himself, Piper. He wasn't having any of me telling him you were okay."

Grizz looked back at Foust and huffed, then barreled into me, knocking me onto my back. He hovered over me, sniffing every inch to make sure I was okay. Or maybe it was the sweet stench of the fey he was investigating. Either way, his fluffy face was a welcome sight.

"Hey now," I said, trying to push him away so I could stand. "All right, all right. You missed me, I get it." I wrapped my arms around his thick neck and gave it a squeeze. "I missed you too. I was worried for a while that I might not get home to tell you that." He yanked his head away and shook it violently. "I know, that outcome would have been totally unacceptable for me too. But it didn't happen, so let's not worry about it."

Didn't happen to me, anyway.

"You can tell the bear all about your harrowing ordeal on the way back to the mansion," Knox said, a weak smile tugging at his mouth. "We need food and rest because the fallout of what we did there hasn't begun yet. But it will... soon. We need to be ready."

As we walked back through the woods, my hand on Grizz's back, I tried not to let Knox's words scare me, but they did. And rightfully so. We'd stormed Faerie and stolen its prisoner, wiping out a slew of its sentinels in the process. I'd never met the queen of the fey, but I'd heard enough stories to know she wasn't to be trifled with. Her wrath knew no bounds, and she was cunning and patient. If we weren't diligent, we'd never see her retribution coming.

And Jensen's death would be the first of many at the hands of the fey.

9

I'd fallen asleep on the floor of my room, Grizz's massive body wrapped around me like a fortress, when Jase knocked on my door. He eased it open and popped his head around. Grizz growled at the vampire until I shushed him. I was starting to think the bear really didn't like anyone but Kat and me.

"It's time," he said, his voice weighed down by the gravity of what we were about to do. Sending a vampire into the ether was a sacred ceremony, one that would be heavily attended, including by the king himself. I wasn't ready to face him yet—not after everything that had transpired since we'd last spoken—but I had no choice. My attendance was required as well.

I nodded to Jase and he closed the door, leaving me to get changed. Grizz looked on, wariness in his expression like I'd seen before in Alaska. It was the expression he wore when he wasn't comfortable with a plan, or when he could see that I wasn't.

"It'll be okay, big guy. Nothing is going to happen to me

in this house." The bear looked unconvinced and let out a sigh to better convey that fact. "Keep it up and I'll make you stay here while I go down there and face the king." Grizz shot up onto his hind legs and let out a sound that would have made a lion proud. Maybe an alpha werewolf too. "Point made, now knock it off. You can't be acting like that tonight. This is important. You need to be on your best behavior, and if you can't do that for me, then do it for Kat. She needs us."

He landed with a thud that shook the chandelier hanging over my bed, the crystals tinkling like bells. Knowing time was of the essence, I grabbed a simple black dress out of my closet and threw it on, then wrapped my hair up into a top knot. Some quick red lipstick and I was ready to go.

Grizz walked beside me as we made our way down the hall and outside. The burning of the body happened behind the mansion where a pyre of sorts was set up just for that particular purpose. We'd only had to use it once since I'd arrived at the mansion. But this time was different. This time it was a friend.

The entire corps of enforcers was there, with the vampire king standing ready to address them. Normally the mate of the fallen vampire would have been standing next to him, but Kat was nowhere to be seen. I searched the crowd for the brothers and Merc, hoping to find out what was going on, but Knox intercepted me as I approached.

"She's not here," he said quietly.

"I know. She's supposed to be up front. Do you know where she is?"

"She bolted when they brought the body out."

I swallowed hard, thinking about the pain she was in.

"Can you follow her? Keep your distance, but make sure she doesn't do anything crazy."

"Already on it. Foust and Brunton are tracking her around the property. They'll howl if anything gets sketchy."

"Thank you," I said, letting my eyes drift back to where the king stood before the body, which was laid out on a marble slab surrounded by twigs and branches and things that burned. "I have to go now." He nodded, letting Grizz and me continue on to the group. Grizz got more than his fair share of looks as we wound our way through the crowd to join Merc and his brothers. Merc looked over at the bear with morbid curiosity, and the grizzly peeled his lips back to expose his teeth, silently snarling at the vampire. Merc leaned closer and flashed his fangs in return.

Grizz didn't flinch.

"I think I'm starting to like the bear," he said under his breath. I patted Grizz on the head to set him at ease just as the king began to speak.

He went on and on in the old language, leaving me in the dark, but I recognized Kat's name when he said it. Ekaterina rolled off his tongue so beautifully that I wished his expression when he said it had matched. I could see his disdain at her absence.

He did little to hide it.

As the flames grew higher, the smoke billowing up into the moonlit sky, I heard a cry in the distance, which was soon echoed from all around the property. Kat's howl would not stand alone. The pack joined in, their voices carrying through the air like one. It was haunting and beautiful, and I felt the tears I'd been holding back let loose at the sound: Kat's final goodbye to Jensen.

I wiped my eyes as the king finished the ceremony and

turned to walk away. Then I heard my name called out from behind me, and I froze. The king was approaching.

I hadn't seen him since my return.

It appeared he wanted to remedy that.

Merc stayed at my side, unwilling to leave me alone. Whether that was out of concern for what the king might do or what I might say, I couldn't be sure. Either way, his hand found the small of my back and anchored me in place. I took a deep breath and plastered on a funeral-appropriate smile. Even though Jensen was dead, the king would expect a cordial greeting.

"Your grace," I said, fully equipped with a small curtsy.

"I see that your return has not been a mundane one, Piper. It's so unfortunate that chaos seems to trail you like a lost puppy."

Another deep breath.

"It is not the return I had hoped for, sire. That's for sure."

"You risked everything going to retrieve your mate—including one of my valued enforcers."

"Jensen volunteered, sire," Jase said, stepping up to flank Merc. "We all did."

"Without consulting me first," the king replied. He didn't bother to hide his irritation.

"Time was of the essence," I added.

"Was it, now...? And here I thought it was I who made such decisions. Not you."

"He's my mate, your grace." I bit those words out through gritted teeth. Teeth bared in a serpent's smile. "I didn't know I required your permission to go after him."

"He would have required it to go after you when you suddenly disappeared in the middle of the night, had he come to ask for it," the king said, leaning forward. He was close—so close that he could have pressed just a wee bit closer and had his teeth at my throat. I felt Merc go stiff beside me, preparing for God only knew what. I had no intention of finding out. "And I would not have given it to him."

"Then why did you send Kat?"

The king pulled away to look at me, his eyes bright with amusement.

"Because I didn't give you permission to leave, Piper. I don't care for insubordination. I care less for desertion. After all I've done for you, that was how you chose to thank me? By bonding to one of my enforcers, only to run away? It's disgraceful."

"I gave her no choice," Merc said, his voice so cold that I actually shivered.

"The circumstances are irrelevant," the king replied, dismissing Merc with a wave of his hand. "She has returned." He looked over his shoulder at several of the pack members emerging from the woods. A disapproving frown pulled the corners of his mouth down. "And she's brought a harem of wolves along with her." The king turned to Merc, stepping so close that they were almost nose to nose. "I wonder how she managed that." They stood silent, letting the tension grow between them until the king smiled and walked away without another word.

Once he was far enough away, I let out the breath I was holding.

"What the fuck was that?" Dean asked, walking around Jase to stand in front of us.

"I don't think he likes me very much," I deadpanned.

"Ya think? Jesus... he's pissed the fuck off."

"He won't be a problem," Merc said, watching the king disappear around the front of the house.

"Because you're going to make sure of that, or...?" I

asked, honestly scared of his reply. "You know what? Don't answer that. I don't want to know."

Grizz nudged my arm, signaling that he wanted us to get out of there. I agreed with that idea and turned to walk back toward the mansion, but Merc's unexpected words stopped me short.

"I never thanked you, Piper—for coming to Faerie. For rescuing me."

I looked over my shoulder at him and forced a smile.

"Leaving you there wasn't really an option."

"It was. You chose to not let it be. *Why*?"

I contemplated that question for a moment, not really knowing how to answer. The simplest reply would have been that I wasn't ready to lose him forever. We had issues—massive understatement—but I wanted to work through them, if for no other reason than I owed him that much. Letting him be a prisoner in Faerie didn't really lend itself to that. But that answer actually wasn't simple because it opened a floodgate of grey area and emotions that I wasn't up for discussing—not yet, anyway. That was definitely a problem for another day.

"Because after everything that happened between us, you were there for me when I needed you—when I asked you to help Knox. I needed to return the favor."

"But I told you not to come, that it wasn't safe."

I shrugged.

"Maybe I've learned to handle myself since I left the mansion."

A dark smile ghosted his face before disappearing.

"I think you might be right."

The intensity in his eyes was more than I could handle, so I walked away, Grizz at my side, to the sound of howling wolves, the stench of smoke and ash, and the knowledge that tomorrow might not bring change with it, but that not all was lost because I still had hope.

I prayed that hope wasn't in vain.

10

Our time in Faerie seemed to have taken a toll on me.

From the moment we'd returned, my body had seemed desperate for sleep. Maybe because we'd technically been gone for two Earth days. Maybe because I'd used a ton of magic while there. Or maybe because I was still exhausted from everything that had gone down in the weeks prior. I just couldn't tell.

Regardless, I soon found myself in my favorite place to go when I needed to be alone in a home full of others. I wanted a moment of peace and quiet and, more importantly, coffee. Lots and lots of coffee. But since the arrival of the pack, my former sacred place was no longer. I couldn't count on it being empty like I always could before. Except for that night. The pack was still off keeping tabs on Kat, so I had the kitchen all to myself.

I started collecting everything I needed to make coffee—a ritual that I loved. One that I had sorely missed.

I looked over at the stereo, wanting to turn it on, but I knew better. If I had, I would have drawn attention to my whereabouts. Someone would have come to make sure I was okay, and I just wasn't up for that. I continued to prepare my liquid breakfast in silence, making quick work of the process. Once it was brewing, I went over to the cupboard with the mugs and opened it, reaching for the first one I saw. Then, looking at the one I was about to grab, my hand stopped short.

So did my breath.

Down on the lowest shelf was an exact replica of my *Morning Princess* mug; the one that had been smashed to bits the day after Kingston had sent a tornado to kill me. The day after Merc had saved my life—the first time. I gently took it down and turned it over and over in my hands. It had always been my favorite.

And now it was back.

I felt Merc's presence behind me, looming at the far end of the room. The déjà vu of the moment was undeniable. Taking care not to destroy the treasure I'd just uncovered, I put the mug down on the counter and pushed it back against the wall for safekeeping. Then I turned to face my blood-bound mate.

He stood across the room, looking every bit as formidable as he had the last time we'd found ourselves in that position, but this time there was an air of unease that wasn't due to my lack of clothing, or the warning his brothers had given me, or the way Merc stared at me as though he were looking right into my soul. This time there was a clear divide between us that I feared might never be closed, regardless of our bond. The thought made my heart drop into my stomach.

"What's wrong?" I asked, wondering what had changed so quickly since our interaction outside.

He took a step forward and I froze for a moment. His

erratic moods made me nervous. They reminded me of the dark times I would have loved to have forgotten.

Seeing the tension in my body, he stopped.

"I'm scaring you."

"Why are you acting so differently?" I asked, doing my best to keep my voice calm against my rising anxiety.

"I just had a talk with the king. It has done nothing for my mood."

"Oh."

"He wanted to know all that happened in Faerie—what the fey wanted with me. He was displeased with my lack of answers."

"He thinks you're withholding information from him." A statement, not a question. Merc nodded in response. "Well... are you?"

His dark eyes narrowed, making him look more menacing than he likely meant to. Mention of the king seemed to make him either angry or suspicious. As of late, I felt the same.

"Yes, but not directly. I have answered his questions to the best of my ability."

"But you're not offering up information willingly." He shook his head. "Merc—"

"He will not be a problem, Piper."

"He could be a pretty big problem if he finds out, Merc."

"I suspect he already knows what I have not told him. He just does not know that I know."

"And is that a problem? Or could it be?"

His hesitation made my unease grow.

"Potentially, but by then I don't suspect it will be an issue anymore."

"You need to be careful with him."

"I am aware of his duplicitous nature, if that is what

concerns you. I see him for what he is." *I see you...* The manic words he'd spoken to me the night he tried to kill me slammed against my mind so hard that I took a step backward, bumping into the counter. "Piper?"

"I'm fine," I said, throwing up my hands to deter his approach. "It's just something you said to me—that night." His tight expression fell to one of regret. "You said something similar. That you saw me, like that meant something far more ominous than it should have. Did you think I was conspiring with the king against you?"

His chest rose and fell before he answered.

"Yes."

"Do you know something about him that I should know?"

"No. Not yet. Not for certain."

"Will you tell me? When you know?"

With small, tentative steps, he walked toward me. The desperation in his eyes when he was right in front of me was so plain; it was impossible to look at. Instead, my eyes fell upon the mug that had been replaced. I picked it up and cradled it in my hands. "Did you... did you replace this for me?" When I heard nothing in response, I dared to look up at him. He nodded once. "Thanks." My reply was sheepish and weak, accurately portraying how I felt in that moment. There was so much I needed to tell him—so much I needed to say—but I just couldn't organize my thoughts enough to force the words out. Instead, I let the pregnant pause in the conversation grow until it filled the room, practically pushing me out of it.

That would have made it all so much easier.

"It was your favorite, was it not?"

My turn to nod.

"When did you get it?"

I watched as his jaw flexed, holding back an answer he seemed pained by the idea of giving me.

"A while ago."

"Oh..."

"I wanted to be prepared should you choose to return home."

"Oh..."

"I wanted you to have a sense of normalcy—to feel safe and secure."

"Mhmmm..."

"Could you please answer me in actual words, Piper? I cannot read your responses. I cannot figure out what errant thoughts might be running through your mind, and it unnerves me."

"I'm fine, it's just—" I stopped myself short, uncertain of what to say. It had been clear the night that Merc saved Knox that he still loved me. That he would never forgive himself for what he'd done to me, even though it was not his fault. To have said what I wanted to in that moment would have done little more than fuel his guilt further, and that was something I didn't want to do. "I didn't expect to see it, that's all. It surprised me. In a good way."

The corner of his mouth twitched as if a smile dared to avail itself to me. Then, as quickly as it came, it disappeared.

"To answer your question, yes, I will tell you once I know for certain. Understand that this is not about unwillingness to share this with you. It's about needing to confirm my suspicions first. To tell you before that could put you in danger should the king learn of my treachery."

"Okay."

"Are you certain of that?"

"Yes. It's okay. I can handle that."

His smile finally escaped.

"Then I will leave you to your addiction while I work to put my suspicions to rest."

He hovered for a moment before turning and making his way out of the kitchen.

"I'm not addicted, you know! I could quit anytime I wanted," I said in my defense. Half joking, half not.

He looked over his shoulder at me, not an ounce of playfulness in his expression.

"We cannot so easily quit the things that we depend on. The things that we love."

My body went numb at his words, my arms limp. And for the second time, the sharp sound of porcelain meeting marble echoed through the kitchen as my *Morning Princess* mug shattered into tiny pieces. I prayed it wasn't a metaphor for what was to come between us.

I hoped it didn't symbolize what I might do to his cold, dead heart.

11

I abandoned my coffee idea for the promise of escape that sleep would bring me. My mind was too exhausted at that point for even coffee to help anyway. After I cleaned up the fragments of my mug and threw them away, I made my way up the butler's staircase to the second floor and my room. Grizz was waiting for me, curled up on the rug at the foot of my bed.

"Hey buddy. I feel the same way. Too tired to function." He exhaled, letting his lips flap dramatically. The gesture made me laugh way harder than it should have, but I embraced the small moment of levity as much as I could. The way things were going, I didn't know if or when I'd have another like it. "This is why I keep you around, Grizz. Comedic value."

He shot me a sidelong glance that told me how much he appreciated my assessment of our relationship, then closed his eyes and went back to sleep. A few minutes later, while I was getting ready for bed, I heard my bedroom door gently close. I came out of the bathroom to find Kat standing in front of it, her eyes wide and empty. She looked like hell—

clothes dirty and torn—and I wondered if she'd picked a fight with the entire pack.

It sure as hell looked that way.

"Jesus Kat!"

She stepped forward, letting the light of the room envelope her, and I realized what she'd done. She'd lain down in Jensen's remains. She was covered in soot and ash.

"Oh Kat," I said, rushing to her side. "We need to get you cleaned up." As I ushered her toward my en suite, she turned and looked at me. Those empty blue eyes of hers would haunt me for years.

"Can I stay here tonight? With you?"

I pressed my lips together to hold back my swell of emotions and nodded. Instead of talking, I rushed about, drawing her a bath. Once I had her situated in the tub, I woke Grizz and told him to keep an eye on her while she bathed. I hurried down the hall to her room to find her some clothes, then rushed back, not wanting to leave her alone for too long. Forlorn Kat was not a version of Kat I'd seen or understood, and I worried about what she might do. What she could be capable of. Even with Grizz at her side, fear grew in my heart.

Thankfully I returned to find Grizz with his massive head propped on the side of the tub, his muzzle buried against Kat's neck. She scratched his ear absentmindedly, her gaze firmly set on something far away in the distance; something beyond the marble that surrounded her. For a moment I wondered if I'd ever get the Kat I'd known back again, or if she, like me, would be forever changed by an event in her life that was too devastating to ever put into words.

I knelt down beside the bear and grabbed the clean washcloth I'd put on the side of the tub.

"Let's get you cleaned up and into bed," I said softly, not wanting to pull her out of whatever faraway place she was in. With gentle strokes, I washed away the remains of her spouse—the water growing darker with every pass—until I could no longer see her body through the murkiness. It took a little effort to haul her lithe but dense frame out of the bath, but I managed with Grizz's aid. I wrapped her in a towel and walked her into the bedroom, sitting her down on the edge of the bed. I went to collect her clothes and returned to the room to find her naked under the sheet, her back toward me.

"Will you hold me?" she asked, her voice so soft that I could barely hear her. Grizz looked up at me with warm brown eyes, then walked around the bed to rest his head down in front of her.

"Of course I will," I replied, crawling in behind her and wrapping my arm around her shoulder. "Because I've got your back."

I HAD no idea what time it was when I woke up, but neither of us had moved. Kat was still curled up in my arms. I tried to inch my way out of the bed so as not to disturb her, but that proved impossible.

"Are you going coyote-arm on me, Piper?"

I choked on a laugh.

"It was that or I wet the bed. I can stay if you want, but don't blame me for the wet spot."

"Wouldn't dream of it," she said, stretching her arms above her head as she rolled over to face me. Her normally sassy expression was heavy with things unsaid. But it was lighter than the night before, which was the glimmer of hope I needed to see. "About last night—"

"Kat, please don't explain yourself."

"Thank you," was all she said.

"Of course. Anything you need."

She looked over at Grizz then smiled.

"How about a shirt? The bear is side-eyeing my tits and it's freaking me out right now."

I laughed, grabbing the shirt I'd pilfered for her while she was in the tub. I tossed it to her and she pulled it over her head, covering herself—likely for my benefit. Kat didn't care about being naked, and really, she had no reason to. Her body was ridiculous.

"You hungry? Want me to go make you something to eat?"

"Don't do that," she said, snapping at me. "Don't treat me like a wounded animal."

"I'm sorry. I didn't mean to."

She sighed hard, raking her hands through her short auburn hair and down over her face.

"I'm sorry. This is hard for me in so many ways I don't even know where to start, Piper. I need something to stay the same. Does that make sense?"

It did. It really, really did.

"Got it. So you're saying you'd like sarcasm for breakfast with a side of go-fix-it-yourself?"

A smile tugged at her lips.

"Yes. That. I'll have a shit-ton of that."

"That, my friend, I can do."

I walked away, my bladder demanding to be released, and gave Kat some space so she could finish getting dressed. When I emerged from the bathroom, she was standing by the door to my room, looking ready to face the day.

"Tell me you have something for us to do today? Something dangerous and frowned upon that's likely going to lead to me kicking someone's ass. I need a distraction. Maybe plural."

I opened my mouth to give her the bad news—that I didn't have anything above and beyond the war to offer her—then I snapped it shut. In my periphery I could see the sparkle of light hitting gold. I turned to see the broken amulet on my dresser, begging to be picked up. Finding its former owner was a huge part of why I'd returned to NYC, and the search for him was certain to be embroiled in chaos.

I walked over and picked it up, dangling it off the tip of my finger for Kat to see.

"I think I can keep your mind—and your fists—busy for a little while."

She smiled across the room at me, a real smile that made her eyes sparkle with mischief.

"I do love a manhunt."

"Me too. Especially when I'm not the man being hunted."

Her smile widened.

"Let's get out of here before we pick up any tagalongs. Your alpha boyfriend is a pain in the ass to shake."

Didn't I know it.

"Agreed. Road snacks, then out the door."

"Exactly what I was thinking."

She opened my bedroom door and peeked out. Once she gave the all clear, she waved at me to follow her out.

"I'm going to grab pants. I'll meet you at the car."

She took off down the hall, leaving me with a pissed-off grizzly bear staring at me.

"Not this time, buddy. I need you to stay here and keep tabs on what's going on while I'm gone. I promise I'll be fine.

I just have to track down a friend." He quirked his brow at me, calling bullshit on my explanation. "Fine. He's not exactly a friend, but I need to find him. I'll be back later. Be good, okay? Don't start a fight with the vampires." He gave no indication that he wouldn't, but I didn't have time to argue with a bear. I needed to sneak out of the house undetected and attempt to find Reinhardt. I had no idea if he was in New York, or even alive for that matter, but I had to try. I'd put all my eggs in his basket, and if I was going to be of any use in the growing war between the supernaturals, I needed to get a grip on the depths of my powers. Reinhardt was the only one capable of helping me do that, providing he still had a pulse.

And providing he didn't try to kill me instead.

12

We stood on Broadway, neither of us knowing what to do next. We'd gotten out of the mansion alone under the guise that we were running to get groceries, which was a feat in and of itself. But when faced with the task of actually hunting Reinhardt down, we were at a total loss. Kat's irritated expression let me know that our cluelessness wasn't really working for her.

She was going to do something half-cocked for sure if we didn't find a solution soon.

"Remind me not to go on covert missions with you anymore, Piper. They suck."

"I know. I'm sorry. I guess I was so worried about getting out of the house alone that I didn't think much about what finding Reinhardt would require."

"It might require a shovel and a whole lot of digging if your hunch about him being alive is wrong." She eyed me tightly. "Tell me we're not going on a body search. Please. I'm clearly not dressed for that."

"I don't think we are."

"Right. I get that, but what I don't get is *why* you think that. You have no proof. Kingston said he eliminated him, and he had the amulet to prove it. You don't think Reinhardt just handed it over because Kingston asked nicely, do you?" I shook my head. "And really, would it have mattered even if he had? Kingston still would have killed him just to cover his tracks."

I wanted to refute what she was saying, but I couldn't. Her points were valid, and under normal circumstances, probably correct. But there was a niggling in the back of my mind that I just couldn't escape. Something that told me I needed to find him; that I needed to learn the truth about what had happened. Whether Kat could accept that or not didn't matter. I'd find him on my own if I had to.

"I can't explain it, Kat, but I don't believe he's gone. I need someone to teach me—to make sense of all that stuff I did against the warlocks. If anyone can, it's him. He's my only shot."

"If he's alive..."

"Only one way to find out if he is."

She sighed heavily.

"I can't believe that what you're saying somehow makes sense. But we're still no closer to finding him. Has inspiration struck you yet? Can you use those handy powers of yours to track him?"

I scoffed.

"I doubt it. I tracked Merc down because of our bond. That's not going to work so well for us with Reinhardt."

She narrowed her eyes at me, taking a step closer.

"Did you even try?" I shook my head. "Then maybe you should."

Realizing she was right, I reached into my pocket and pulled out the amulet. Then I stood on the sidewalk in the middle of Manhattan and closed my eyes, focusing all my attention on the world around me.

"Lead me to the one this belongs to," I whispered, my arms reaching out from my sides slightly, inviting nature's guidance to me.

A gust of wind blew my hair in my face, turning us in the opposite direction. Above us, sitting on top of a lamppost, a raven stared down at us. It cawed once as if to tell us to follow, then flew off. I could feel the breeze urging me to follow, so I did. Kat was at my side, the two of us running down the street, dodging pedestrians and traffic along the way. We kept the wind at our backs and the raven in our sights, switching directions as needed.

We ran for longer than I thought I could, fueled by adrenaline and the hope that we were nearing our target. That Reinhardt really was alive and still in NYC. Soon we would learn all too well that he was.

And he was not very happy to see us.

13

When our guide disappeared, we found ourselves standing outside a dilapidated building that had once been under construction—probably an attempt to create an up-and-coming apartment building. It looked like the project had been halted midway, leaving little more than a glorified set of beams and collapsing walls covered in graffiti; all gang related tags, from what I could tell.

"Well this is charming," Kat said under her breath as she scanned our surroundings. "I can see why he'd hide here."

"It makes sense, doesn't it?" I whispered. "Who would look for him here?"

"Who looks for a dead guy in the first place, Piper?"

She had me on that one.

"Fair point, but you see what I'm saying."

"I see trouble, that's what I see, and I'm starting to rethink my need for a distraction. Let's get this shit over with fast. I don't think you're invincible, and I hate getting shot, so I'd like to spend as little time as possible here."

I swallowed hard, looking at the wreckage we were

about to enter. It was dark in there and horribly dangerous. The chain-link fence surrounding it, with warnings posted everywhere, told me as much.

"Show me the way," I muttered under my breath. A moment later the enormous black raven landed on the fence only feet away from us. It looked at me curiously, cocking its head from side to side as though it were assessing me. It probably thought I was as crazy as I felt, knowing what we were about to do. For a moment I started having second thoughts. The raven cawed at me then took to the sky, circling us once before flying into what remained of the building.

Without pause, I followed, with Kat on my heels.

"Anything seems sketchy and we're bolting, got it? Something about this just feels off to me..."

"Understood."

"The last time I went somewhere with you alone, my car ended up in the East River—with us in it." She flashed me a smile to try and settle my nerves a bit, but even she couldn't hide her reservations. And Kat rarely had any.

"I know, Kat," I groaned, trying to keep up with the bird as it flew deep into the dark building. I could barely see what was around us, the shadows nearly consuming us. It was unnerving to feel so blind, but I pressed on anyway. I had to know if he was there.

I had to know if my plan could work.

The raven had long since disappeared from sight, but I could hear its calls from the bottom of a staircase, beckoning me to the basement. Every hair on my body stood at attention at the thought of going down there. Kat and I stood on the landing looking down into the dark chasm. Judging by what little I could see of her expression, she didn't seem excited about our next move.

"I'll go first," she announced before taking the first step down. "I'm starting to think that maybe bringing your overbearing boys with us wouldn't have been such a bad idea."

"Too late now," I countered, following close behind her.

"I'm well aware of that, thanks."

Her acerbic tone was duly noted.

With each step down, I could feel the tension building, the anticipation growing. It was almost too much to bear. I feared my lack of connection to nature down there. I wondered if what little power I seemed to have control over would be lost entirely in the concrete dungeon in which we'd soon be immersed.

Then, without preamble, I stepped onto the floor of the basement, greeted by the engulfing darkness. Seconds later Kat made a self-deprecating sound, followed by a weak beam of light coming from her direction.

I forgot she had a damn flashlight on her keychain.

"Can't you see in the dark?" I asked her, shielding my eyes from the light.

"Yeah, but this is too much for even me."

The beam was too weak to fully illuminate the vast space, but it gave us an advantage that we needed. Huddled together, we made our way through the vandalized space, careful not to trip on debris or walk into the crumbling support columns.

"I don't see anyone," Kat said under her breath. "But I hear them."

"Them?"

"Heartbeats. Plural."

It was then that her ray of light fell upon a far corner of the building, illuminating what could best be described as a colony of sleeping bags. Homeless—or addicts—had taken up residence in the building. Maybe both. The drug paraphernalia strewn around them most definitely spoke to the latter.

"Human?"

She sniffed the air.

"Yes..."

"But? I hear a 'but' in there somewhere."

"But something about the air in here is off. Can you feel it?"

I closed my eyes and tried to connect with what she was saying—tried to find a dissonance in the air around me. I came up short.

"I can't. Where is it coming from—"

A blast of power or wind or magic blindsided Kat and me, knocking us back until we found ourselves pinned against the cold basement wall on the far side of the room. I tried to move against it, but my efforts were futile. Kat's seemed to be as well, which spoke volumes.

"I think we found what you were looking for," she growled in the darkness. Unfortunately for us she'd dropped her mini-light with the force of the blow that now held us in place.

"And what, pray tell, would that be?" a male voice called out. His words echoed through the basement, filling the space with his power.

"Who are you?" I asked, doing all that I could not to sound as frightened as I felt.

"I think the better question here, my dear, is who are *you*?"

"My name is—"

"Don't tell him!" Kat shouted, cutting me off.

"I can see you're going to be a problem." He spoke those words just before Kat was ripped from my side. I felt the breeze she made as her body flew past me, swallowed up by the vast, dark space.

I never heard her cry out. She was just gone.

"Now I will ask you this only once more: who are you?"

I swallowed hard against my rising fear.

"Piper. My name is Piper. I've come here looking for someone."

"And who might that be?"

"Reinhardt, former lord of the warlocks."

Silence.

"Reinhardt is dead." His tone was as cold and rigid as the corpse he told me I sought.

"I need to see him."

"Then I suggest you find his body, wherever Kingston left it to rot."

"I have something for him."

"What could you, muddled mess of magic that you are, have to offer him, if he were indeed alive?"

"Why should I tell you? What I have is for Reinhardt alone."

Laughter boomed through the basement.

"She fancies herself brave," he mocked. I could hear his heavy footfalls get louder as he approached me, and my chest tightened. I desperately wanted light in that moment. I needed to see the face of death that stalked me.

"Let me see him," I whispered under my breath, doing all I could to focus on that request and not the ever-nearing supernatural who seemed determined to harm me.

I heard the raven caw in the darkness before a slow-burning orb of light began to glow from that direction. It was as if a small part of the sun had broken off and fallen into the basement where I found myself trapped. Soon it turned the entire space from pitch black to the warm golden hue of dawn just as the sun peeks over the horizon.

I could now see my captor.

Shrouded in layers of filthy, tattered clothing stood a tall, formidable man with a wildness in his grey eyes that sent shivers through me. There was a paranoia in there; one I had seen in Merc just before he'd nearly beaten me to death. If this man before me was indeed the warlock I sought, I started to have second thoughts about my plan.

A lot of them.

"So now you can see me," he said, eyes narrowed to slits in anger. "But I can also see you. And what I see tells me so very much."

"You are Reinhardt, aren't you?" I ignored his taunting and tried to ascertain that he was indeed the one I was after.

"Tell me something, Piper. You say you have something for the former warlock lord. What could you possibly have that he would want? Your little parlor tricks don't impress me."

"Something I got from Kingston."

His eyes went wide at the mention of that name. Reinhardt had unwittingly taken the bait.

"Where is he?" he snarled, lunging toward me.

"*Dead*."

That word stopped him cold.

"Not possible."

"I think he might argue that point, if he could. But that's hard to do when you're buried somewhere near the Earth's core."

His expression turned from anger to disbelief.

"That would take an immense amount of power to do. I can think of only a handful of beings capable of it. So tell me, Piper... who did it?"

I paused for a moment, wondering if telling him the truth would bite me in the ass. I could practically hear Kat screaming at me in the back of my mind to play dumb—be evasive. Do all the things I used to do to survive. But as he pressed nearer to me, I did the one thing I knew I shouldn't.

I told him the truth.

"I did."

His laughter ricocheted off the walls of the dank basement. The sound was harsh and loud and terrifying.

"You must think me a fool. Do you, Piper? Do you think I'm a fool?"

His hand wrapped around my throat, and fear pierced every cell in my body. He sounded like Merc had once. And I had no doubt that he intended to accomplish the very thing that Merc nearly had.

I was about to die.

With my vocal cords trapped under his vise grip, I could not speak the words I wanted to—anything to call something forward to save me. As I dangled from his extended arm, the force previously holding me against the wall no longer in play, I reached into my shirt and pulled forth the shattered amulet: the one that had once belonged to Reinhardt.

The second he laid eyes on it, he released me.

Gasping for air, I pulled the chain up over my head and clutched the talisman in my hand. I tried to stand to face him, but the lack of oxygen proved too much for me, so I cowered against the wall, crouching down beside it.

"I said... I had something... for Reinhardt," I wheezed, trying my best to speak between breaths. "I took this... from Kingston. Right before... I killed him."

He looked from the amulet to me, and back again. Then

he took a step in retreat, his confidence in the situation temporarily shaken. I'd scared him with the truth.

"You are the one he was after," he said, his voice as distant as his gaze. "You are the one that started all of this."

"I never wanted any of it," I told him, finally able to push myself up to stand. "I just wanted to be left alone. But Kingston couldn't let it go. He had to best me. And he died trying." I held out the pendant, offering it to him. Again he looked at it, then me, then back at the source of so much power. Power that was now broken. "You are Reinhardt, aren't you?"

His expression hardened instantly.

"You did not come here just to give him this. You want something in return. What is it?"

"To be trained."

He inched closer to me, leaning his face toward mine.

"If you are powerful enough to destroy Kingston while he was in possession of this, then you don't need Reinhardt."

"I do need him. I can't fully control my powers. I don't know how. I can manage the small things without issue. Maybe even some midlevel magic. But the big things—like what I did to Kingston—they nearly consume me. I need a mentor. I need someone to teach me focus and control before the power I have burns me to ash one day." I let my gaze fall to the floor. "I almost let it once. Twice, actually. I can't afford to let that happen again."

He eyed me tightly.

"Not my problem. Maybe you should hunt down your parents and demand they train you. You'll either succeed in getting the mentorship you seek or die in the process. Either way, your problem will be solved."

"I'd love to do that if I knew who they were."

He pulled away from me to assess me.

"Interesting..."

"What's interesting?"

"I'll make you a deal, Piper. I'll tell you something about your parents if you act like this day never happened. You never came here. You never spoke to me. Sound fair?"

"Since you haven't admitted who you are, that seems easy enough."

He shot me an incredulous look before leaning in close to me, his lips at my ear.

"You have warlock blood in you."

He pulled away and smiled at me. It was a smug and evil contortion of his mouth that let me know that there was no good in him to be found. Not a charitable bone in his body. He may not have confirmed my suspicion, but I knew he was Reinhardt. I also knew he would never help me.

"How do you know my father is a warlock?" I asked, grabbing him by his sleeve to halt him. My gesture earned me another blast of force that drove me once again into the wall behind me.

"Because this amulet was imbued with the power of my kind. Only my kind can wield it because only the blood of my kind can hold it."

I let his words sink in deep, past my fear and anger and loathing of the being before me. My father was a warlock. My warlock father had abandoned me. And one of his kind had hunted me for years in an attempt to wipe me from the face of the Earth.

That could not have been a coincidence.

"As for Reinhardt, I'll be sure he gets this," he said, turning to walk away from me for what I could only assume would be the last time. "And remember, Piper. This day never happened." Those words had a weight to them that settled on my mind uncomfortably.

Minutes later I found myself standing in a dark basement, frightened out of my mind.

And I had no idea why.

14

I made my way out into the daylight to find Kat waiting for me on the opposite side of the chain-link fence. When she looked at me, I could tell she was just as confused as I was.

"What the fuck are we doing here?"

"No clue."

"Did we come here for a reason? Are we lost?"

"I have no idea, Kat. I keep trying to think of why I was just in the basement of this rundown building, but my head just hurts when I do and I don't come up with an answer."

"Yeah. Me too."

"Do you remember where the car is?"

She looked thoughtful for a moment.

"Hmm... kind of. But I can smell our way back if I need to."

"Great. Let's get out of here. This whole thing is creeping me out."

"My sentiments exactly... except I'd have added a swear or two for good measure."

I laughed through my unease. Kat had always had a way

of settling me down when little else could. The girl was inappropriate humor and lack of tact all rolled up into one.

I adored her for that.

About twenty minutes later we found ourselves beside her newly restored car: the one I could remember plummeting into the East River just as plain as day. That memory was clear. What we'd just been doing in Manhattan, not so much.

"Is your memory getting a bit clearer?" I asked Kat over the hood of her Boxster.

"Yes, but damned if I can remember what we were doing in that building."

"Yep. Same problem here."

"Somebody's fucked with us, that much I know. How and why and who, though, remains a mystery."

I rolled that thought around in my mind for a moment.

"For now," I mused, thinking that there had to be a way around whatever magic had stolen our memories. I closed my eyes and muttered to myself, "show me what my mind can no longer see."

A flash of memories assaulted my brain, accompanied by an excruciating headache.

The final image I saw was Reinhardt walking away from me. The self-satisfaction he felt was evident in his swagger. He thought he'd bested me. He was in for a rude awakening.

Kingston had thought he'd bested me too.

I thought of how much I'd enjoy wiping that smug look Reinhardt had worn right before he'd erased my memory of him clean from his face. I vowed right then and there to do just that. If Reinhardt thought he'd seen the last of me, he was sadly mistaken. I was born of a warlock father. I had the power to show for it. And he'd just given me a taste of that power that I yearned to control. If anything, he'd made my desire to find him again even stronger.

"What's going on, Piper? Where'd you go? You've been zoned out for the last minute or so, not answering me when I called you."

"I remember why we came here. Why we were in that building."

"Great! Care to share?"

"Get in the car. We need to head back to the mansion."

"Tell me. Now." It wasn't a request.

"We found Reinhardt and the bastard wiped our minds of the whole thing."

"Except he didn't bank on you being powerful enough to override him." The smile on her face as she realized that truth was priceless. It held pride in me and vengeance for him all at the same time.

"I plan to use that hubris against him, but we need to get home before the boys call bullshit on our grocery cover and completely freak out."

"I'm pretty sure they'll call bullshit when we walk in with no food, Piper. And we do need to restock the kitchen."

"Really? You want to go grocery shopping right now?"

"Hell no," Kat said with a wink before hopping in the driver's side of the sports car. "Send your wolfy boyfriend out for them later, since he seems to know this city so well. We've got a warlock to hunt down."

"God I love you," I said, climbing into the passenger's side.

"It's a rough job, but someone has to do it."

Though she sold her joke well, I could feel the undercurrent of truth she believed it held. Kat knew the inevitable was coming; that she would be ousted from the home she'd shared with her fallen mate. It was why she was ecstatic about putting off her return.

"Kat—"

"It was a joke, Piper. Relax."

"You don't have to leave," I said softly. "There's a way for you to stay."

"Yeah? What's that? Bind myself to Dean? He's hot as hell, but something is not right with that one."

"No, I don't mean bind yourself to Dean."

"Then what do you mean, Piper? Because I think you know all too well what's going to happen to me."

"You could join Knox's pack. He and I already talked about it—"

"You did what?"

She shouted at me so loudly that pedestrians on the street stopped and stared at us.

"I simply mentioned what would happen to you. That's all."

"And he said what? That he'd save me?"

"No, Kat. I told him you don't do white knights."

"Damn right I don't. I don't need a male to protect me. I'll do just fine on my own."

"I know you would, Kat. That's not what I'm implying. I'm just saying that, if you're not ready to leave the house for whatever reason, there's a way around it. One Knox is open to."

"He's using me as a pawn to get into your pants again, Piper."

"I think that's a bit harsh—"

"And I don't. I know he was there for you when you needed someone on your side, and I'm thankful for that. I really am. But there's something about him I don't trust, and I can't shake that feeling."

"I don't want you to go, Kat," I whispered. "I need you."

She let out a heavy sigh.

"I need you too, but I also need you to pull your head out and read between the lines."

"You didn't trust Merc either. Do you trust anyone?"

"You. Jase and Dean... Jensen..." She paused for a second to collect herself. "As for the guys you sleep with, it's not looking good."

"Just consider it, okay? For me?"

She fired up the car's engine, revving it a few times to calm herself down.

"I'll consider it."

"Thank you."

"Don't thank me yet."

She pulled out into traffic, squealing the tires as she did. We drove through the city, headed where the wind blew us, all to find the warlock that didn't want to be found. An epic game of cat and mouse was afoot. But this time I wasn't the mouse.

And I had no intention of falling into a trap.

15

We wove through the city on an epic goose chase for two hours before we reconsidered our plan. I wondered if Reinhardt had used some spell to throw off my magic tracker. There was no way he could have covered that much ground on foot. It seemed odd to have done that, given that he'd made sure we didn't remember anything. It made me wonder just how paranoid the warlock was. Regardless, our manhunt was cut short until we could figure out a better way to corner the warlock and make him see reason.

That training me was in our collective best interest.

Kat and I had blatantly lied to the boys when we'd left, and I wondered if they'd sent out a search party in our extended absence. I pulled out my phone to see how many messages I had. Right on cue, it began to buzz with an incoming call from Knox.

"Hey, we're on our way home now."

"Did you buy the whole store? I mean, I know we need a lot of food, but that's some impressively thorough shopping."

Kat flashed me a sidelong glance that told me it'd be better if I came clean now rather than when we got back. I was inclined to argue that point but didn't. She'd have snatched the phone out of my hand and told him herself.

"About that..."

"What? I'm not going to like this, am I?"

"Nope."

A growl.

"Truth..."

"Kat and I might have lied a bit when we told Jagger and Foust that we were going to get food."

"Go on." He managed to keep a lid on his growing rage, but I knew it was there regardless.

"Remember that amulet of Kingston's—"

"Of course I do."

"Well... we thought we'd see if we could track down its rightful owner."

"The dead warlock?" he asked, his tone incredulous. "You went out to find a dead guy?"

"Yeah... except it seems like he's not so dead."

"Are you saying you found him?"

"Kinda. I can't guarantee that we did for sure, but it looks that way."

"I feel like there's another 'but' coming my way."

"There is, in the form of 'but he took the amulet and wiped our minds clean of the whole thing'. He didn't bank on my power being strong enough to override it, but by the time that happened, he was long gone. We couldn't track him after that."

"So he just disappeared into thin air?"

"Yep."

"With the amulet?"

"Bingo."

"... Fuck."

"I'll get it back. I still need to find him and convince him to help me with my powers."

"Doesn't sound like he's too keen on that idea."

"Keen or not, I have to make him see that I'm valuable to him. Somehow."

"No. No way, Piper. You don't hand yourself over to some half-cocked Magical without more of a plan than that. You know nothing about this asshole other than what you just learned and that sure as fuck doesn't seem very promising."

"He's hiding out, Knox. He's either scared or smart enough to know that he needs to keep a low profile after everything went south between the warlocks, and I just threatened his ability to do that. We're probably lucky he didn't try to do worse."

Another growl.

"We'll talk about this when you get back. I need to go kill something in the meantime."

"Not the bear!" I shouted at him.

"The bear's safe. Can't make promises about anyone else," he said, then promptly hung up the phone.

"I think he took that well," Kat said dryly.

"You're the one that wanted me to tell him over the phone!"

"And this outing was your idea."

"You said you wanted a distraction! A chance to hunt something down."

"True, but it was still your idea. I just agreed to go. To have your back."

"Doesn't seem like you've got my back with Knox," I mumbled under my breath. She merely shrugged in response. "Traitor."

"Nope. I'm just not in the mood for a testy werewolf, so I'll be avoiding that shit when we get back. If he comes at me hard, he's going to find out how unpleasant I can be when pushed."

I exhaled hard.

"Fine. You're right. It was my shitty idea. I'll take the heat for it."

She smiled, staring out the front of the car while her hand rummaged around for something in her pocket.

"It wasn't a shitty idea. It was a great one. And I don't think all is lost." She turned that smile directly on me. It was wry and rebellious and promised to get us into more trouble than we already were. She pulled her hand from her pocket and held out a piece of soiled grey fabric. "Recognize this?" I looked at it with a scrunched expression, my nose turned up at the smell. "I may have swiped a chunk of that asshole's nasty clothing. I found it while you were talking to Knox. Reinhardt might be able to jam up your tracking system, but he can't fuck with mine. And if you play your cards right, I think you could convince that pack of yours to help us hunt him. Maybe he can hide from the two of us, but not from fifty werewolves."

"You're a genius, Kat!"

"Yep. Now you need to get Knox to play ball, because we're not doing this shit again without reinforcements."

"I'll get him on board."

"Merc too?"

I sank back into my seat.

"One step at a time, okay?"

"You haven't talked to him about things, have you?"

"When would I have done that, Kat?"

"I heard you two in the kitchen."

"Yeah, well... that was short-lived. We are overdue for a long conversation, but I don't know about bringing this up. It just seems like another distraction—one that I don't know how to navigate because he'll want to help, and then I'm right back stuck between him and Knox. It's so stressful. I don't want to hurt anyone, but I think that's all I do when they're around each other. And that hurts me."

She was silent for longer than I expected. I was prepared for a potent comeback about sucking it up and picking between them. About ripping off the Band-aid and moving on with life. When I didn't receive it, I turned to look at her somber profile as she stared straight ahead. With every second she didn't speak, my unease grew.

Kat wasn't one for contemplation, or thinking before speaking, for that matter.

"I think you have to take care of yourself, Piper. Maybe that's selfish, but you can't afford not to be. I'm looking at your situation from a very different perspective now, and I see just how difficult it must be for you. I know you have feelings for both of them: genuine feelings. And I know you didn't ask to be in this position. In fact, you're about the only female I know who wouldn't relish being stuck between those two, but that's just not who you are. You care deeply for those you love. Just make sure that you don't get lost in that equation. Remember that at the end of the day, without them, it's you against the world."

"So choose wisely." She nodded. "I'll tell Merc," I said quietly.

"Good. Just make sure I'm not around for that either."

She turned and flashed a playful smile at me.

"I hate you sometimes," I groused, folding my arms over my chest like a pouting child.

"Mission accomplished."

By the time we reached the mansion, I'd resigned myself to the fact that I was about to have not one, but two horribly awkward conversations. Necessary, but awkward nonetheless. Full disclosure was the name of the game from that point on. Brutal honesty the plan.

And it would be brutal.

16

"One of you start explaining," Knox said the second we walked through the door. He and a few of the others were waiting for us on the grand staircase that led upstairs out of the foyer. I looked over at Kat, who shrugged at me and started down the hall toward the kitchen.

"I said you were on your own," she said over her shoulder.

"You really are a traitor!" I yelled after her. A laugh echoed back toward me, her only response to my outburst.

I took a deep breath and turned back to face Knox, who was now standing right in front of me, Jagger and Foust flanking him. Foust wore a patronizing expression, while Jagger looked deeply concerned by my actions. Knox, not surprisingly, just looked pissed off.

The conversation promised to be every bit as much fun as I'd expected.

"Tell me again why you lied to them and then went off on your own to do something totally reckless with the loose cannon in the kitchen?"

"Would it have been reckless if Reinhardt were actually dead?"

"Piper," Knox groaned, rubbing his hand over his face. He was trying his best to tamp down the frustration he felt, but it looked to be taking almost every ounce of energy he had.

"All right, all right!" I said, exhaling hard. "What do you want me to say, Knox? That it was easier for me to go with Kat? That I wouldn't get a lecture about danger before being shut down? That I knew Kat would be down for finding the hopefully-not-dead warlock? She's been through hell—one I hope to never understand. I knew she needed an outlet for the emotions she won't process any other way, so when I saw the amulet sitting on my dresser, I thought that maybe, just maybe, we could kill two birds with one stone. Find Reinhardt and get answers—preferably by force, for Kat's sake."

Knox's blue eyes practically burned through my skin as he stared at me, assessing my words.

"Truth."

"Yes, well, I am capable of it from time to time, but you seriously need to bring it down a notch or five, Knox. We're fine. I know I'm not in full control of my powers, but I'm far from helpless." My words came out a little more heated than I'd meant for them to, but I had a point. One he needed to hear.

Judging by his response, it wasn't one he enjoyed.

"This was so much easier when you needed me," he said to himself, running his fingers through his hair until they interlaced behind his neck. He craned his head back until he looked up at the ceiling, exhaling hard. "I don't know how to navigate this new dynamic, Piper. It goes against everything in my nature to stand on the sidelines, especially when it comes to someone I care about—someone I view as mine to protect."

"I do need you, Knox." My words were soft and true, and he looked down at me with hopeful eyes when he heard them.

"You have to understand why I'm frustrated with you."

"Of course I do. I knew you would be the second we drove off. In the spirit of honesty, the truth is I hoped you wouldn't find out."

"But I did—"

"Because I told you."

"Because you got caught."

"Minor detail."

Jagger pressed his lips together in a weak attempt to hide his amusement with our argument. He failed miserably and let out a childlike giggle that made me smile despite the angry alpha looming before me. Knox looked over his shoulder at Jagger and silenced him with a single glare. His freckled cheeks burned so bright they almost matched his hair.

"So what else do you have to report that you haven't already told me?"

I ran through our brief conversation in my mind and realized I'd left out at least two major things.

"Kat snagged a piece of fabric from his clothing so we can hopefully track him down," I said, trying to sell that fact as the positive it was in an otherwise shitty scenario. "All of us."

"Anything else?"

I took a deep breath, unsure how to say what I was about to say with any amount of tact. Eventually I gave up and just spit it out. Maybe that approach would be appreciated.

"I'm half warlock..."

The three wolves pulled away from me, shock on all their faces.

"Come again?" Knox said, eyes narrowing to scrutinize me more closely.

"The guy we found—the one that may or may not actually be Reinhardt—he said I had to be part warlock to handle the amulet."

"Well fuck me running," Foust said on an exhale. "I did not see that coming."

"Maybe he's lying," Jagger offered, looking uncertain as he said it.

"Maybe he's not," Knox replied, his eyes still fixed on me. "Which just makes the whole thing with Kingston that much more fucked up. Why would he try to kill the daughter of his own kind?"

"Maybe because the problem wasn't that she was part warlock," Foust said, drawing all of our attention to him. "Maybe it was the other part that freaked him out."

"Whatever it was, he's dead now," I said, the bitter note in my voice plain. "And I don't see why this warlock in particular would lie about that. He didn't seem to know who I was in the least. He'd have no reason to lie."

"Warlocks are good at finding a reason to lie," Knox countered. There was something unsettling in the way he said those words, like he knew what it was like to be dicked over by one as well. Another thing we had in common.

"Either way, we need to find him. Whether he's Reinhardt or not—and I think he is and is just trying to hide his identity—I need to talk to him again. I need to get him to mentor me somehow, and if I'm half warlock, that only makes him a better candidate for the job."

"I don't like this," Knox replied, raking his fingers through his hair.

"I don't love the idea, but I can't control my power at its extremes, Knox, and you know it. You've seen it yourself!" His lack of argument was duly noted. "I don't know what else to do. If you have a better idea, please, I'm all ears. If not, we follow through with this idea—harebrained or otherwise. We need to find the mystery warlock."

Maybe it was the desperation in my voice or the beseeching look I gave him—the childlike need to find someone to help me fulfill my potential—but either way, Knox caved under the pressure.

"Okay. We'll find him, but not until I can do a little digging around myself first. Deal?"

I nodded.

"Deal."

"Good. Now you and I need to have a little chat about the bear."

"Grizz? Why? What'd he do now?"

Again Jagger let loose a giggle that alerted me to the fact that whatever Knox had to tell me wasn't ominous. In fact, quite likely the opposite. And I really needed a little entertainment in that moment.

"He took a dump on Knox's bed." Jagger barely managed to get the words out before he broke out into full-on hysterics. He collapsed to the floor at Knox's feet, holding his stomach while tears rolled down his freckled cheeks.

"Oh boy..."

"He seems to be unhappy with something I've done," Knox said, shooting a scathing look at the wolf on the floor before turning back to me. "I was hoping you could figure out what so that it won't happen again."

I let out the breath I was holding.

"So you didn't hurt him?"

"I said I wouldn't, didn't I?"

"Yeah, but... that was before he shadoobied on your sheets." Foust let out a chuckle at my comment before trying to cover it up with a cough. "You know what," I continued, "doesn't matter. I'll talk to the surly bear. I think he's just super frustrated at being left behind all the time."

Knox's expression soured.

"I completely understand."

"You know what? I think I'll go find him right now. And then I'll clean up your room."

"Don't bother," Knox replied. "I think Ginger McGiggles over here has earned that honor."

Jagger's laughter quickly cut out.

"Aww, c'mon Knox."

"Not so funny now, is it?" The alpha let a half smile curl his lips before walking up the stairs. I was close behind him, breaking away to go look for the rogue bear leaving presents for the alpha. I wondered if I was going to have to search Merc's room for gifts from the grizzly.

My day kept taking the most bizarre turns.

17

Grizz was nowhere to be found.

Whether he was pouting or hiding, I couldn't be sure. But what I did want to make sure of was that he hadn't given Merc's bed the same treatment and gotten himself killed because of it. At that hour I wasn't sure if Merc would have been in bed or not, so I took a chance and sneaked into his room just to give myself some peace of mind. His room appeared empty when I pushed the door open enough to stick my head in. Though it was dark, I couldn't see a figure in the bed, so I tiptoed across the floor to search it quickly for bear droppings, letting out a sigh of relief when I didn't find any. Knowing that Grizz was no fan of the vampire, it made me question exactly what Knox had said to him to make him so angry.

With that thought in mind, I turned to sneak back out of the room and ran right into the person I had hoped to avoid. I couldn't see Merc's expression in the darkness, but I imagined it was a mix of concerned and curious. He wore that one a lot around me.

"I can explain," I said, the words falling from my mouth in a hurry.

"You don't need to. This room is far from off limits to you."

"I just—well, you're not really going to believe this when I say it, but—I came to see if Grizz pooped in your bed."

The pause that dragged out between us made me fidget. I really wished I could have seen his face.

"I'm not certain I want to know the answer to this, but why would he have done that?"

"Because he did it to Knox."

"Interesting..." he said, walking back toward the door. He flipped on the light switch, then dimmed them so they weren't so harsh. "I thought the bear liked the alpha."

"He does, but they tend to have differences of opinion."

"I can empathize with your furry friend on that one."

I let out a sigh, not loving the direction our conversation had taken. I knew Merc and Knox didn't like each other. That truth was seared into my brain; I didn't need a reminder.

"I should go," I said, heading toward the door.

"Piper," Merc said, stepping in front of the me. "I'm sorry. I know this is not easy for you. I don't mean to make you more uncomfortable with my comments."

"I have to go find Grizz."

"The bear is fine. He's in the kitchen with Kat. She's hand-feeding him grapes."

"Oh. Okay... thanks." I waited for him to step aside. When he didn't, my chest tightened a bit. Unable to meet his eyes, I stared at the door beyond him. "What do you want, Merc?"

"To tell you something I've been meaning to since you returned home but have not had the opportunity."

"What's that?"

"How proud I am of you."

My heart stopped for a beat.

"Why?" My reply was just a whisper. I pulled my gaze up to his eyes and locked in on them. There was a depth of sincerity there that I'd only seen once before—when we were bonded by the king. I had to turn away from them so I could think.

"For escaping me. For surviving. For finding a safe place to start over," he said as he moved toward me. I could feel the pull with every step he took. "You are so strong, Piper. So much stronger than even I dared believe. You did what no one else could have done. You not only escaped me, but you escaped our bond. And because of that, you lived." He stood so close behind me that I knew if I leaned back a fraction of an inch, our bodies would touch. I resisted the desire to be connected.

"Why did you leave that night—in Alaska? Why did you just disappear?" I asked him, shifting my weight backward a touch.

"What choice did I have, Piper?" he countered softly. "After all I did to you..." He cut his reply short, then exhaled heavily. The gentle breeze it caused ruffled my hair.

"I was right," I said aloud. "You left out of guilt." I turned to see if my assumption was plain in his expression. Not surprisingly, it was. From his sad eyes to the slump of his shoulders, Merc wore his guilt like a cloak of shame.

"Of course. Why else would I have gone?"

"I don't know, I just—"

"I laid my hands on you. Beat you. Paralyzed you, if only for a moment. Had the others not come, and had you not fled, I have no doubt in my mind that I would have succeeded in what Kingston had planned."

"You would have killed me..."

"Yes," he growled, his tone laced with self-loathing.

"What you did to me... it wasn't your fault," I said, fighting hard to maintain eye contact with him. The depth of grief in his eyes was almost too much to bear.

"I did those things—no one else," he argued, his expression bleeding to the mask of indifference he defaulted to.

"Because Kingston *made* you do them. I know you would have never hurt me otherwise. Even when I ran—when I was running—there was a tiny part of me that doubted you would kill me."

"I'm glad you ignored it."

"It seemed as though the farther apart we were, the easier it was to push those niggling feelings away," I explained. "And the dreams kept the fear alive."

"Dreams?" he asked, the shifting of his weight behind me causing the wood floor to creak in protest.

"Of you... at the top of the staircase. The boys were holding you back."

"The night you ran."

"Yes."

Again, I felt the floor groan beneath me. Merc was agitated. On edge.

It made me wonder.

"It surprised me how vivid they were. And how they were always the same." I looked up at him and was met with his stoic stare. But there was something behind it; something lurking just below the surface. A knowledge. An understanding. I could see it in his steel-blue eyes.

"They weren't dreams, were they?" Silence. "You," I exhaled. "You sent those visions to me. You wanted me to run. Wanted me to be afraid."

"I wanted you *safe*," he corrected. "And safe was far away from me."

I stood there, jaw sagging slightly at the knowledge that Merc had been spurring me on the whole time.

He reached his hand up as though to touch my face, but dropped it just shy of making contact.

"I've lived in solitude for so long, both self-imposed and otherwise, that I fear language is no longer my ally. The spoken word no longer serves me as it once did. With you, I resorted to sharing my feelings in a different way."

"I don't understand..."

"The night after we were ambushed in the alley, do you remember it?"

Remember it? That was an understatement. I'd dreamt of him and me going at it like rabbits. The next day when I saw him in the kitchen, I was still blushing.

"Yes."

"Did you dream of anything memorable?"

"Yes," I replied, my tone breathy and low.

"I thought so. I could see it in your eyes the next day. There was an intimacy to your stare that only someone who has shared themselves with another can hold."

"Are you saying that that was actually your dream? That I dreamt your dream?"

"You dreamt my fantasy until reality intervened."

"Kat," I muttered under my breath. "Kat came into my room and woke me."

"And your conscious mind broke the connection."

"You wanted me to want you," I said, my tone almost accusatory.

"No, Piper. I wanted you to know that I wanted you," he said, stepping closer. "My brothers had told me of your past —your trials. I knew you had been hurt beyond measure, and yet you sat before me in the club that night virtually unafraid. Even after the warnings you were given, you saw me more as a curiosity than something to fear. There was something so alluring about that. And then in the alley, faced with impending death, you feared more for Jase and Dean than yourself. You ran toward the battle when you should have already been miles from it."

"You made it stop that night. Kingston figured that out. That's why he did what he did to you."

"I felt the bars of the door behind you in that alcove giving way under my grip. I could not lose you to the storm." His expression fell, sadness overtaking it. "And yet I lost you anyway. Kingston still succeeded."

"You haven't lost me," I whispered. His eyes widened for a moment, then narrowed. "You think our bond has been severed—that mine has, at least—but it hasn't. I still feel the pull to you just as strongly as I did the night the ceremony was carried out. The night I drank your blood."

Once again he reached for my face, this time cupping it gently. Reverently. The hopeful look in his eyes was more than I could take. I closed mine and turned toward his touch, pressing my skin more closely to his.

"I thought..." he started, cutting himself off. I could hear the trepidation in his voice. "I thought that perhaps, given what you are, that the ties were not as strong for you. That I would be bound to one who was no longer bound to me."

"Not true," I assured him. "I still feel it. There was just so much—"

"Shhh," he said, soothing my rising anxiety. "You owe me no explanation."

Unable to bear the separation any longer, I threw my arms around him and pressed my face tightly against his chest.

"Maybe I don't owe you an explanation, but I do owe you something," I said, my voice muffled by his body. He pushed me away just enough to stare down at me with a piercing gaze. Before he could stop me, I continued. "I forgive you, Merc. For everything. All of it."

"You can't," he breathed, his eyes wide with surprise.

"Yes, I can. And I just did."

"Piper—"

"No, I mean it. And if I can forgive you, then you can forgive yourself. Those crimes were not your own, Merc, and they died with Kingston." He stared at me, silent. "You once told me that my scars are a map of my past. That they tell my story. What happened between us—it's now part of *our* story. Good or bad, it doesn't matter, because we're here. We're alive."

"But not together."

I frowned for a moment. The sadness I felt at his words nearly undid me.

"Merc—"

"Your choices are not to be apologized for either. I left you little choice in the matter. You did what you needed to in the moment. I cannot fault you for that."

He kissed me lightly on the forehead before turning to walk away.

"I came back because I needed to see you. Because I needed some kind of resolution."

He paused, his back still facing me.

"And have you found it?"

"No," I whispered, my body a ball of nervous energy. I had no idea what I was doing; all I knew was, if I let Merc walk out of that room, it would mean so much more than it appeared to.

He turned around.

"What do you need to achieve it?" I could hear the need in his voice as he spoke, the low, husky tone one I knew all too well.

I was breathing hard—too hard—and he could see it. The change in his demeanor was plain. Without further provocation, he stalked back to me, stopping only inches away.

"I had given up hope on this," he said, fighting hard to restrain whatever urge had risen within him. "Given up on us. Should I, Piper? Should I walk away? If you tell me to, I will. For the crimes I committed against you, I would do that. But if you say no—if you tell me to stay—then I will fight for you. Whatever has developed between you and the wolf, I will eclipse that in a heartbeat. What will you choose, Piper? Which future do you want?"

I stared up at him, my heart in my throat. He had just laid it all out there, leaving it all on me. My mind raced, trying to filter through too many variables at once. Splitting pain shot through my skull. Then I felt his hands on my face, pulling me away from all of it—grounding me in the here and now. My strength. My rock.

"MERC!" a voice shouted from deep within the house. "We've got a fucking situation!"

He growled in response.

"We're about to," he said under his breath, leaning in toward me slightly. "You and I will continue this conversation later." He stormed out of the room with me hot on his heels. We didn't make it far before running into Jase and Dean, both wearing the same concerned expression.

"It's the fey," Jase said. "The queen is demanding an audience with those of us that trespassed in her world—her words, not mine."

"What does the king have to say about this?"

"He's not stupid. He doesn't want to go toe-to-toe with her any more than we do. He said to meet with her on neutral ground and see what she wants."

"Neutral ground?" Merc repeated, his tone incredulous. "Exactly where would that be? Does such a place exist at the moment?"

"That's what I want to know," Knox called out as he approached, Foust, Jagger, and Brunton flanking him. "If everything with the treaty has gone to shit, then there is no such space to have a meeting."

"She's up to something," Dean said, stating what seemed to be fairly obvious. Merc's eyes fell heavily on me.

"I think she wants a better look at the little Magical that shut her people down."

"You mean the assassin who killed her sentinels," I replied, swallowing hard. "Somehow I don't think she's going to be especially gracious about that."

"No," Merc said, still staring down at me. "I don't imagine she will."

"Then it's simple. We don't go," Knox declared, in his mind resolving the issue with that statement.

"It's not that simple," Jase countered. "Merc, do you remember anything from when you were taken? Anything that might tell us what she's after?" Again my blood-bound's eyes fell upon me.

"I have my suspicions."

"Me," I said softly. "You think she's after me."

He nodded once.

"I think news of your existence—your power—and your return has reached her spies. What better way to draw you to her than to take your mate?"

I could feel Knox bristle at the use of that word in reference to Merc and me.

"That makes no sense, though," I argued, trying to puzzle out why the queen of the fey would have wanted to come for me before I'd done what I did in Faerie. After, I understood, but before I killed her people? I couldn't put it together.

"Maybe Kingston was in cahoots with her," Dean said, offering up a solid motive.

"Possible, but not likely," Jase countered. "The queen has never favored the warlocks. She barely tolerates them. I don't think she'd have trusted Kingston if he'd come to her with information about you. Besides, she could have stolen his glory and taken you out herself. He'd have never risked forfeiting his chance."

"So we basically have no idea what she wants," I said, exhaling hard.

"Only one way to find out what the whore of Faerie wants," Kat said, striding toward us down the hall. "I say we go."

"Kat," Jase said, the sympathy in his voice so plain that it made me cringe. I knew he cared about her and how she was doing after Jensen's death, but he didn't know her like I did. Instead of gratitude for his concern, she was about to serve him his ass on a platter with her middle finger in the air.

She turned murderous eyes on him until he stepped back a pace.

"If you ever speak to me in that tone again, I'll cut your balls off while you're sleeping, got it? Jensen didn't coddle me, and I sure as fuck don't want you—or anyone else in this house—to do it on his behalf. If I want to walk my ass out of here and start shit with the queen of the fey, I'll do it because it puts a goddamn smile on my face, got it?"

Jase had the good sense to just stand there silently and

weather her storm. She was in rare form, even by Kat standards. More reckless than usual.

Exactly the type of person we didn't need with us when we met with the queen.

"So, like I was saying," she continued, acting as if nothing had just happened. "I say we go and see what she wants. She's on our turf now. If we bring enough iron with us, I don't think she'll be a problem."

"That is because you don't know her like some of us do," Merc replied, looking across the congregation to stare at Knox. To the alpha's credit, he didn't wither under Merc's stare. "She will have prepared for that."

"By what, wearing a tinfoil hat?"

"No. I imagine she will come here without actually coming here."

"The mirror..." Knox said. Merc nodded.

"It's her only safe play, so it really matters not where we meet. She'll send her guards, but she will not be with them."

"And we can't kill them?" I asked, thinking of how beautifully terrifying they had been when I'd last seen them.

"It would be unwise unless they make the first move." Merc's eyes drifted to Kat. "Can you contain yourself?"

She shrugged.

"Probably, but if she says something to piss me off, no promises."

"When are we supposed to meet her?" I asked.

"As soon as we pick a place, the king will get word to her."

"Central Park," I blurted out, clueless as to why. I didn't exactly have fond memories of the place, given what Kingston and his cronies had done to me there. Regardless, I'd put it out there and the others seemed fine with it, so Jase called it in. Moments later the king gave us the okay, with a note to be on high alert. Seemed the king trusted the queen about as much as I trusted him.

Not a great sign.

An hour later we all filed into a caravan of SUVs and made our way through the city to our predetermined location. Apparently Jase knew where we were headed, so we all followed behind him, silent and on edge. An ambush wasn't out of the question; I wouldn't have put that past either the king or the queen.

We walked until we reached a remote corner of the park. Jase flagged us over beyond a copse of trees. Knox and Merc followed him, with Kat and me right behind them. Everyone else pulled up the rear—except for Jensen, of course. He wouldn't be making the appearance for the queen.

With that grim reminder, we came around a bend in the path to find ten fey sentinels shrouded in darkness. They stepped forward, weapons drawn, when we appeared. In the center of their ranks stood a single fey holding a raw, unframed piece of mirror the size of the back of a chair. Merc had been right; the queen was smart enough to stay away.

"Well that sucks," Kat muttered under her breath.

"And here I thought it was a blessing."

From deep within the mirror came a glowing light. It illuminated the shaded area we stood in, highlighting each of us in its unearthly beam. The regal being I'd seen in Faerie during our escape stood in the center of it, her robes of blood red contrasted by the brightness. It was the queen that had come for us just before we'd escaped Faerie. She looked like an angel of death, standing amid her minions on the other side of the portal; and I imagined that wasn't too far off.

"You came," she said by way of welcome. "I so hoped you would."

"We were under the impression that our attendance wasn't optional," Dean said, doing nothing to hide his contempt for the bitch responsible for those that had taken his brother-in-arms. Jase put his hand on his brother's shoulder to calm him, the two of them sharing a silent conversation that ended with Dean giving Jase a tight nod. Then they both looked over to Merc, who stepped forward toward the fleet of fey the queen had sent.

Closer to the mirror.

"There you are," she said to him, her voice playful, like she was speaking to a child playing hide-and-seek with her. "Are you prepared to return now? Will you come willingly, I wonder, or will you cause the death of another member of your little group? This should prove interesting."

The glow of bloodlust and madness in her eyes was terrifying.

I felt Kat move beside me, and I clamped my hand down on her wrist as tightly as I could. I didn't want to use my magic in front of the queen again—something about doing so felt dangerous—but I wasn't about to let Kat start a fight she couldn't win. I had no idea what kind of tricks that bitch had up her sleeve, and I had no intention of finding out by serving Kat up to her and her minions.

"Stay put," I whisper-shouted at her. A low growl was her only reply.

Merc continued to stare down the queen, not saying a word in response to her, and it made me wonder whether he'd pulled the mute routine with her as he'd done with so many for so long. Maybe that was why she'd come back—she hadn't gotten whatever information she was after when she'd taken him.

The queen's feigned pleasantness fell rapidly from her face, leaving a façade of stone in its place. Her irritation grew with his insubordination, and I would have sworn that I could feel an icy breeze coming through the mirror.

"He's not going anywhere," Jase said, acting as Merc's spokesman. "We came to talk, not hand over our own."

"I think you might change your tune once I'm done with you, enforcer."

Her words were ice, and the blanket of cold enwrapping me felt like it was getting tighter by the second. Something bad was brewing. We needed to get out of there.

"Doubtful," Dean said, stepping closer to Merc. "And if you try to take him, you'll have a front row seat for the slaughter of your pretty fairies here."

"You must be the dumb one," she said, drumming her fingers on her leg. "Too bad. You look like you'd be fun to play with. Maybe if I sealed you mouth shut..."

"Enough bullshit," Knox growled. "If all you came here to do tonight was demand you get the vampire back, that ain't happening. Time for you to go, your fucking majesty."

"Now now, there's no need for such language, Trevor Knoxville. No need at all. In fact, I have to say I'm hurt by your tone. After all we've done together—after all we've done for each other."

All eyes fell on Knox, the tension in the air so thick I could barely breathe. Or maybe that was the fear that I was about to learn something about Knox's past that I couldn't unhear. Something I might not be able to overlook.

"Our past is our past. I didn't come here for a trip down memory lane. You wanted to see those that came for Merc, so here we are. And like I said, if you want us to hand him over, it's not going to happen. Period."

A wicked smile stretched so wide across her face it

looked as if someone had slashed her with a knife, leaving the wound to gape open. Nothing about it was human in appearance. Nothing about it was comforting.

"I think you might change your mind about that, *Trevor*." The queen leaned to speak into the ear of a fey next to her. He walked toward the mirror until suddenly he was standing in front of us. Just like that—there he was. The mirror itself was a portal.

My hair stood on end.

"Her majesty wants to see the girl."

"Good," Kat said, stepping forward. "Because I have a few things I'd like to show her."

"Not the wolf," the fey said, his androgynous voice floating over us like a leaf on a breeze. "The other. The Magical one."

Years of obedience reared its ugly head and I took a step forward, walking until I was wedged between Merc and Knox. I did what I could to look confident, but the queen's icy stare, even from a world away, made it impossible. I could feel my shoulders hunch and my chin begin to tuck. Knox slipped his hand up to the small of my back to calm me, and I could feel Merc's heavy gaze on me, so I looked up to meet it. With a single nod of his head, he told me all I needed to know. I could do this. I would be safe no matter what.

"Come forward," the queen said with a wave of her hand. "It's not like I'm going to bite."

I worked hard to keep my smart retort at bay as I took another step forward to the head of the group. The fey she'd sent was only paces away, staring at me with wide, inhuman eyes that looked curious and hungry and something else I couldn't quite place—and didn't think I wanted to.

"Call off your dog," I said, jerking my head toward him.

With a noise that sounded suspiciously like a whistle, the fey retreated back through the mirror until he was at the queen's side. She patted him on the head like a prized animal. My stomach rolled as I worked to keep the disgust I felt from my face. There was no way in hell Merc was going back there to be her prisoner—or an addition to her menagerie.

"Better?"

"What do you want?"

"I wanted to invite you to come and visit me. I'd like to know more about this creature who laid waste to twenty of my sentinels. I would love to know how you did it, but you didn't leave any alive for me to ask."

"Maybe if they hadn't attacked us in the first place, that wouldn't have happened."

"Maybe you shouldn't have invaded my realm uninvited, and I wouldn't have sent them for you."

I took a step closer to the mirror. Almost close enough to touch it.

"Piper..." Knox cautioned from behind me.

"I know," I replied in placation. "I just want her to see the look in my eyes when I say this. So that there's no confusion." Turning every bit of hatred I had for those that had killed Jensen on the queen, I spoke. "And maybe if you hadn't taken something that didn't belong to you, you wouldn't have forced our hand. If you try to take him again, I can assure you it won't end any differently."

The queen's dark eyes brightened and she laughed wildly while those around her stood like stone.

"Take him? I can assure you I did no such thing."

"I don't believe you," I replied, my words little more than a snarl.

Her laughter cut out in an instant.

"Perhaps you should ask him. Maybe he'll be more forthcoming with you—his *mate*."

Though I tried not to let doubt seep in, its icy cold hand was winding its way up my spine, stiffening it with every inch. I looked over my shoulder at Merc, who stood stoic as always, giving nothing away.

"Is that true?" I whispered. "That she didn't take you?"

"He didn't have a choice," Jase called out. I looked over at him as he stared at Merc, embroiled in a silent conversation. "He chose to go without a fight. He thought it would be easiest." He paused for a moment to look at me. "He thought it would be best—for you."

That icy hand of doubt clenched my heart, stopping it cold. Merc had given himself up to the queen for me. Because he'd thought we were truly over. Because he wanted me to be happy.

And he didn't think he was a factor in that equation.

With a deep inhale, I turned back to the queen, who couldn't have looked more pleased with herself if she'd tried.

"That changes nothing. You can't have him."

"Can I have you, then? Would you come in his place? It would give us such a wonderful opportunity to get acquainted."

"Not a fucking chance," Knox snarled, lunging forward.

"How interesting, Piper. Could it be that you have two alpha males wrapped around your curious little finger? Perhaps I've underestimated you. And as for you, Trevor, I suggest you remember who you're dealing with. Who you've dealt with in the past. I wonder if your new little toy would be so doe-eyed when she looks at you if she knew your dark secrets like I do. If she'd still stand by your side." Then the queen dropped her human face like a curtain, leaving behind an alien beauty that was nearly impossible to look upon. But I didn't look away. No way was I taking my eyes off her as she stormed toward the mirror. "Tell me, Trevor, did you run away because of what you did? Was the guilt so pervasive that you tried to escape yourself, running away to the backwoods like a coward?" She stopped right in front of the portal, her black eyes piercing as she stared right through me. "Or did you run because you never kept up your end of the bargain? I wonder..." Knox went stiff beside me. "Let me say this in the plainest terms, so that you all understand me. One of you will be returning to Faerie, and you will be doing so in one week's time, or there will be consequences. Severe ones. I'll leave you three to choose amongst yourselves, but this will happen." She turned her back to us and walked toward her entourage. "I'm sure you have a lot to discuss now, so I'll leave you to it. I'll be in touch."

With a flick of her wrist, the mirror went dark, then the reflective silver you'd expect of a mirror. The sentinels remained behind for a moment, still standing in their statuesque way. Then they filed through the mirror one by one until the final fey holding it drew it down over his body, the mirror itself disappearing the moment he was through. The whole thing was unsettling to watch.

A gentle hand on my shoulder drew my attention, and I turned to find Merc behind me, staring at me with concern in his eyes.

"What the fuck just happened?" I asked, the shock I felt thick in my voice.

"The queen's famous manipulations."

"I hate that bitch," Knox grumbled under his breath.

"So this really didn't have anything to do with us coming to get you, did it?"

"I would say not," Merc answered. "I was unable to reach her mind through the mirror, but something much more insidious is going on here. I'd bet my life on it."

"Well that's good because it might come to that," Knox said, starting off toward the park entrance. "She'll make good on her word. She's coming back for someone, and if we don't have someone to give her, shit will get serious real fucking quick."

"A fact I'm well aware of, *Trevor*."

Knox stopped dead to turn and stare down Merc.

"You got something you want to say, *Mercenary*?"

"I'm just curious as to how well acquainted you are with the queen."

"About as well as you are, by the look of it."

The two stared at each other for a moment before Knox turned and walked away, disappearing into the night. Merc didn't move.

"It will come to a choice between the two of us," he said gently. "Whatever the queen has up her sleeve if we don't go along with her plan is undoubtedly grand and devious."

"What are you saying?"

"I'm saying that either Knox or I will be heading to Faerie—and likely not returning."

Every ounce of blood in my face drained away.

"There has to be another way—"

"We have a week to find it. If we don't, I'm afraid that is the reality of the situation." He gave me a sad glance before looking away. "You cannot go. That much I know. The queen can never take you."

There was such finality in his tone that it piqued my interest. He knew something I didn't; something that made him fearful.

"What aren't you telling me, Merc?"

"It could be something; it could be nothing. Either way, your ignorance will help keep you safe, Piper. You must trust me."

Not waiting for my argument, he too walked off down the path, leaving me shrouded in darkness and surrounded by my growing anxiety and the fear that we wouldn't find a way out of the mess we were in. What I did know was that neither of them was going to Faerie to be the queen's prisoner. Come hell or high water, I was going to find a solution to our problem.

And that solution would come in the shape of a sketchy warlock who thought he'd bested me. He'd soon learn that I was so much more than he'd bargained for. He'd soon learn that I was a thing of nightmares.

18

"Kat!" I whisper-shouted at her, shaking her arm as she slept. "I need your help."

"Wha?" she mumbled, still deep in slumber.

Time for plan B.

Knowing it might not end well, I made sure I was far away from the bed when I launched a bucketful of water at her: ice-cold water. She shot off the bed in a flash, claws out, ready to kill.

"It's just me," I said, putting my hand out to stave her off. "I need your help."

"You need to start running," she growled at me, shaking the water from her hair.

"We can play chase later, Kat. You and I need to go find Reinhardt. Now. I think he might be our solution to the whole nobody-going-to-Faerie thing."

She stood on her bed, breathing hard, visibly trying to calm herself down. She'd always been edgy, but it had gotten worse since Jensen's death, which was understandable. She didn't have the protection of her bond anymore, and Kat was a survivor. I'd always admired her for that. I'd tried to learn from her—to be more like her in that regard.

"You know I'm going to kick your ass for that little stunt later, right?"

"I would expect nothing less. Now, can you go change and come with me?"

"What about the boys? Weren't we going to use them to help us find your elusive warlock?"

"Yes, but I want to try something else first."

"Try what?" she asked, still sounding annoyed. She hopped off the bed and walked over to her closet, snagging a towel from the doorknob. A second later she was naked, toweling off.

"I can't seem to track him for whatever reason. But maybe I can track the amulet."

She looked over her shoulder at me, curiosity in her eyes.

"Go on."

"Reinhardt—or maybe-Reinhardt—said that I could only handle the amulet because I had warlock blood in my veins."

"Interesting—"

"And I'm the one that broke it. Maybe I have a connection with it that we can exploit."

"Sounds like a possibility. I still think we should bring the others with us."

I exhaled hard.

"If I tell them what I want to do, I'll have to argue my point for God only knows how long before they might agree. And if they don't, they won't let either of us out of their sight, so the whole plan is botched."

"And you think he can help us out of the Faerie debacle."

"I think he's our best option, yes."

Kat pulled a tank top down over her body, skipping the bra option altogether.

"Okay, here's what we're going to do. We'll go to Knox and tell him that we have a plan that he can go along with or not, but either way, we're going."

"Um, Kat? Are you high? You have met Knox, right?"

Something dark ghosted over her expression before she pulled it back to her trademark shit-eating grin.

"Oh, I've met him all right. And that's exactly why he's going to go along with our plan."

"You're not making any sense right now."

"I'm making more sense than you want to know about," she countered, slipping her tight pants up and buttoning them. "More than he'll want to realize too."

She slipped on her favorite black boots and headed for the door. Grizz was waiting dutifully in the hallway for us. She gave his fur a tousle, then stomped her way down the hall, headed for the guest room that held Knox, Foust, Jagger, and Brunton. Instead of knocking, she kicked the door open in true Kat fashion and walked right in. The four of them were on their feet in a flash, eyes glowing in the darkness.

"Good. You're up," she said, standing in the middle of the room. Her eyes drifted over to Brunton, who must have been having one hell of a dream, and she smiled. "Some of you are *really* up..."

"Start talking before I start swinging," Knox growled. Apparently he was about as much of a morning person as Kat.

"We're going on a little scavenger hunt. Your services are requested—and by requested, I mean required."

She turned on her heels and walked back toward the

door, smiling down at me as she passed. Her hellion streak was out in force, and I couldn't help but wonder if we'd even make it to the vehicles without an all-out brawl breaking out. She still hadn't settled things with Brunton. I made a mental note to not let them sit anywhere near each other in the SUV.

"Piper?" Knox called to me. His tone was more even, but he was still pissed for sure.

"Just get dressed and meet us outside. I'll explain on the way."

I stepped out of the room and closed the door behind me. Grizz was right in my face, his big brown eyes shooting daggers at me. He knew he was about to be left behind again, and he was clearly not thrilled about that. His need to be at my side was starting to stress us both out because there was no solution to the problem.

I couldn't exactly take a grizzly for a walk down the street—not even in NYC.

"I'm bringing the boys with me this time, so don't worry." He nudged me with his nose, a low grumble escaping him. "I know it's not the same as you coming too, but you know the wolves won't let anything happen, right?" He let loose a wet snort that coated my arm with something I didn't want to think about. Instead, I wiped it off on my pants. "We'll figure out a way for you to help soon, buddy. I promise.

"Don't look at me that way! It's not my fault. You know it's not my fault." Judging by the look on his face, he didn't. "May I remind you that you're the one that insisted upon coming here?" He snorted in objection. "Well of course I wasn't planning to leave you behind, but you volunteered before I could say a thing about it. Don't put this all on me."

He sat back on his haunches with a harrumph, looking at me with sad eyes.

"This would be so much easier if you were supernatural, you know? You wouldn't feel so out of place all the time. I know you don't like staying here while we go out, and I really know how much you despise Merc. You've made that point well known, thank you very much. But still, I don't know what you'd have me do."

Grizz launched to his feet, leaning far back until he stood bipedal, blocking out the sun with his massive form. Then he growled loudly.

"I know you can fight. You were the main reason I was able to stop Kingston. But I can't have you get hurt, Grizz. I'd never forgive myself."

Cocking his head to the side, he dropped down to all fours and walked to me, nuzzling the side of my face with his own. It dwarfed mine in comparison.

"You'd never forgive yourself if something happened to me, would you, buddy? That's what you're telling me." He pulled away just enough to pin sad eyes on mine. With a sigh, I hugged him as well as I could. "We'll figure something out. I promise. Okay?"

He shook his head and walked away from me, clearly unhappy with my lack of a plan. I wanted to chase after him, but I had neither the time nor the words to make it better, so I made my way down the stairs and outside to join Kat, hoping that the boys would be in a better mood by the time they emerged from the mansion.

Kat still looked pretty pleased with herself, leaning against one of the black SUVs in the lot. The enforcers weren't back yet, but the sun would be rising soon enough, and I wanted to avoid crossing their paths if possible. We might be able to strong-arm Knox into coming along, but if Merc found out what I was up to, he'd throw me over his shoulder and take me back into the house.

"I think that could have gone better," I said, sarcasm thick in my tone.

"Really? I thought it was pretty spot-on, myself."

I opened my mouth to argue, but the slamming of the front door cut me off. I looked over my shoulder to find four rather irritable-looking wolves headed our way. I took a deep breath and prepared for the argument I knew was about to go down.

"Kat's sorry," I said.

"No I'm not," she replied.

"She's just on edge about what we're going to do—"

"The fuck I am—"

"So now that we've got the apologies taken care of—"

"You're going to tell me what this is about?" Knox asked.

"Yes. That." I stalled for a minute, trying to think how best to break my plan to him.

"We're going after the warlock who isn't really dead," Kat blurted out. I shot her a death glare and she smiled at me. "Not sorry."

"Clearly," I muttered under my breath. "She's right, though. I think that maybe Reinhardt could have an answer for our mess with the queen."

Knox's eyes narrowed.

"Why would you think that?"

"I don't know... because he seems to be one hell of an expert at disappearing. He's surviving under the radar. Surely he has to be sly enough to have some information that could help us."

"Piper, you don't even know who this asshole is, let alone his capability or willingness to aid in this."

"Well I'm not a hundred percent sure he's actually Reinhardt, but does that matter? He's a sneaky, conniving bastard who jumped us in that basement. That's exactly the kind of person who might be able to outsmart the queen. Plus he's got the amulet—and that's how we're going to track him."

"And then what? We'll ask him really nicely to help us out of the goodness of his heart?"

"No... not exactly. I hadn't really ironed out a plan for that yet, but I think if I can actually show him what I'm capable of doing this time, he might actually volunteer to train me. Like it would be in his best interest to have me as an ally and not an enemy."

"This is sketchy at best, Piper."

"I know that, Knox, but our options are limited. What else can we do? We need a way to shut down the queen because you're not going to Faerie with her, and Merc isn't either."

"Fuck... this is insane," he said to himself, raking his hand through his hair.

"Maybe it's not," Jagger said. Knox turned and pinned murderous eyes on the ginger-haired wolf, and he took a step backward. "I'm just sayin', Piper's no joke in battle. Maybe she could stand against the queen—with our help. And the help of this douchebag warlock."

"And maybe she'd get her ass handed to her," Brunton said. "There's no way to know what the outcome would be."

"I think it's Piper's call to make," Foust added. "And whatever she chooses, I'm with her."

Knox turned on him.

"Even if it's against my direct order?" The challenge in his tone was plain.

"You know I can't go against your orders, but I'm hoping it doesn't come to that."

"Can we just go find this shady fucker before the vampires show up and cause even more drama than you four are?" Kat groused. "I'm not in the mood for it."

"Knox," I said softly. "We're going either with you or without. What's it going to be?"

"I'm in," Brunton said, striding past Kat to the driver's side of the vehicle. The two glared at one another, the challenge clear in their gazes.

"Me too," Jagger said, following behind him.

"Knox?" Foust asked, looking to his alpha.

"Fuck!" Knox shouted in frustration. "Yes, fine. Let's find Reinhardt, or whoever he is, and get him to do whatever it is you think he can do for you, Piper."

"He'll help me," I said, lacking the confidence I'd hoped my voice would hold.

"I think you're putting a bit too much weight in your lineage there, Piper," Kat said, pushing off the back of the SUV. "But I hope you're right; that being part warlock will be enough."

Knox's eyes narrowed at me while Kat disappeared around the far side of the vehicle.

"You know this is crazy, right?"

"No crazier than anything else we've done over the past couple of days."

"Maybe crazier than you think," he said under his breath before storming off to the vehicle.

"Knox!" I called after him, but he wasn't having it. He kept walking and yanked open the passenger's side door, slamming it behind him. I stood there for a moment, staring over at Foust. "Am I missing something here?"

He shook his head.

"I don't know, Piper. But I think we're about to find out."

That was the understatement of the century.

Our search was remarkably uneventful; where it led, however, was less so. It wasn't long before we found ourselves in the same block as the portal to Faerie in Chinatown. I highly doubted that was a coincidence.

"Anyone else's hackles up right now?" Kat asked as she climbed out of the vehicle.

"Yep," Brunton replied.

The rest of us emerged a block away from the restaurant that held the portal to the queen. Looking around, I scanned the area for Reinhardt, but saw nothing.

"Help me find the amulet," I asked. The familiar caw of the raven was the response to my call. Sitting atop the nearest streetlamp, he watched us expectantly, as if waiting to make sure we were ready to follow. One nod in his direction and he was off. The six of us ran after him as he flew off toward the sunrise in the distance. We wound our way through some tight alleys and corridors, soon finding ourselves at a dead end. The concrete wall before us was at least ten feet high.

"So where is he?" Knox asked, frustration tainting his tone.

I closed my eyes and focused. I could hear the raven above me, cawing. He'd not led me astray last time, and I trusted he hadn't now. Reinhardt was there. I just had to force him out of wherever he was hiding.

When I opened my eyes, I looked up to the bird, whose focus was behind us on the building's brick wall. I turned slowly, making it look like I was still at a loss as to where he was, then started to pace back down the alley. Just as I was about to pass the spot the raven had shown me, I lunged toward the wall. Instead of meeting rough brick, my hands connected with fabric: fabric hidden by magic.

Fabric that belonged to Reinhardt's clothing.

He appeared in a flash, his grey eyes wide and angry.

"You again," he growled at me before flicking his wrist and sending me flying across the small divide to slam against the adjacent building. That time I definitely met brick. It dug into my back as I slid down it to the pavement.

"Drake!" Knox shouted, running to my side.

The warlock looked surprised to see the alpha. Almost sheepish.

"What are you doing here?" he asked, looking over as the rest of the crew approached looking none too happy.

"What are *you* doing here? And why do you have that?" Knox asked, pointing to the amulet. I awaited the answer as Knox helped me up. My head was reeling with questions and disbelief. He really wasn't Reinhardt. He hadn't been lying.

"You know her?" Drake, aka 'not Reinhardt', asked, ignoring Knox's question.

"Yeah, and if you fucking pull shit like that again, we're going to have a problem."

"She didn't say anything about you."

"You didn't exactly give me a chance last time we met," I countered, rubbing my back. "You were pretty big on being a creepy asshole at the time. An unhelpful—and ungrateful—one at that."

"You really were," Kat added. "I think you should apologize." She cocked her head, staring at him in the way she did right before she lost her shit on someone. Not-really-Reinhardt needed to tread lightly.

The warlock's lips pressed to a thin line of irritation.

"I apologize for our last meeting. Had I known you were —*attached*—to him," he replied, jerking his head in Knox's direction, "I would have behaved differently."

"If I'd known it would have helped, I would have led

with Knox's and my connection." The snark in my tone was hard to miss. "And why would knowing Knox matter anyway?"

Drake's eyes fell upon the alpha, full of curiosity.

"He and I have history."

"Of course you do." I looked over at Knox, my irritation with his secrecy written all over my face. "Is there anyone in this city you don't know? Have 'history' with?" He seemed amused by my use of air quotes.

"A few."

He clearly had no intention of elaborating on that, so I let it go. For the moment.

"Great! Now that we have that not at all ironed out, how about we get down to the other matter my friend came to you about," Kat said, continuing on as though he hadn't just apologized. "She needs training. She's part warlock. You're a warlock. I think you see where I'm going with this..."

"Yes. Training." Drake looked over at me, assessing something about me—something he didn't seem to really like, judging by the way his expression soured. "I will train her. On one condition."

"What's that?" Knox asked, taking a step toward Drake.

"That she fix this," he said, extending the amulet toward me.

"Me? I have no idea how to fix that thing."

"Then we have no deal."

"Do you understand what training is?" I asked, storming toward him. "It means I need help controlling my power. It means that you just asked me to do something that I don't know how to do—couldn't possibly do, even if I wanted to."

"Show me that you are worth training," he replied, meeting my approach until we were almost nose to nose.

Anger the likes of which I'd rarely felt boiled inside of

me—just as it had the night that I killed Kingston. It shot out from somewhere deep inside me, bleeding through my veins until my body no longer felt like my own; until my mind cared about little more than revenge.

"You want to see what I can do?" I asked, placing my hand on his chest. "Make him burn." A flame erupted on his chest—blue like the fires Kingston so loved to use—and started to engulf his clothes. He spewed forth spell after spell, the panic in his voice rising with every moment nothing happened. His eyes were wide with fear as he stared at me through the flickering flames.

"Piper," Knox called. "He can't help you if you kill him."

I wheeled on the alpha, pinning deadly serious eyes on his.

"Maybe I don't need him after all."

"I'll do it!" Drake shouted, his voice pinched with terror. I watched the flames dance around his face a little longer, mesmerized by their beautiful but deadly movements. "I said I'll do it!"

Though I didn't want to make them leave, I fought the urge to watch them engulf and destroy him.

"Make it stop!" I yelled, shaking my head to clear the dark thoughts away. Like the fire had never even happened, it disappeared, leaving Drake unharmed. With a couple of deep breaths, I felt more like myself, only terrified that I had been about to let a being burn before my eyes—that I'd wanted it to happen. "So am I worth training or not?"

Drake nodded his head frantically, his salt-and-pepper hair falling into his eyes.

"We can start immediately, but I fear I will need something in return—not for me, but for you. That power... it runs so deep. I don't have enough to keep it in check." He pulled the amulet out from under his shirt, the jagged vein running through the stone glimmering in the sunrise. "We need this."

"Fine. Let's get it fixed. What do we need... another stone?"

"No. We need someone to heal it."

"There's a catch in here somewhere," Kat said, taking a step closer. "What is it?"

"There is only one who can do such a thing," Drake said, his eyes willing me to see the truth he felt was so plain.

"Who?" I asked, afraid of the answer.

"She who made it. The queen of the fey."

Shit.

"That's kind of a problem since that's who I'm trying to get control of my power to face."

His expression went dark.

"I see no other way, Piper. I fear I cannot do what you ask without it."

"Surely not all your magic is tied to that thing—warlocks must be powerful without it. I mean, Kingston nearly killed me without it more times than I can count."

"Oh I have power, make no mistake about that. But yours is wild and untamed, and without the amulet, it will be nearly impossible to help you harness it." He smoothed his hair back and straightened to his full height, which was taller than I remembered. "The amulet was created with one purpose—to help the warlocks become even more powerful."

"Why would the queen do that? Wouldn't she be screwing herself somehow?"

"No," Drake said plainly. "Her powers are strongest in Faerie. Here she is no more powerful than I. The amulet was a gift to Reinhardt—a bargaining tool. She wanted an ally on Earth and chose to align with him."

"But that goes against the treaty," Kat said, realization dawning in her expression. Her eyes widened as she put the pieces of the puzzle together. I, however, was a step or two behind.

"Yes. It does."

"Did the vampire king know this?" Knox asked, an edge of anger in his voice.

"That I cannot say. But I know the king of the vampires is no fool. He has his spies, as we have ours. I have little doubt that he knew of their alliance."

"This is all great information, but it still leaves us with a broken amulet that we need fixed and a queen highly unlikely to help us."

"An impasse, I'm afraid," Drake said, looking as though he pitied me, if only a little. "I cannot promise that I alone can help you gain control."

Silence fell upon the group for a moment before Knox offered a plan B. One I hadn't considered.

"What if I can help?" Knox looked down at me with hopeful eyes. "Maybe our connection will help balance her."

Drake shook his head.

"I fear it might be quite the opposite. I'll need to work with her more to know for certain."

I pondered Knox's idea for a moment. It was solid but for one element. Knox seemed to help ground me in my power so I could pull forth more. Merc, on the other hand, seemed to be the one capable of pulling me away from it. I didn't need the wolf.

I needed the vampire.

"Merc can do it," I said, shying away from Knox's stare. "He's pulled me from the darkness before. He can do it again."

"Mercenary?" I nodded in silence. "You keep strange company, Piper."

"She's bound to him," Kat said. "I'd keep that in mind, if I were you."

Drake's eyes narrowed.

"I will indeed."

"So," I started, feeling awkward under his gaze. "You're willing to try, even though you think training me won't work?" He nodded. "Great! When are we going to start? Because I'm on a timeline here."

"I'll be in touch very soon," he said, exhaling hard. "And tell the vampire we may need him."

THE RIDE HOME was thick with tension. The six of us sat in the vehicle not speaking for the better part of the ride. It wasn't until the final few moments that Kat broke the silence; and she did so with a whopper of an observation.

"Anyone else in here thinking that it's an awfully big coincidence that Merc returned just before everything went to shit with the treaty? Because I can't stop pondering what that shady fucker Drake said about the alliance between the queen and Reinhardt. If they really were in cahoots, then that would threaten the fuck out of the king. Enough so that he might bring out his secret weapon."

"That would be a pretty big fucking coincidence," Brunton said in agreement.

"It also begs a question that can't leave this vehicle," she said. She looked over her shoulder at me in the back seat for a split second before looking back at the road in front of her. "Did the king have something to do with Kingston usurping Reinhardt?"

My blood went cold at her words.

"But if he did that..." I couldn't finish my thought, the scramble of ideas in my brain making it impossible to focus.

"Exactly," Kat replied.

The male wolves looked around at one another in confusion.

"What are we missing?" Foust asked me. I could feel his stare on the side of my face, but my mind was still reeling too hard to speak.

"A potential conspiracy," Kat said, looking at him in the rearview mirror. "One I intend to get to the bottom of."

"Not alone," Knox added. "You can't stand against the king on your own."

"Fuck no," Brunton added. "She doesn't get to have all the fun by herself."

"Piper," Jagger said from the seat to my left. "Are you okay? You don't look very good."

"I'm fine," I whispered, sounding anything but.

"Lie." Knox turned around in the passenger seat to face me. "What are you thinking?"

"If... if the king joined forces with Kingston, then he never cared that Kingston tried to kill me. He didn't do a damn thing to try and stop him."

"Or worse," Kat added before growling so loudly that it eclipsed the hum of the engine.

Her subtext slammed into me hard, knocking my breath away for a moment.

"You think he was a party to it..."

She merely nodded in response.

"But he took you in," Jagger said, trying to make sense of the nonsensical. His freckled face scrunched up in confusion before he looked at me with a fire in his eyes I'd never seen before. "How could he betray you like that? You of all people?"

"Power," Knox answered on my behalf. "It always comes back to power."

"But I had none then," I argued. "Why take me in at all? Why waste his time on me?"

"Maybe that was the problem. Maybe he thought he'd picked a winner, then finally decided you were dead weight." Knox's words were harsh but not improbable. "Maybe your death was what he offered to Kingston in return for overthrowing Reinhardt."

Silence fell upon us for a beat while that probability sunk in.

"If that's true," Kat said, her words little more than a snarl, "I'll tear his fucking head off with my bare hands and impale it on a stake while I burn his corpse."

"Do you think—" I swallowed hard, not wanting to believe what I was about to suggest. "Do you think anyone else knew?"

"Like Jase and Dean?" Kat suggested.

"Yeah."

She shook her head.

"No. No way. But that said, we can't risk discussing this anywhere in the mansion—not even when you think it's safe. We don't know if there are traitors in our midst. We can't risk alerting the king to what we think is going on."

"Agreed," Knox said. "We keep this between us and no one else. Not until we know more. Not until we can confirm his involvement."

"And if we do? If we can prove he did it?"

Knox's eyes glowed yellow as he turned to pin them on me.

"We do a little overthrowing of our own."

19

When we got home, I grabbed a snack and went straight to my room. I wanted a hug from Grizz and to sleep for twenty-four hours straight. I wasn't sure I'd get both, but either would have sufficed.

Instead, I got the cold shoulder from my fuzzy buddy and a visit from Merc in my dreams.

Not long after I drifted off, Merc appeared beside my bed, looming above me. I scooted backward to make room for him, and he sat on the edge, looking down at me intently. A mix of apprehension and concern swirled in his dark eyes, making my heart race. Even though it was a dream, our dreams were never just that. They were a meeting place of sorts.

A place where secrets could be divulged.

"What you did—going after Reinhardt—you should have told me."

How did he know?

"I didn't cut you out to hurt you. I did it because I didn't want an argument."

"You would not have gotten one," he replied, the intensity of his stare almost pinning me to the bed.

"You think I was right to go?"

"I think you need a mentor, and he was your best bet. You had something to leverage him with—something of great value to him. I think it was a well thought-out plan—except for the part where you left me out."

"I didn't want to spook him," I said in my defense. "I don't know your history or what might have happened between you two in my absence. The last thing I wanted was to drive him away because of my entourage."

His lips pressed to a thin line as he considered my argument.

"A fair point but a moot one, it seems, given that the warlock you sought isn't the one you found."

"What do you know of Drake?" I asked, hoping to get a bit of insight into the warlock I'd just attached myself to.

"He is Reinhardt's second—was Reinhardt's second."

There was a sadness in his eyes as he said it that made me wonder if he'd been close to the warlock lord. If once again there was something he wasn't telling me.

"You believe he won't try to trick me? Harm me?"

"I believe he won't. Especially not after you set him on fire because he angered you." A small smile curled the corner of his mouth. "Kat filled me in on everything. I think I would have enjoyed seeing you put Drake in his place."

"It smelled bad. You might be glad you missed it."

The bed shook as he fought to retain his laughter.

"Perhaps another time." The amusement in his eyes faded, giving way to lust burning in their depths. "Piper—"

"Wait!" I said, throwing out my arm. "I need to tell you something before you do whatever it is you're thinking of doing."

"It must be terribly important," he said, the pull of a smile tugging at his lips again.

"I didn't want to say anything about this—we all agreed not to—but I think you should know. For some reason, I think you may already suspect it."

"What is this secret?"

I took a deep breath, preparing to play a card I couldn't take back, dream or not. Once Merc knew my suspicion, there would be no unknowing it. And, if his allegiance was still with the king, it could end badly for me.

Like the last time I mentioned the king in his presence.

"It's about the king." When his expression didn't devolve, I continued. "We think he might have known about Kingston's attacks on me. That he might have enlisted the warlock for that very task."

"To what purpose?" he asked, the words clipped and tight as they left his mouth.

"In exchange for usurping Reinhardt. Kingston could never have accomplished that on his own, or he would have a long time ago. He was always obsessed with power. I'm sure that's why he attached himself to me. He thought I could provide it for him, which really just further supports my argument. He couldn't have known what I was. Not unless someone told him."

"Someone like the king."

"It makes sense of so many things, Merc. Like why the king took me in. Why he allowed Jase and Dean to endanger themselves to keep me safe. He thought it would pay off for him one day." Merc stood up to pace the room, his anger visible in his coiled muscles and furrowed brow. As he did, another realization dawned on me; one I hadn't fully grasped until that second. "But that would mean that the king has known who I am all along..."

Merc stopped wearing a track in my carpet.

"Yes. It would."

I flew out of the bed to stand before him, staring up at his harsh features; features tight with knowledge that would frighten me to no end. That would change everything for me.

"Piper, I must tell you something," Merc said. My body went still, my breath cut off for fear he might change his mind about telling me what he was about to divulge. "I believe the king has always known who and what you are. It is why I have mistrusted him from the moment I met you. It is why I have silently questioned his every move since I returned."

"But how?" I asked, the pleading, childlike tone of my voice cutting through the growing tension in the room. "How could he know, unless..." I slapped my hand over my mouth to squelch the scream that threatened to escape.

"He knew who you were born of."

My knees gave out from under me, and I staggered back a step or two before Merc caught me, steadying me with his strong arms.

"He's always known." My whisperings were rhetorical, but Merc nodded in response anyway. "Knowledge is power."

"Then why would he let Kingston kill me? Why would he let him take me out if I was such a great prize?"

"Perhaps he doubted who you were because your powers had not emerged. Maybe you were the only leverage he had to push Kingston to remove Reinhardt from power."

I opened my mouth to ask him why, then snapped it shut again. Drake had said the amulet was a gift to the warlock lord: a way to increase his power on Earth while binding him to the fey queen. Together their power could overwhelm any other race of supernatural being, should it come to such a thing. If the king learned of this covenant between the two parties, he would surely want to end it.

And with the treaty about to fall...

"He knew he'd lose if it came to war between the races," I said, stating what Merc obviously already suspected, if not knew. He nodded again. "But... but wouldn't it have been easier to just destroy the amulet to break their bond? Letting Kingston have it couldn't have been an improvement."

"It would have if Kingston had allied with the king over the fey queen."

"Could that have happened? I mean, could he have just broken that bond if the amulet is of her making?"

Merc pulled me closer.

"Magic is driven by honor. It is swayed by the heart. Kingston's allegiance would lie with whoever could provide him with what he desired most. And that was your death. I do believe the bond between the queen and the warlocks could have fallen with Reinhardt's demise."

"Shit..."

"But Kingston is dead and the amulet is broken now. That changes many things."

"Yeah," I replied absentmindedly, my mind still reeling over the revelations.

"Is there something else?" he asked. He sounded like he hoped I wanted to ask him something. Like he wanted to tell me something that he couldn't—not unless I asked him directly.

"Maybe," I said, thinking of everything Kat had said in the car. The girl had been borderline paranoid since Jensen's death, but that didn't make me question her logic. In fact, everything she'd pondered seemed more valid than I wanted to admit. “Kat said something on the way back—about your return.”

“Yes.” He stared down at me with sharp eyes that begged me to see what was right in front of me. A mystery waiting to be unlocked; a soul waiting to be unburdened.

“She thought the timing was suspicious. That it was convenient that, just before the treaty fell, the king’s greatest weapon returned without explanation.”

“What is it you wish to ask me, Piper? I need you to be specific.”

“Why were you sent away? And why did the king bring you back?”

“I was sent away because of information I’d obtained.”

“Information about what?”

“Not a what.”

“... Who?”

“I knew of a child that was not to be. For that, I was punished—for eighty years.”

I could feel my eyes go wide, fear spreading through my veins like ice.

“Eighty years...?”

“Yes.”

“Whose child was it?” I asked, terrified to hear the answer.

“A child of the fey queen, which could not have been because it has long been established that the fey king is sterile.”

“But—”

“This is why the pregnancy was hidden. Why my knowledge of the child could not be tolerated for fear of that knowledge being used as a weapon at a later date.”

“Who punished you, Merc? The king or the fey queen?”

Silence.

"Both. The king agreed to detain me indefinitely to spare my life. Releasing me was in breach of this covenant with the fey queen."

"But Kat said you were sent away because your mind broke."

"A convenient story filled with enough truth to be believed, but not enough to be accurate."

"Oh my God." I exhaled those words as I wrapped my arms around his waist. The thought of being imprisoned for that long was unthinkable to me. A fate far worse than death.

"I am here now. Do not fear for me."

"But the queen—she can't take you back, Merc. If she does—"

"She won't."

The knot in my stomach was far less confident in his safety.

"The child," I started, pulling away from him enough to look up at him. "What about the child?"

He smiled down at me.

"It seems she survived."

"How can you be certain?"

"Because you are standing here before me. You have the power of the fey queen in your veins, Piper. And all that goes along with it."

Those words slammed into my chest, stopping my heart for a moment. Was I this forbidden child? Was I the cause of Merc's incarceration? No, I couldn't be. The eighty-year timeline didn't allow for that to be true. But that didn't mean I wasn't born of that child; that the bastard child of the fey queen didn't provide my DNA. That I wasn't blood of her blood. Bone of her bone.

"Merc... were you brought back to confirm who I was?" I

asked, my heart in my throat. "To wade through my mind to determine my lineage?"

He nodded, and my heart plummeted to the floor.

"But I could not, for obvious reasons. And because of that, I fear I set events in motion that led to your fate with Kingston—and with me." The pain in his eyes as he spoke made my already wounded heart hurt more. "It is also why I went with the queen when she came. I wanted to keep you safe—to make amends for failing you at every turn."

"Wait," I said, trying to catch up with my runaway thoughts. "You really did let her take you away to a fate known only to her crazy ass?" He merely nodded in response. "Holy fuck, Merc! Why? Why would you do that? And don't say to keep me safe, because I don't believe for a second that was your only motivation. You went there to punish yourself, didn't you?"

"It seemed a just fate at the time, but that was before we last spoke. Before you gave me hope that not all between us is lost."

"I want you to hear me when I say this, and I mean *hear* me: you are no longer allowed to punish yourself or martyr yourself because of me, got it?" That familiar twitch at the corner of his mouth showed itself. "Do not make me go all fire-breathing dragon on you."

"I haven't seen that particular trick yet," he replied, snatching me closer to him. "But I think I might like it."

"I think there's already enough heat in here, don't you?" My voice betrayed my emotions, its husky tenor doing nothing to hide what his proximity did to me. What it had always done. Maybe it was the balance between life and death that called to me, or maybe the cliché of opposites attracting. All I knew was that, anytime that male hovered over me, I couldn't think straight. Speech failed me. Breathing was erratic and shallow.

And when he touched me...

His hand drifted up to palm my face, his thumb stroking tentative circles on my cheek.

"I know your predicament here troubles you, Piper. I can see it wearing away at you in the quiet moments."

"Thankfully we haven't had many of those."

"But we will eventually, and I worry about what will happen to you when you have to face what you're running from."

"If I were running, I wouldn't have come back here. Back to where I knew you'd be."

"Your body is here, but your mind is not. I may not be able to hack into it as I can everyone else's, but I can read you nonetheless. It's written all over your face. I think it's why you seek to do things without me or Knox."

"What would you have me do, Merc?" I asked, pulling away from him to do a little pacing of my own. "I hate that I feel the way I do about both of you. I feel like a horrible person because I'm not supposed to feel this way, and yet I do. It's wrong to hold what you did against you, but that event led to me meeting Knox and the pack. To me turning to him and him being there for me when I needed him the most. Should I throw you aside so I can be with him? Or do I turn my back on him because your mind was restored? Whatever I do, it won't be fair to someone—someone I owe so much to. Someone I love..."

"Torturing yourself over this isn't fair to you," he pointed out. "I will never force you to choose, Piper. Knox should not either."

"But we're still bonded, Merc. If I were to walk away

from you forever, where would that leave you? I don't think I could do that."

"I don't wish for you to choose me out of pity," he said, his dark eyes narrowing. The intensity in his gaze made me squirm. He wasn't angry—I could tell that—but he wanted to make sure I heard him and heard him clearly. "That would be far worse than you leaving me." I nodded my head in understanding, unable to speak with his heavy stare weighing me down. "Now... since we're here and finally alone..."

His intense expression slowly turned to one full of heat and lust and a hint of something else I couldn't quite place. He took a step forward to once again close the distance between us, and I held fast under his approach. My skin alighted as he dragged a fingertip along my arm up to my shoulder. It continued to my neck, taking my breath away with it. By the time it reached my jaw, my heart was racing wildly in my chest, pounding against my ribs so hard I feared it might come flying out.

"I can hear your heartbeat," he said with a mischievous quirk of his brow. "And your cheeks are all flushed."

"It's hot in here..."

"But it's only a dream, Piper."

"A hot one."

Silence.

"It could be," he replied. "Say the word and we can be as we once were: entangled in the bedsheets, my name escaping your lips as I bury myself inside of you. We could have that here. No shame. No guilt." He wound his fingers into my hair, pulling my face closer to his. "No expectations."

"Merc—"

"I'm not asking you to choose, Piper. I'm asking you to let

go of what's eating you inside." His head dipped closer, his lips grazing my ear. I inhaled sharply in response. "Tell me you don't want to let go—tell me and I'll leave you now."

"I can't," I whispered, barely able to think clearly.

He pulled away long enough to stare down at me, his dark eyes swallowing me whole.

"Good."

Without hesitation, his lips crashed down upon mine, the press of them harsh and desperate and everything I wanted to feel in that moment. He scooped me up with ease and placed me down on the bed. My body cut it in half horizontally, leaving my legs to dangle over the side. Standing between them, coaxing them wider apart, stood the enigmatic being who had saved me from myself and bound himself to me for an eternity. The male I'd once fallen in love with.

My body ached for him as I watched him pull his shirt up over his head, revealing what I'd already known was there but was all too happy to lay eyes on again. His body was pale perfection. By the time his pants hit the floor, I felt like I was going to explode.

His hands skimmed along my legs, continuing up past the hem of the oversized shirt I had worn to bed. With a simple tug, he had my underwear off and flying across the room. I never got a chance to see where they landed. Instead, I felt those same hands grab me by the hips and drag me further toward the edge of the bed. Merc was there to meet me, more than ready to do what he'd promised. The hard press of him against my core made me moan, my eyes rolling back in my head.

Without hesitation, he buried himself deep inside of me. As he worked me into a frenzy, I tried to hold on to that feeling—just like I remembered from the first time we had been together, when our blood bond sang in my veins and my body cried out for him. The feeling eclipsed everything that had happened between us, all but erasing it from my mind. In that moment—that dream—we truly were bonded, and I knew it could change things between us if I let it. With every thrust, I could feel my body choosing for me.

"Be as loud as you want," he said, his body driving into mine. "No one can hear you here."

That turned out to be a fortunate truth.

My screams could have woken the dead.

I STARTLED awake in my bed, sweat coating my body. My breaths came ragged and hard—like someone who'd just had sex until she couldn't stand anymore—which made sense. Kind of. The intricacies of my dreams with Merc were complicated at best. Should I feel guilty for having a sex dream? Even a magical one that may or may not have actual real-life implications? He and I had wandered into the greyest of grey areas that night, and I feared it wouldn't lead to anything good.

My guilt had already started to creep in.

I picked up my phone to see what time it was just as it sprang to life, vibrating with an incoming call. The number wasn't one I knew. I took a deep breath, then hit the talk button and waited for a voice on the other end to speak.

"Hello?" the gruff male said.

I let out the breath I was holding.

"Drake. How did you get this number?"

I could hear him scoff on the other end of the line.

"I would not be much of a mentor if I couldn't manage that simple a task, Piper."

Fair point.

"What do you want?" I asked, ignoring his jab.

"I didn't want anything. You wanted training."

"And we're starting today?"

"No, we're starting right now. Hang up the phone and come outside. Alone. Let's see how well you follow instructions."

"But—"

The line went dead.

"Good talk, Drake," I said to myself, pushing off the bed and away from the sweat-stained sheets. A problem for another time.

I figured he wouldn't be pleased if I took a quick shower, so I changed my clothes and pulled my hair up away from my face. When I stepped out of my room, I found a very curious and slightly smug-looking bear waiting for me.

"What?" He looked past me to the bed and then back at me again. "Oh for fuck's sake... how can you possibly know that?" After I asked that question, I immediately wanted to take it back. The sounds the bear made at me in mocking were likely accurate and a hundred percent unnerving. "Stop! Please stop! Promise me you'll never do that again. Ever. Or I'll take you back to Alaska." His amused expression fell away, leaving a grizzly with his teeth bared staring me down. "Well now you know how serious I am," I continued, ignoring his menacing stare.

I walked past him, and he fell into step behind me. The bear had zero intention of letting me wander unchaperoned, though I didn't know why. He couldn't have heard my conversation with Drake, could he?

I opened my mouth to tell him that I had to go alone, then snapped it shut. The poor bear had been shut out of everything since we'd arrived in NYC. Was there really any harm in letting him go outside with me, providing that's where Drake actually was? The more I thought about that, the more it seemed unlikely. The enforcer pad was so magically warded and glamoured and God only knew what else that other supernaturals didn't even know where it was. I groaned with the realization that the warlock was likely about to send me on some magical wild goose chase, and I was not thrilled at the idea.

The sun was high in the sky when I stepped out into the front yard. Grizz barreled past me, sniffing the air like a crazy beast. Then he stopped, having caught a scent, and turned slowly toward the side of the house and the woods that lay beyond. He let out a low growl of warning before stalking away in that direction. When I moved to follow him, he turned and snapped at me, telling me to stay put until he said otherwise. In short, I'd just been parented by a grizzly bear.

"He can't possibly be here," I said, just as my phone vibrated with an incoming text. It simply read, "strike one."

As a jolt of dread shot through me, I looked over at Grizz, who was in a full sprint toward the woods. I took off after him, worried that Drake would take his frustration out on my buddy. And if he hurt one tiny patch of fur on that bear's head, I'd send him down to be with Kingston.

And likely burn myself out in the process.

"Grizz!" I screamed as I ran, hurdling the shrubs that lined the border of the woods. Branches bit into my flesh as I chased after him, but I couldn't catch up. Supernatural or not, that damn bear was fast. "Grizz!"

A roar unlike anything I'd ever heard erupted through the trees, sending birds flying. I ran toward what they were escaping. By the time I reached the spot, I was winded and terrified. Hovering over the gorge, held there by magic alone, was Grizz. Drake stood on the bridge, his arm extended toward the grizzly, a wry smile on his face.

"I take it this one is yours?" he asked. His smug expression told me he knew damn well that the bear was mine.

"Don't hurt him!" I shouted, lunging toward the bridge. Grizz dropped three feet with my approach.

"Would you like him back?" I nodded frantically, afraid to say the wrong thing. My tongue was held captive by my fear, which probably wasn't such a bad thing in reality. "Then come take him."

"But—"

Grizz dropped another ten feet, and I screamed.

"You have to fight for what's yours!" Drake shouted at me, snapping me out of my near-meltdown. "Stop being a scared little girl and start being the force of nature you are! You are not a victim. Stop acting like one!"

Like a slap to the face that I desperately needed, his words jarred me from my fear, letting anger take over. He'd attacked one of my own—the bear who'd helped me stop Kingston—and that was unacceptable at best.

At worst, it was a death wish.

"He is mine!" I yelled, reaching my hand out for Grizz as if I could grab him. "Bring him to me!"

Wind from nowhere whipped at my face, blowing the suspended bear toward me. Focused solely on him, I kept my hand extended, reaching for him. I would not be satisfied until I ran my hands through his fur.

"Then take him," Drake said, his voice cold and low. With a drop of his arm, Grizz plummeted toward the bottom of the gorge, taking my heart along with him.

"NO!" I cried, dropping to my knees by the gorge's edge.

"Take him!" Drake's voice roared in my ears, crashing through the panic swirling in my mind.

I shot to my feet and grabbed the bridge's railing, steadying myself.

"BRING HIM TO ME!"

I felt the ground beneath me rumble in response. The water below Grizz churned wildly, collecting into a white, frothy mass that shot up toward him like a geyser, catching him. It fired him up to me like a cannon, landing him right at my side. My fear barreled through my anger, keeping me from a meltdown of epic proportions. All I wanted to do was throw my arms around the bear's neck and squeeze him tight and erase the memory of what I'd just seen from my mind.

"You're okay," I said over and over again, uncertain whom I was trying to convince of that truth.

"Lesson number one," Drake said as he walked toward us. "Never let fear overtake you. You cannot fight from fear. You die from it."

I glared up at him as I soothed Grizz (or myself).

"Lesson number two is going to be how to nuke a warlock who fucked with my bear," I replied, my words little more than a growl.

"Now you've got the spirit." He had the gall to smile down at me as he spoke. "Anger is your weapon, Piper. You have to learn how best to wield it. Your love and concern for the bear snapped you out of it this time, but that will not always be the case."

"Anger as a weapon?" I said as I stood up, putting myself between the warlock and the bear. "That shouldn't be a problem." I moved to lunge for the warlock, but Grizz was having none of it. He pushed past me to snarl and stamp at Drake. My mentor looked down at the bear with curiosity, then smiled.

"Well I'll be damned." He bent down and stared into the

bear's eyes—which seemed a suicidal move at best—then laughed.

"I'd bring that down a notch, Chuckles. The bear took on an entire lodge full of werewolves because he thought my virtue had been compromised. I don't think he'd bat an eyelash about removing your face right now—especially not after the stunt you just pulled."

Drake uncurled himself, standing at his full height before me. He somehow looked taller than before. Larger too.

"That stunt was part of your training, which you specifically asked me for. And perhaps if you had followed my instructions and come outside alone, I wouldn't have used your *guardian* in your lesson."

I opened my mouth to argue, then shut it. There was something about the way he'd said 'guardian' that raised my suspicion. There was a weight to that word that I couldn't ignore.

"My guardian...?"

He nodded, looking down at Grizz with amusement.

"He's an unusual one, but one nonetheless."

"And what exactly does that even mean?"

"Witches and warlocks have familiars—animal guides that come to them when called. That help to protect them." Grizz and I looked at one another, confusion plain in our expressions, then turned back to Drake. The humor in his eyes bled to annoyance. "Surely you didn't think he was a pet."

"I didn't give it a lot of thought, Drake. He just kinda showed up and—" I cut myself short, realizing what I was about to say would only further support Drake's theory.

"And what? What did he do?"

I took a deep breath.

"He protected me from Knox."

The warlock's smile returned. I wanted to slap it from his face.

"Anything else?"

Another deep breath.

"Yeah. A few things."

"It's fine, Piper. You don't have to illustrate all the obvious reasons he is what I say he is. I'll save you that embarrassment. But for ease of future revelations, if you could just accept my word as gospel, it would really speed up your training."

I looked down at Grizz and buried my hand in the thick fur of his neck.

"Guess you really were supposed to come to New York with me, huh?"

Grizz snorted as though I'd just realized the obvious.

"I can only assume that Knox's presence and your connection to him called forth your familiar."

"Yeah, I guess."

He eyed me tightly, leaning closer to me.

"Have you had another? Has another animal come to you when you called?"

I contemplated that question for a moment before answering.

"Sort of..."

"Sort of, how?"

"In Alaska—I was healing one of the wolves, and Grizz was trying to tell me how to do it. By the time I'd tapped into enough magic to do it, half a forest's worth of animals were lined up around us, including the entire pack."

"Your call is strong, Piper. Very strong."

"Oh! I almost forgot the raven!"

His eyes narrowed at me as he took a step closer.

"The raven?"

"Yeah. Here in the city. When I asked for helping finding the owner of the amulet. It brought me to the building we found you in." Drake stood silent for a moment, then shook his head as if to pull himself from his thoughts. "What does that mean?"

"Nothing—just that your call is strong, as I said." He forced a smile at me that looked foreign on his face, then stepped past Grizz and me, heading toward the house. "Your lesson is done for today."

"What aren't you telling me?" I called after him, trying to catch up.

"Your wolves are coming," he replied, ignoring my question. Then, with a snap of his fingers, he disappeared into the ether.

But not before I heard the familiar caw of a raven and saw a flash of black feathers land on his shoulder.

20

"I've got bad news," Jase said, barging into the kitchen. I yelped and nearly dropped my plate, startled by his outburst. The wolves around me shot me a curious look, then turned their attention back to Jase. "The king has called for a meeting, disguised as one of his soirées."

"Aw shit," I groaned under my breath. "He's still doing that crap? With everything going on?"

"I have my reservations about it too, Piper, but we don't have a choice. Our attendance is mandatory, as is yours."

"Looks like we're about to party with the vampire king," Brunton said, his voice full of disdain. "Can't wait." He took a big bite of his sandwich and chewed it slowly, showing Jase just how not excited he was about going.

"When is it?" I asked, dreading the dress search I knew I was going to have to do.

Jase's expression hardened.

"Tomorrow."

"Tomorrow?" I shouted. The king's parties were always scheduled well in advance. To announce an event like that with a day's notice didn't sit well in my mind. Something strange was going on. Something very, very strange.

"Wear something you already have. Act normal. Try your best to get through the night without incident. Merc is going to try to get to the bottom of this before tomorrow night."

His pointed stare begged me to read between the lines—that Merc was going to try to search the king's mind for the truth. Not a safe plan, given his history with the king of the vampires. My heart started to race at the potential implications.

"Yeah. Okay... sounds good. I'll let Knox know."

"Do that. I'll keep you posted if anything changes."

I nodded in response, and he walked out of the room, leaving me with a curious pack and a growing sense of dread. The king was a creature of habit, if nothing else. Changing his party-throwing M.O. made me nervous as hell—for good reason.

❧

THE NEXT DAY I rummaged through the stash of dresses crammed into the back of my closet to see if I could find something reasonable to wear to the king's party; something that wouldn't earn me the judgmental stares of everyone there. My hair bristled at the thought of the bitch squad—a reflex a long time in the making—but then I remembered that I could lay them to waste if it suited me, and I smiled. No more cowering in a corner for me.

No more trying to make myself invisible.

I found something ruffled and black at the very back and pulled it out to see if it would work, holding it up against me. As I admired it, I heard a voice from out in the hall that made me jump. I turned to find Jagger lurking in my doorway, hesitation in his eyes.

"Jesus, Jagger! You scared me."

"Sorry..."

"What's up? You need something? Something for the party?"

He looked up and down the hall before stepping into my room and closing the door. I didn't know if he was looking to make sure Grizz didn't ambush him, or if he was worried that either Knox or Merc wouldn't appreciate him being in my room, but I didn't bother asking. He was wound so tightly I was worried he'd blow a gasket.

It reminded me of how he'd acted right before we'd left Alaska to return to NYC.

"I have to talk to you."

"Okay..." I gestured to the bed before moving to sit down on it myself. My hope was that he'd come sit next to me and calm down; his tension was beyond visible, from the set of his shoulders to the muscles clenching in his jaw. Instead, he paced the room like a dog in a cage. "Jagger, you're freaking me out right now. Tell me what's going on." He continued to pace, raking his hands through his hair and tugging on it. "Have you talked to Knox about—"

"No!" he shouted, wincing the second the word left his mouth. "I'm sorry, Piper. I didn't mean to yell at you. It's just —" He cut himself off, stopping in the middle of the rug. His eyes were unfocused, staring past me to the window of my room like something outside of it called to him.

With my luck, that was likely happening.

"Why can't you talk to Knox, Jagger?" I did my best to use the voice Jase used to employ on me when I'd come back after being attacked by someone and wouldn't tell him who.

"Because he'll try to fix things like he always does, and he'll get himself killed in the process."

That got my attention.

"What needs to be fixed?" I asked, standing up to join him. I approached him like the wounded animal he resembled. I didn't want to spook him.

"I fucked up so hard, Piper," he said, choking on the words a bit. "I didn't want to come back here—this is why I didn't want to come back."

"Jagger." I took his hand in mine to get his attention. Like a child, he turned his genuflected eyes to mine, but barely. He was so ashamed of whatever it was he'd done. It made my heart hurt to see him that way. "Tell me what you did."

He took a deep breath, letting it out in one big huff. It seemed to calm him a bit, but just enough to keep him from twitching.

"Will you hate me? Once I tell you?"

"Of course I won't, Jags. I could never hate you. You could never do something to make me hate you."

His jaw worked hard, clenching his teeth to keep in whatever ugly truth he was determined to unload on me. Apparently it was against his better judgment.

"I left New York because it changed me. I didn't like who I'd become. How much of myself I'd lost being here." He let go of my hand and walked around the bed to the far side of the room. He looked out the window, unable to look at me, and unburdened his soul. "It's a long story, but the short of it is this. When I came here, I didn't have a pack. The pack I eventually ended up with... well, let's just say that they had their own version of Kingston, and I got roped into his shit."

I held my breath and prayed he'd continue. Nothing was more important to me in that moment than his story.

"Mack loved all things illegal: drugs, trafficking girls,

black market guns… and magic. For a werewolf, he was obsessed with Magicals—especially the fey." He turned his head as if to look at me, but his eyes never reached me. "He was amazing at sniffing out the lower fey that lived on this side of the veil." Silence. "So were a few others—including me.

"At first he made it a full moon game of sorts. I didn't even realize what I was doing until it was done. I killed a young female fey masquerading as a hooker. He'd denied us fighting or girls for two full moons; by the time I got to her, bloodlust had already set in." He turned to look back out the window, bracing his hands against the casing. "He took the body—acted like he was doing me a favor by covering for me. I didn't realize for months that that had been his intent all along. That he wanted the body. He used the guilt I felt and the threat of telling our alpha to keep me under his thumb.

"I don't know how many fey I tracked for him before I learned of Knox's pack in Alaska and escaped the city to join him. If it weren't for Knox, I'd probably still be hunting for Mack—or dead."

I did my best to school my expression, but it was a challenge. Jagger—sweet, fun-loving Jagger—had demons the size of Texas. Demons that tore him up inside. No matter how I felt about what he'd done, he clearly felt far worse.

"We've all done things to survive, Jags—"

"But don't you see? I didn't do it to survive! I did it because I was weak." He turned to pin ferocious eyes on me; eyes full of guilt and self-loathing.

"Jagger," I said, stepping around the bed to approach him. "He used you. I know a thing or two about that. Do you remember what you said to me after you learned about Kingston—about all that had happened between us?"

His expression softened to one of sadness when he thought about that conversation.

"I told you it wasn't your fault."

"Yes. And not to blame myself."

"But all those fey that died because of me—"

"Would have died because of Mack eventually." He pressed his mouth into a thin line in an attempt not to argue. "Now, I need you to tell me how you 'fucked up', or I can't help you."

His shoulders slumped forward and his head hung low.

"The other day—when you and Kat were supposed to be going to the store but decided to go on a Reinhardt-seeking mission instead—you came home empty-handed. So I thought it would be helpful if I took one of the cars and ran to the store to get some food. I know my way around the city. It seemed like such a harmless errand." His eyes drifted back out the window, so I walked over and wedged myself between him and his mental escape, demanding he look at me. What I saw in his expression, I would not soon forget. His demon had found him. "I was loading up the car when I heard someone call my name. I knew the voice instantly. My hair still stands on end just thinking about it."

"Mack."

He nodded in affirmation.

"I don't know what the odds are of him being in that neighborhood right when I was, but it can't be a coincidence, Piper. He didn't even look surprised to see me. He looked... *amused.*"

"What did you do?"

"I threw the shit in the car and peeled out."

"Did he follow you?"

"Yeah, but I lost him eventually. There's no way he could have tracked me back here."

"Unless he already knew where 'here' was..."

What a sobering thought that was.

"Piper, I swear I would never have done it if I'd thought this would happen. This is exactly why I didn't want to come back."

He resumed his pacing of the room, complete with hair pulling. I wondered if he'd have any hair left by the time we were done formulating a plan.

"Jagger," I said, using as firm a voice as I thought he could handle. "Knox said he'd take care of things when we were back in Alaska. You have to tell him this. He'll know how to handle it."

"No, he won't, because he told me not to leave the mansion alone!"

Shit.

"Was it an order? Like a direct, he-was-all-pissy-about-it-when-he-said-it order? Or was it more of a suggestion?"

He contemplated the difference for a second before replying.

"'He was somewhat casual about it when he said it."

"If it was a direct order, you'd *have* to follow it, right?"

"Well yeah... but..."

"Jagger. He's gonna be pissed, but he can't blame you for wanting to help. That's like blaming Grizz for being a bear."

"I guess."

"We need to tell him. If you want I'll do it for you, but he has to know. He can't fix something he doesn't know about."

"I'm not sure there's any fixing this at all."

"Well you can start by not doing any more solo food runs, okay? Your heart was in the right place—"

"But my brain wasn't."

I smiled at him.

"Maybe not on this one. But you're not alone in that. I've

done some stupid shit for good reasons in my time. You're in good company."

His eyes lit up with a genuine smile, and he pulled me into an embrace.

"I'll say. Best company ever."

We stood like that for a moment, enjoying the calm before the storm. I was about as excited to tell Knox about what had happened as Jagger was. Knox wasn't a big fan of surprises.

However, our chat with the alpha went far more smoothly than I could have imagined. Sure he freaked out for a hot second, but then he settled down, realizing that, in the grand scheme of issues, Mack was pretty far down on the list. As long as Jagger stayed put—unless the whole crew was going out—he'd be fine for the time being.

Later was a problem for another day.

For now, we had a party to go to.

21

The ball was everything I remembered and hated. Snobby, uptight vampires filled the room with an air of superiority that I wanted to set ablaze. Even after my time away and everything that had changed, I could feel my shoulders rounding, my body taking on its invisible posture. The one that had kept me safe for so long.

Then I saw someone on the other side of the room that made my back stiffen.

"I'm going to kill her," I muttered under my breath as I started across the room. I heard others calling after me, but the sounds of their voices were swallowed by the rush of blood pounding in my ears, blocked out by the singular thought repeating itself in my mind.

Revenge.

Sylvia—Kingston's lover and traitor to vampire-kind—had the nerve to stare at me, the smug upturn of her lip forming more of a snarl as I approached. She didn't know what I was capable of, but she was about to find out. Too bad she hadn't been in on that little secret ahead of time.

She would have risked the king's wrath and not attended his party if she had.

"You..." I spat the word at her like a missile. "You nearly killed everyone I love." As I sped toward her, rage burning in my eyes, her expression fell. She took a step back in retreat, but there was nowhere for her to run that I wouldn't find her, and she knew it. To her credit, she stayed to face me. "Why did you do it?" I asked, stopping just before her. She said nothing in reply, just stared at me with indignation she didn't deserve—not after how she'd sold out Merc and the rest of us. No, she'd be humbled if I had anything to say about it. She'd beg for mercy by the time I was finished. "Tell me!"

Still she remained silent, her perfectly lined eyes glaring at me.

I could feel the shift within me this time. I knew my magic was coming to me hard and fast. The angrier I got, the more swiftly it heeded my call. Before I realized what was happening, blue flame engulfed Sylvia. Everyone around her stepped back, not wanting to catch fire themselves; not wanting to come to her aid, not that they could. With her mouth wide open, letting loose a silent scream, she collapsed to the floor and tried—to no avail—to extinguish what was destined to consume her.

I bent down beside her, the heat and stench of burning flesh assaulting me. But I didn't care. I wanted to be close to her when she finally cracked and gave me what I wanted: answers.

"Tell me why you did it and I'll end this," I said, my voice soft and calm and everything I didn't feel. I was chaos and madness and elemental wrath loosely bound by skin. "Tell me because I know you're not smart enough to have done it all on your own."

"Piper—" Knox warned. I could feel him looming somewhere behind me, but I didn't bother to look back. He knew enough not to come closer. He'd inadvertently make things worse.

Then I heard the voice of the one who could shut me down, and a small piece of me came back to myself. He whispered low and in my ear where no one else could have heard him speak. What he said was for me and me alone.

"Don't let him see." Though his statement was vague, I knew exactly what he meant. The king hadn't arrived at his own party, and Merc didn't want him to witness what I could do. Not firsthand, at least. Rumors would reach him sooner rather than later, but how much weight he'd give them would remain to be seen. Merc didn't want me spilling my magical beans to the one who couldn't be trusted.

"She deserves death," I replied, unwilling to look away from the pale blue flames.

His hand pressed against the small of my back, and I inhaled sharply before scrambling back to my feet. The inferno flickered for a moment, then burned out entirely, leaving Sylvia's dress in ruin and her skin blackened. She would heal slowly, but she'd also know that I could do that to her again.

A lesson worth noting.

Hateful, hardened eyes stared back at me from her soot-covered face, and I lunged for her again. This time, however, I was stopped before I could even start. The king's voice boomed through the ballroom, stopping me cold.

"What is the meaning of this?" he asked, staring down from the floor above. His face was calm, but it clearly belied his growing rage. He didn't like interruptions—especially not at his parties. And he sure as hell didn't seem to like them coming from me. "Piper...? Would you care to explain?"

"I wanted to know why she told Kingston what she did—why she'd side with him over her own."

"And?"

"And she won't tell me because she's still an evil whore." I turned my attention back to her, grabbing her by what remained of the strap of her gown. "Jase should have killed you when he had the chance."

"Jase would have been punished had he done that," the king said, drawing my eyes up to him yet again. I let go of Sylvia, shoving her and her charred dress away from me as I walked to the center of the room. I had his full attention, whether I wanted it or not. But really, what did I expect after causing a scene like that? It was almost as if a small part of me had wanted that very outcome.

"So she goes unpunished? After all she did?"

"She has been punished," he replied, steadying his expression so as not to give away just how irritated he was with me in that moment. I didn't need to see it to know. I was pushing his buttons, and that game wouldn't be suffered for long. "The reason Sylvia cannot tell you what you want to know is that I made sure she could never betray her kind again," the king said, daring a glance over at Sylvia before returning his glare to me. He leaned forward, his body bending over the railing. "I cut out her tongue, Piper. That's what I do to those who would act against me as she did."

I couldn't help but feel a wave of nausea roll over me. Sylvia deserved whatever she had gotten after spilling vampire secrets to a warlock, but still—that was a gruesome punishment. Death seemed kinder. I'm sure that's why he hadn't granted her that.

"What about me? What about my vengeance?"

"She did not betray you."

"She betrayed my mate!"

The king's eyes danced with delight for a moment. His attention turned slowly to Knox, making a spectacle out of his point, then back to me.

"Which one?"

I felt Merc's hand on my back, cautioning me to choose my words wisely, but I wasn't sure I could. Even with his steadying force, I couldn't help but think about how amazing it would feel to watch the blue flames that had just engulfed Sylvia swirl around the king's beautiful face until it melted away...

"Piper!" The king snapped at me, drawing me from my dark thoughts. "Which. One?"

"Well, given that I didn't know Knox at that point in time, I think the answer should be obvious. Don't you?"

I felt Jase go still beside me. Not a good sign. But I already knew I'd stepped out of line with my response. The question my behavior begged was: would I leave the party with my tongue intact?

"Were you actually a vampire," the king began, carrying on as though my insolence hadn't fazed him, though I knew better. I knew what lay behind that cold, ambivalent expression he wore. Death. "I might be persuaded to allow you to continue your theatrics, but you are not, so you may not. And if you choose to take it upon yourself another time to finish whatever it is you started here this evening, there will be consequences."

"Big ones, I'm sure."

"So glad to see you learned something in your time with my enforcers. Something other than how to sleep with them." My hands flexed wildly at my sides, begging to unleash the storm brewing within. Outside I could hear the thunder rolling in like a tide of magic ready to rain down upon everyone there. I leaned back against Merc's hand, hoping to quell the power I could not contain on my own. "Speaking of that," the king said, turning his attention toward the wolves—and where Kat stood among them. "I'm surprised to see you here this evening, Ekaterina. Your presence is no longer necessary at these events, for obvious reasons."

I looked at where Kat stood steadfast, weathering the king's insults like a pro. She'd known they'd come one day. She didn't look at all surprised that that was the night.

"She's here with us," Knox said before Kat could get a word out. Though I knew she'd hate him speaking for her, I was glad he did. It kept me from saying something worse.

Or did it?

"And why are you here at all, Alpha?" the king asked Knox.

"Because he's with me, as you so kindly pointed out," I countered, stepping away from Merc's grounding touch. "And I'm blood-bound to him." I looked over my shoulder at Merc to make my point. Merc's stern expression warned me to stop before I dug my hole any deeper. I smiled back, which let him know that I had no intention of stopping. The king and I had unfinished business. Business I was about to air for all to hear. "It is my right to be here."

"I tolerate your presence—"

"As I tolerate yours," I said, cutting him off. I heard snickering from the pack, but I didn't look back. I'd have recognized Jagger's poorly stifled laughter anywhere. Brunton's too. "It's hardly like anyone actually enjoys coming to these uptight parties of yours, but the mandatory attendance or death thing tends to make them show up regardless." His eyes went wide at my insult. I half expected him to jump down from the second-floor balcony and rip my heart out with his bare hands, but he didn't move. He remained where he was, towering over me from above, and glared. And that made me wonder...

Was he afraid to come down and punish me?

"You think you can hide behind your bond to my enforcer—that it makes you untouchable—but you cannot. It does not. And you would be wise to remember that." I could hear the groan of wood beneath his hands as he choked the railing, presumably like he wanted to be choking me. In fairness, I couldn't fully blame him. The fact that he hadn't tried yet spoke to his composure.

"I don't need to hide behind anyone," I argued. "I do just fine on my own now. But I don't think that should surprise you all that much." I winked at him, letting him know that I was in on the big secret—the one about him knowing exactly whom I was born of. That fey blood ran through my veins. Warlock too. "And as for this party, I think I'll show myself out." I looked over my shoulder at Kat, who was staring at me with wide eyes filled with disbelief. "Feel like going for a swim?" I asked her. "Shallow end only, of course." A smile spread wide across her face.

I turned without being dismissed and cut my way through the crowd that parted as though I had something contagious they didn't want to catch. Kat fell in behind me, and the pack behind her. By the time I made it to the glass doors at the back of the mansion, I had a full-on entourage accompanying me. It was then I realized why the king had stood back and allowed my show of defiance. Bringing an attack on me would have brought the wrath of Knox's pack down on all in attendance. At best, it would have meant another war on his hands. At worst, it would have been a total bloodbath.

Most of the king's enforcers were out fighting the real war at hand.

With a grand pull, I threw both doors open and strutted through the young vampires partying outside. They stared at me like I was a god—like I'd just done the impossible. Maybe I had.

But maybe I would die because of it.

I didn't care about that right then. I was too busy basking in the rush I felt. Unlike the last time I'd run out into the backyard of the king's property, I wasn't fleeing anything. I wasn't ashamed. I wasn't afraid.

While I looked up at the clouds above awaiting my command, music began to blare all around me. Apparently Kat had already hijacked the sound system. The bass rattled like my chest when I let loose the nervous laughter it withheld. The sky opened up and a gentle rain fell upon me like an old friend. I reached my arms up to greet the droplets, letting them roll down my face. Rain, not tears, stained my cheeks that night.

And it felt amazing.

I didn't have long to bask in the feeling, though. A knock on my shoulder from a naked blur running past me jarred me from my thoughts. By the time my eyes focused on who it was, Kat had launched herself into the air above the pool, tucking herself into a ball. A tidal wave shot up into the air, and for a moment, panic shot through me. Werewolves were too dense to swim (as our stint in the East River had taught me), and I couldn't see if she'd landed in the deep section of the pool or not. Seconds later her head popped up, a self-satisfied grin gleaming back at me in the moonlight.

I let loose the breath I was holding.

"I thought you said we were going for a swim!" she shouted at me across the lawn.

Who was I not to make good on a promise?

Though I was far more bashful than my werewolf friend, I ripped my dress up over my head and threw it aside, darting in my bra and underwear toward the pool that spanned the better part of the backyard. I could feel the pounding of footfalls shaking the ground as I ran, and I knew I wasn't alone. Just before I jumped into the air, a redheaded streaker and his dreadlocked friend flew past me, hitting the water before I even had the chance.

I went under, the water swallowing me up before spitting me back out again. When I stood up, I had to close my eyes at what I saw. Men running naked were just too much for me. With hands over my eyes, my body rocked with the waves the wolves created as they all jumped into the shallow end of the pool.

"I don't know what just got into you," Knox said from behind me, his lips brushing my ear. "But I think I really like it." He pressed himself closer to me, and I gasped. He must have really, *really* liked it.

"The king's a liar," I said, spitting the words out like they were poison.

"Yes," he agreed. I could feel the rumble of his growl reverberate through my back right to my core, and my breath hitched in my throat. "He is."

I turned to look at his eyes, the soft golden hue of them telling me all I needed to know. Knox would go after the king if he had the chance—or if the king came to make good on his threat against me. To remind me that I was not untouchable.

Before I had a chance to reassure Knox that it wouldn't come to that, a ruckus drew my attention. I looked to my right to find Kat standing, in all her naked glory, with Brunton held high above her head. The smile on her face told me exactly what she had planned.

She was standing next to the deep end.

"What the fuck?" Brunton yelled, trying to wriggle (naked) out of her overhead press.

"I believe you and I still have a score to settle," she replied, unfazed by his anger.

"Kat..." I said by way of warning. Her smile only widened.

"Maybe he can float," she said with a shrug. Without skipping a beat, she tossed him into the twelve-foot section to find out. Brunton's slew of curses was quickly swallowed up by the water, just as he was. Scrambling hard against his weight, he never even made it up for air. He sank to the bottom and braced himself against the pool floor before shooting up through the water with a massive jump. He rocketed up out of the water, nearly his whole body emerging. His trajectory had him headed toward the pool's edge, where I imagined he hoped to get a hold of something—possibly even Kat. But she was waiting for him with the pole from a pool net. With one swing, she batted him back into the water.

"This is kind of fun," she said, giggling as he sank yet again. "Like that whack-a-mole game."

"Enough!" Knox shouted, but not before Kat had poked the net end of the pole down into the pool to jab at Brunton. I knew the boy had beaten her badly when she'd arrived in Alaska unannounced, but he hardly deserved to drown for it. Kat had made her point. It was time to shut her down.

"Help him swim," I said under my breath. Seconds later bubbles erupted all around us, emanating from the bottom of the deep end. Brunton's body rose with them, riding the air pockets to the surface. I swam over to where he hovered just above the water, cushioned by the massive bubbles beneath him. "Now I think it's about time you two worked your shit out without trying to kill one another." I shot Kat a nasty look over my shoulder. "Are you done? Are you even now?"

She exhaled hard.

"I don't think I'd say we're even—"

"Not even close," Brunton said, interrupting her. I looked back at him and found the devil in his eyes.

"I can do this all night," Kat countered, waving her pole around in mocking.

"Not if I get out of this pool."

"*If*," she said, leaning forward to meet his challenge. "*If* you get out."

"Brunton," I started, turning my attention to the one I hoped might listen to the voice of reason. Kat wasn't exactly known for that trait. He lifted his head at an awkward angle to look at me. "Please..." The rage that burned in his eyes faded away. "Can you please let her have this win?"

"It's not a win," he said, clarifying that fact for all in earshot—basically everyone outside. "But yes, I'll let it go if she does."

Kat stared at him hard, her sharp eyes searching for the catch: the trick that would bite her in the ass somehow. She was always ready for the other shoe to drop, and for good reason. Maybe she needed to see that, just this once, it might not.

Much to my surprise, she slowly extended the pole toward him, and he grabbed it with equal hesitation. After a pause to see how he'd react, she started to pull him on his raft of bubbles toward the edge of the pool where she stood. The orbs of air lifted him until he could step down onto the concrete—right next to Kat. The two of them stood there—naked as the day they were born—and stared at one another. It was as if they were having one of Jase and Dean's silent conversations, but I knew they weren't. They were waiting to see who, if anyone, would make the first move to break their minutes-long truce.

When Brunton moved to walk around her, Kat quickly shifted herself away from the edge of the pool and watched him like a hawk as he strode away, never touching her.

"Enjoy the view," he called back to her, not bothering to turn and confirm that she was watching him. He could probably feel the weight of her stare on his back—or wherever it fell. Her eyes looked a little too low for that, but I didn't bother overthinking it. I mean, Brunton did have a great ass.

"Keeping the peace yet again," Knox said, walking toward me. I leveled my eyes on his and tried to ignore everything below. I failed miserably, but I deserved points for trying.

"I thought after almost starting a war, it would be good for my karma."

He smiled at me, the wry curl of his lip letting me know that I was in trouble.

"We'll see about that later. For now," he started, heaving me up over his shoulder. "Back into the pool with you."

I sailed high into the air, laughing along the way. I embraced that feeling of joy as I crashed into the unforgiving surface of the water, sinking down deep to where the darkness lay. It was a sobering reminder that even though—at that moment—the pressure we'd all felt since our arrival in NYC had abated, something ominous waited for us. A decision that would change my life forever.

I knew there would be no escaping that fate.

I knew that, no matter what we did, we'd lose someone to the fey realm.

❧

WE'D BEEN in the pool for about five or ten minutes before I realized that none of the brothers had joined us. Merc, Jase, and Dean were all still inside. It seemed an ominous sign at best.

My concern for them grew, driving me from the pool to gather my dress and try to pull it down over my soaking wet body.

"What's wrong?" Knox called, climbing out of the pool. I had to turn away from the show he was giving me. It wasn't time for those kinds of thoughts.

"The brothers—they're still inside. I need to make sure they're okay."

Though I was fully expecting Knox to blow off my concerns, he never said a word in rebuttal. Instead, he whistled once, and the pool cleared out in a flash—except for Kat. She shot me a look that silently asked if I needed her.

All I could do was shrug in return.

The pack threw on clothes quickly, the lot of us looking like a bunch of drowned rats as we approached the king's mansion. But before we could make it inside, Dean intercepted us, closing the door behind him.

"Not a good idea, Piper," he said, his palms out to halt us. "Merc is... you know... fixing things at the moment. I don't think you walking in on that would be a such a good idea."

I nodded, my mind reeling with the potential consequences of my mate's actions.

"Is Jase with him?"

"Yeah. He's keeping him on a tight mental leash, but I

don't know... Merc isn't being especially subtle at the moment."

"Shit!"

"Don't panic. It'll be fine. It's just going to take a while." He looked past me to the pack at my back. "Not to be a dick, but it might be better if you guys head out. If the king sees you, it might undo what Merc is trying to accomplish."

I nodded again, at a loss as to what to say. I was the reason Merc had to mindfuck the king; my insolence had driven me to throw the gauntlet at him. I'd known there'd be no going back from there, and I'd done it anyway. Not the smartest move I could have made.

But damn was it satisfying to have had the upper hand with him for once.

To have him know that he didn't hold my life in the palm of his hand.

"It's fine, Dean. We'll go." I looked over my shoulder at Knox, and he nodded in agreement. "We'll be at home. Call me and let me know everything is okay when you leave, okay?" I hugged Dean tightly, and he squeezed me back the way he always had. He really did give the best hugs.

"Straight home. No snack stops. No pee breaks. Nada, got it? Shit's getting crazy again. If something's going to go down, I want to be there."

I forced a smile at him.

"I solemnly promise not to singlehandedly start another war in the city." I crossed my heart for effect, and he laughed.

"That's my girl. Now get the fuck out of here."

He turned and opened the French doors to head back inside. He was swallowed up by the crowd soon thereafter, and I couldn't help but wonder if he was telling me everything; if he was holding back about what was going on with the king. He hadn't outright lied, or Knox would have called him on it, but there was a niggling somewhere in the back of my mind that said he was leaving something out. Something that might have scared the shit out of me if he'd told me.

I walked back to the car playing worst-case scenarios over and over in my mind. Jagger's arm around my shoulder helped calm me a bit, but even the goofy redhead couldn't soothe my growing unease about what might be going on inside the king's home. Merc's gifts came at a cost—even without Kingston's magical meddling—a cost that I'd both heard about and seen. If undoing the mess I'd made took too much of his power, I shuddered to think of the consequences.

Losing him to his madness was not an option.

22

Our trip home was completely uneventful. A small mercy indeed.

We all filed into the mansion in relative silence and split up once inside. The better part of the pack made their way to the kitchen while the rest of us headed for our rooms. I wanted to find Grizz and let him know I was okay.

I found him asleep on the floor of my room. He looked peaceful and content, so I backed my way out, not wanting to disturb him. I eased the door closed behind me and turned to find Kat exiting her room down the hall at the same time.

She made her way over to join me.

"You wanna talk about your little outburst at the party?"

"Nope. Not at all."

The left side of her mouth curled with amusement.

"You wanna pretend it never happened and watch a movie?"

"Yes! That. I want to do that." It was the perfect escape

for my mind until I heard from the brothers. "Can I borrow some clothes? The bear's sleeping. I don't want to wake him up."

"You mean you don't want to deal with his silent interrogation."

"That too."

Kat shook her head and led the way back to her room. I threw on a pair of comfy sweats, tucking my phone into the pocket so I could feel it vibrate, and a hoodie. She had on the same, but she somehow made it look far sexier. The girl just had 'it'.

We walked down the hall until we hit the media room. Totally exhausted from the night's events, I flopped onto the corner of the massive sectional sofa and slumped down until my head was barely visible over the back of it. Not that I was hiding.

There was hardly any point in that.

Kat joined me, taking up the right side of the couch. She grabbed the remote and started flipping through the channels until some "underrated" comedy popped up. Her expression lightened immediately. I watched her as she smiled at the TV, thinking just how good it was to see her like that. She'd smiled since Jensen had been killed, but they weren't real smiles; they were smiles full of mischief or malice or the promise of pain. Not a real lights-up-your-eyes-and-crinkles-your-nose kind of smile.

I loved seeing it on her face once again.

"You do realize that you're being super creepy right now, don't you?"

Busted.

"And you're smiling."

She shot me a sidelong glance.

"The movie's funny."

"Good. Laugh it up. You deserve to."

Her smile fell in a heartbeat.

"Do I?" she said softly. "Because I don't feel like I deserve to. Jensen's been gone for what—a few days—and I already feel his memory fading in my mind. What kind of mate lets that happen?"

"One that's been dodging bullets since he died."

"I've intentionally put myself in the line of fire and you know it," she said, turning to face me. "You know me."

"I do. That's why I know you needed to do it."

She nodded before looking back at the TV.

"I loved him so much..."

"I know that too."

"Then why am I not holed up in the room he and I shared together, crying?"

"Because you don't cry, Kat," I said plainly.

"True—but shouldn't I over this?"

"You did a little."

"But I still should be. Why aren't I?"

I took a deep breath and crawled toward her on the couch, sitting down beside her so our legs and arms touched.

"Why do you think you're not?"

She clicked pause on the remote, stopping her show, but she stared at the screen as if she were still watching. Kat never put too much thought into what she said before she said it; rapid-fire response was much more her thing. The fact that she wasn't doing so started to make me uneasy. Whatever she was about to say was heavy for sure.

"Do you think that maybe our bond—it wasn't as strong because he wasn't a wolf? Because I wasn't a vampire?"

"Kat, I don't—"

"I mean it! Maybe there really is something to that. Maybe you're never as connected with another kind as you are with your own." She let out a hard sigh and dropped her eyes to her lap, her shoulders sagging. "I was so desperate to get away from where I was when I met Jensen..."

"You loved him, Kat. Anyone with eyes could see that."

"And he loved me. I'm not arguing that point. I'm just saying—maybe it wasn't as visceral as it would have been if we hadn't been an interbreed couple."

I wanted to refute her point, but in truth, I thought it had merit. I'd wondered the same thing when I escaped from Merc and went on the lam. I'd wondered if I would ever escape the blood bond we shared. Maybe the small fact that he'd tried to beat me to death had helped my conscious mind override our subconscious connection, but I just couldn't tell. Having Knox there to distract me had also helped my mind escape my soul's bond. Or maybe it wasn't really as strong as I'd been told because I wasn't a vampire.

"I don't know if that's the case or not, Kat. But I do know that you loved him as fiercely as you've ever loved anyone. The fact that you're grieving how you are doesn't diminish that. We all handle loss in our own way."

"So... I'm not a horrible person...?" She looked at me with earnest eyes that seemed so wrong on her face. Kat was fearless—always had been. The uncertainty plaguing her made me hate the fey even more for making her feel that way. For pulling the rug out from under my best friend.

A cough from someone lingering in the hallway echoed through the room, drawing our collective attention. Foust and Brunton wandered in, the former looking a bit sheepish about what he'd presumably overheard, and the latter sporting his usual stone-faced expression.

Then he opened his mouth and floored Kat and me both.

"How you grieve is your own fucking business," he said, voice gruff as always. "To hell with what anyone else thinks."

I knew my mouth was hanging wide open as I gaped at him, but I didn't care. Had Brunton just said something nice? To Kat, of all people? My mind couldn't handle it.

"Kat," Foust said, stepping closer to the couch. "I don't pretend to know what it's like to be a lone female, but I know it can't be easy—not even in a pack. Whatever your reasons for bonding to your former mate, you shouldn't question them. And you shouldn't worry about what they did or didn't mean." Foust looked so uncomfortable standing in front of us. He kept adjusting the tie that held back his massive dreads, even though they hadn't moved. "I've never met a tougher female than you, and I can't help but think that you'd do pretty damn well on your own. If you chose to bind with Jensen, then I imagine it was for honorable reasons."

I heard Kat swallow hard beside me.

"Thanks..."

"So what are you two up to, skulking around the media room? Are you that hard up for entertainment that you want to eavesdrop on a couple of chicks?" I asked, trying to lighten the mood. Foust looked at Brunton, who shrugged as if to say "you're on your own, man."

"In all honesty, I was hoping to watch the game."

"Which one?" Kat asked.

"Football."

She cringed at his response.

"Hard pass on that one, big guy. But I can offer you two a couple of spots on this obnoxiously large sofa if you're interested in watching one of the best comedies you'll ever see."

"Any nudity in it?" Brunton asked. His steely gaze landed on Kat, evoking her wicked smile; the one that promised pain.

"Sure is."

"I'm in." Brunton hopped over the couch, landing in the corner of the sectional I'd occupied only a few minutes earlier.

"Hey! That's my seat." Another silent shrug from the unmoving werewolf. "Dick."

He leaned back further into the nook of the couch and put his feet up on the coffee table. Kat, apparently finding his antics entertaining, burst out laughing. It may have sounded a wee bit unhinged, but it was infectious nonetheless, and soon had the rest of us joining in, even if we weren't fully certain why. The ruckus we caused seemed to draw wolves from every corner of the mansion. Before we knew it, there were bodies lying around everywhere in the media room. Foust wedged himself between Kat and me, draping his arms around the two of us, while Jagger found some space between Brunton and me to round out that portion of the couch. Kat looked unimpressed but let him have his fun. I thought I heard a growl in response from somewhere off to my left, but I couldn't be sure. It was too noisy in there to tell.

"Guess I found the place to be," Knox said, walking into the room with care. I guess he didn't want to trample his wolves.

"Shut up and sit down. I'm turning this thing back on," Kat said, not bothering to look over her shoulder at his dirty look. She already knew what it looked like. She'd seen it before.

Knox walked around the couch to stand before the spot where I was now wedged between Jagger and Foust. With a bit more room, it would have been cozy; however, being trapped between their imposing bodies felt more claustrophobic than anything.

"Time to find a new spot, Jagger."

"Aw, c'mon. She smells really good—"

"Jagger. Move."

"Fine." Jagger got up with a huff and walked away to find a spot somewhere on the rug. If I hadn't watched him do it, I'd never have understood how he found a place to lie down. Looking at the pack on the floor was like looking at a box full of puppies, all flopped over one another and crammed together. Even though they were technically grown men, it was so adorable. There was something so charming about the pack relationship.

I found it so appealing.

"So what are we watch—"

"SHHHHH!" Kat shushed the alpha without a second thought. He looked down at me, and I took a note from Brunton's book and gave him a shrug. If he hadn't figured out by then that Kat gave zero fucks about most things, I was hardly going to be able to explain it to him.

"One of Kat's favorites," I said under my breath. "I suggest you shut up and enjoy it."

"Damn right," Kat added, turning up the volume.

Knox, either seeing the futility of pressing the issue or realizing that Kat was in rare form, decided to keep quiet and watch the '90s classic without further protest. For the next hour and a half, the pack, Kat, and I laughed until our stomachs hurt. It was a moment of joy in the onslaught of chaos that had surrounded us from the moment we'd returned to the city. As the end of the movie neared, I silently prayed that it could go on a little longer—that we all might enjoy a slightly longer reprieve. But then the credits began to roll, and the boys started to rise and disperse, and the suspicion crept in that our precarious happiness was about to be obliterated with a single sweep of the fey queen's hand.

Possibly sooner than I expected.

23

"I feel like I've said this a lot lately," Jase said, storming into the game room. "But we have a situation." Kat and I looked back over the sofa at him. The pack had gone trawling for food, leaving us to watch a chick flick that only Foust had considered staying for. Apparently his stomach had gotten the better of him instead.

Or his manhood had.

"What is it?" Kat asked. I could practically hear the plea in her voice for him to tell her something ominous. She seemed to have had her fill of happy time and was again ready for a fight.

"We came upon an unlikely scene tonight."

"By scene he means shitshow," Dean added as he entered the room. "Massive fight between one of the werewolf packs and a bunch of witches just outside the Bronx. And in plain fucking sight."

"Shit," Kat breathed, realizing that even she didn't want the consequences that could bring.

"Exactly," Jase replied, his expression tight with the

knowledge that the war that had once been insidious was becoming an out-and-out liability.

"What did you do? Kill them all?" she asked, walking over to him. I followed not far behind her.

"We did what needed to be done." Merc's voice entered the room before he did. When he rounded the doorjamb, he was covered in blood. My heart stopped for a beat. He took one look at the pallor of my face and came to me, putting his arms around my waist. "I am fine, Piper."

"That's a lot of blood."

"And none of it is mine."

"It's primarily the wolves," Dean said.

"They seemed reluctant to comply with our demand to cease their activities," Jase added. "We took out the ones that required it."

"And the witches?" I asked, my long-term hatred of them boiling up within me.

Jase and Dean looked at one another for a moment, sharing a silent conversation. Merc turned to look at them, and their eyes fell upon him.

"That's where things get interesting," Merc said, running his hand through my hair. "I know how you feel about them —how they treated you in the past, Piper—but the only way to ensure that this war does not spill over into the human world is to shut it down. We cannot contain it any longer. Not by force."

"What are you saying?"

"He's saying that the witches were much more interested in a truce. In helping to stop the war—under certain conditions," Jase said, answering for his brother.

"Like what?" Kat asked, her healthy dose of skepticism notable.

Again the three men looked at one another for a moment before speaking—out loud to Kat and me, anyway.

"They do not want to involve the king." The way Merc said those words sent chills up my spine.

"Well at least we can agree on that much," Kat muttered under her breath.

"It seems that we are not the only ones who no longer trust him," Jase added.

"But can we trust them?" I asked, taking turns staring down Jase and Dean. They'd borne witness to what those bitches had done to me during my time living at the mansion. Hell, they'd shut some of them down themselves—permanently. How they thought I could go along with their plan was beyond me. Every fiber of my being railed against the idea.

"I do not know that we can trust anyone but ourselves," Merc said. His double entendre was clear. He wasn't just speaking of people outside the mansion; he was including some of its new residents in that as well.

"I don't think we have much of a choice," Jase said, cutting off my train of thought. "We either work behind the scenes to neutralize the situation before it escalates past the point of control, or the humans find out about us and all hell breaks loose."

"Yeah, and I don't know about you, but I don't really enjoy being hunted all that much. They might not be the brightest species, but they'd figure out soon enough how to eradicate us. They always fear what they can't comprehend," Dean said.

"Agreed. And they wouldn't be able to differentiate between who is friend and who is foe."

"They'd kill at will and celebrate our deaths," Merc added.

"They'd have to find us first," Kat said, defiance in her voice. A challenge for some human to try and take her out.

"They would eventually," Merc replied. "It has happened before. It could happen again."

What a sobering thought that was.

"We've arranged a meeting on neutral ground," Jase said, taking a step closer to me. "We weren't going to tell you at first; I know this won't be easy for you. Maybe you should stay behind when we go."

"Hell no!" I shouted, batting away the hand that reached for me. "You are not going to meet those bitches without me. I don't give a shit how bad things are or how sincere they seem. They can't be trusted."

"And I'll be going too," Knox said, stepping into the room. Damn that wolf was stealthy. A room full of supernaturals never heard him spying. "And as for whether or not *I* can be trusted..." He nailed Merc with a scathing glare. "Maybe it would be worth reminding this crowd that Piper trusted some of you in the past, and that didn't end so well for her. She's never been harmed under my protection. I don't think you all can say the same. So my pack will be attending this meeting, whether you like that idea or not. It's non-negotiable."

The temperature in the room dropped about twenty degrees.

"The wolves were the ones that instigated the battle we happened upon," Jase said. "I highly doubt your presence will put the witches at ease."

"Different pack." Knox bit out those two words with every ounce of annoyance he felt.

"You plan to make up some shirts with that on it before we go so they know that?" Dean countered. "Because I highly doubt they give a fuck otherwise. They see a wolf and they're going to start whipping spells around that room so fast your heads will spin."

"Will the coven queen be there?" he asked, as though the answer to that question would settle the argument.

"It is my understanding that she will be."

"Then we should be good." Knox offered no explanation before he turned and started out of the room. "Piper, when you're done here, I need to speak with you."

"Yeah. I'll be right there."

He disappeared through the doorway, leaving all of us behind in a wake of curiosity and confusion.

"Your mysterious side piece is just full of surprises," Kat said, shaking her head. "You really do know how to pick 'em."

"Yeah," I said in agreement, shrinking under the weight of Merc's gaze. "Are we done here? For now?"

"If you need to go speak with the wolf, we can fill you in on anything you miss later."

I hesitated for a second before turning to leave. Just as I reached the door, I turned back to look at the brothers.

"I'm glad you're all okay."

Then I took off down the hall in search of Knox.

❧

I FOUND him in his room waiting for me. He was alone, so I stepped inside and closed the door behind me.

"What did you want to tell me?"

He took a deep breath before patting the bed beside him, indicating that he wanted me to join him. I obliged, leaving enough space between us for me to look at him without going cross-eyed.

"You're not going to like what I'm about to say to you, but I need you to trust me."

"That word sure is getting thrown around a lot tonight—"

"I'm serious, Piper. Can you do that?"

I paused for a moment, wondering if I could. Serious sounded like a major downer, especially after the news we'd just received. But such was life, so I sucked it up.

"Yes."

"Good. Now, I'm going to answer the question that I'm quite sure is burrowing through your mind at the moment: why does the coven queen matter?"

"Yep, I did wonder that. Friend of yours or something?"

A tension-laden pause drew out so long that it made me want to bolt from the room.

"We are acquainted."

"And that's reassuring regarding your pack's presence at the meeting because...?"

"Because she knows my character. She will not attack us unprovoked."

"Sounds like she'd need to be more than acquainted with you to guarantee that."

Another pause.

"The details behind the whys and hows aren't going to help right now, Piper. I wanted to be as open with you about this as I could for now. This is where the trust comes into play."

I bit the inside of my lip while I contemplated what he'd said. Did I really want to hear about his history with the coven queen? If it was as illicit as my mind was suggesting it could be, would confirming that make me happier? Or was ignorance bliss for the time being?

"You know that's a lot to ask, right? You're at least aware of that fact?"

He took my hand in his and placed it in his lap.

"I am, Piper. Believe me when I tell you that if I thought you needed to know everything, I'd tell you. But there are things about my life in New York that just can't come out yet. Maybe not ever."

"Merc seems to know things about you, but he hasn't said anything."

Knox's eyes narrowed.

"That's because he knows I know things about him. Casting the first stone wouldn't be wise in his position."

"That's not especially comforting."

"I'm sorry," he said with a loud exhale. "I just wanted to try to be up front with you."

"And I appreciate it. I just wish I had more faith in this upcoming meeting."

His exhausted expression slowly turned to one of amusement, his eyes lighting up with mischief.

"Just think, if it goes to shit, you could just open a hole in the Earth to swallow up the witches."

I tried my best to keep a straight face while I tapped my chin, pondering his suggestion.

"That would be incredibly satisfying, given my history with those bitches."

He laughed out loud.

"Easy, girl. Maybe you should stay home."

"Not a chance. If someone is going to wipe those chicks out, it's going to be me."

"Deal," he said before pulling me into him. He kissed me lightly on the mouth, his eyes open to take in my reaction. I stayed connected to him for just a moment, kissing him lightly before my kneejerk instinct to pull away kicked in. It was soft and sweet and welcome. And I could feel my cheeks flush as he pulled away.

"No pressure, remember," he said with a wink.

"And I appreciate that."

"But I gotta say, those sweat pants are sexy as hell."

I looked down at my borrowed clothes and back at him with disbelief twisting my features.

"Men are so strange."

I stood up to leave and earned an ass smack for the gesture.

"What can I say, I like intrigue. It's nice to think about slipping them off to see what they're hiding."

My cheeks rosied even more.

"I'm going to bed. You should probably go have a cold shower."

I opened the door and stepped through it, unwilling to look back at him. I didn't want him to confirm the effect he was having on me.

"Won't be the first one since I met you," he said just as I closed the door.

With that thought in mind, I made my way to my room. I needed sleep before my training with Drake and the meeting with the witches. I hoped my mentor would have more information for me than Knox and Merc had shared. I didn't trust the witches, no matter what Knox said. They made the vampire bitch squad look like the welcome wagon when it came to me.

I highly doubted that had changed much in my absence.

24

I woke up late the next day. The sound of my cellphone vibrating like it was possessed finally got my attention, and I leaped from the bed. I didn't bother looking to see who it was; I already knew the answer to that.

Drake.

I was late for our training.

Fumbling around the room for some running tights and a t-shirt, I finally found some suitable enough to throw on. Grizz stood by the door, his patronizing look telling me that he already knew we were late.

"Thanks for waking me up," I grumbled, bumping him out of the way with my hip. "Drake's going to be such a douche about this."

Grizz huffed in response, as though I deserved what I had coming my way, which I probably did. I didn't really think it was my fault that I'd had a hard time sleeping. I could feel the press of Merc on my mind as I'd drifted off, and for whatever reason, I'd chosen to wake up rather than surrender to his call. I'd spent the rest of the night wondering what that meant. What my avoidance of him in my subconscious could mean.

Apparently it meant I'd get no sleep and be late to train with a crabby warlock.

Fucking fantastic.

I ran through the yard with Grizz nipping at my heels to spur me on. By the time we found Drake by the bridge, he looked ready to commit a homicide. Not a good sign.

"How nice of you to grace me with your presence this morning." He made a big show of looking at his busted-up old watch, then back at me. "Or afternoon, as the case may be."

"Listen, it was a shit night. I'd go into the details, but they'd take too long and you'd get even more pissy, so I'll just give you the highlights if you want them."

"Which I do."

"Great. Fine." I stopped for a second to figure out how best to summarize the night. I settled on a stream-of-consciousness rambling. "The king threw a last-minute party—which he never does—and we all had to go. I got a wild hair up my ass when he wouldn't let me cook Sylvia, the slut who betrayed Merc to Kingston, so I got testy with him and called him out on his shit. Didn't go over well, as I'm sure you can imagine. I then threw a pool party in his backyard, Merc and his brothers did damage control, the wolfpack came home with me to decompress, and then Merc and the boys came home to tell us that they'd happened upon a battle of sorts between the witches and some pack. They stepped in, kicked a lot of ass, and now—for whatever reason—we have a meeting with the witches today, including the coven queen." I looked at his dumb-founded expression and wondered if I'd left something out. If I'd been more incoherent than I'd expected. "I think that's the gist."

"I think that's plenty." He sounded really irritated with me. I knew that taking on the king had been less than wise, but he didn't know what Merc could do: what he'd done to smooth things over. "Tell me something, Piper. Do you think the king will be quick to forgive you?"

"No, but that's not really your problem, is it? In fact, it would free you from our little deal, right? It'd be a total bonus for you if my mouth got me killed."

"Do not put words in my mouth, especially about things you do not understand." He took a step closer to me, and Grizz lunged in front of me, teeth bared. Drake's mouth curled up into a wry smile. "I'm not a threat," he said to the bear, putting his hands up in surrender. "Not to her or you."

Grizz's shoulders seemed to relax a bit, but he didn't move from his spot. Though he apparently believed what the warlock had said, he wasn't willing to relinquish his position between Drake and me.

"He doesn't seem sold on that," I said, sarcasm thick in my tone.

"He should be. I may be one of the only beings in this city not out to harm you."

"Prove it."

"That is precisely what I was trying to do by asking you about the king. I was trying to counsel you on the matter. Warn you about your behavior."

I hesitated a moment before speaking. With every word out of Drake's mouth, Grizz rested back on his haunches, eventually sitting down in a relaxed posture.

"What I did isn't going to be a problem. Not anymore, at least." Drake's eyes narrowed at me. "You're just going to have to trust me on that."

I was starting to sound like Merc and Knox.

"Well I hope for your sake that's true. But that only solves one of your problems—allegedly. You still have another. One more disconcerting."

"What?"

"The coven queen."

"That bad, huh?"

"You have no idea."

"Knox seems to think her presence will be beneficial."

"Then I think Knox is overconfident—as usual." Drake walked away, headed for the bridge, and I followed along, stopping beside him when he finally situated himself along the railing. "The leader of any faction is in that position for a reason, Piper. All of them. Including Knox..."

That was bait I just couldn't leave on the line.

"How do you two know each other?"

He shot me a curious look.

"He didn't tell you after that day in the alley?"

"No. He's been rather cagey about his past in New York. About you... about the queens..."

"Shocking." Drake's sarcasm was thick in his reply.

"Do you know why he left? Why he went to Alaska?"

Drake inhaled hard, then let it out slowly, buying himself time to either compose an answer or decide if he was going to give me one at all. He stuffed his hands into the pockets of his tattered coat and pulled it closed.

"Only he knows the real reason why he left, Piper. But rumors run wild in the supernatural underworld. I have heard many of them."

"Like what?" My quiet words seemed to echo off the trees around us.

"That is something you will have to ask him. His secrets are not for me to share. But I will say this; if he is unwilling to tell you—if he will not answer your pointed questions—then beware. The skeletons in his closet may be scarier than you want to believe." I let that warning rattle around in my brain until Drake spoke again. "Now back to the coven queen."

"Is she as bad as the vampire king?"

"Yes. Maybe worse in some ways. At least with the king, you generally know where you stand. His allegiance does not waver easily. His goal, for the most part, has been to keep the peace. The coven queen, on the other hand... her magic thrives on chaos, and she knows no allegiance. Even if the alpha thinks otherwise."

"So you think she's up to something?"

"I always assume she is, though in this instance, I do not know what."

I exhaled hard, dropping my head down to the railing. We all knew the meeting was a risk; none of us was dumb enough not to consider that possibility. What we didn't know—what we couldn't know—was whether the risk outweighed the benefits of a potential truce with the witches.

We were going to find out either way.

"Where are you meeting?" he asked, drawing my attention away from my thoughts.

"At a nightclub. There will be humans there, so it should keep everyone in relative check."

He considered that answer for a second, then nodded. Even with just his profile in view, he looked somewhat solemn as he gazed out over the gorge. His mind was somewhere off in the distance, so I waited patiently for him to come back to himself.

A couple of minutes later, he did.

"I cannot go with you—to the meeting. I'm sorry."

"That's fine. I would never have asked you to."

He turned his pale grey eyes to me and stared.

"You don't ask much of anyone, do you?"

I shrugged.

"Not really. I try not to. Maybe that's what happens when you're on your own as long as I was. You don't bother asking because there's nobody to ask." He continued to look at me until the silence grew uncomfortable. "But it's fine now. Now I have so many people around to help me it's overwhelming." I forced a laugh to try and lighten the mood.

"Tell me how you came to live at the mansion," he asked, his tone not unkind.

"The king offered me refuge there. At the time I didn't exactly have any better options, so I took it. I know what you're thinking—that I was a fool to trust him so easily—but it really wasn't even a choice. It was either that or constantly look over my shoulder. Hell, I still did that even after I was under the protection of Jase and Dean—Kat too. It's not really a way of life. Not a sustainable one."

"They truly do care for you." A statement, not a question.

"Yes. They have from the day I moved in with them. Jase and Dean have been like older brothers to me ever since. Between them and Kat, they pulled me out of a deepening depression and death sentence. I'm forever grateful to them for that."

"This is why you trust them without question?"

I shrugged.

"They saved my life in more ways than I can count."

He nodded in response.

"And Mercenary?"

"Yes." It seemed the simplest answer, given our history.

"The alpha too?"

"All of them. And they did it without any regard for themselves. They did it when I was weak and knew nothing of my power. They didn't want anything from me. They just wanted me to be safe."

"Loyalty is a quality rarely found in our world, Piper. Never take it for granted." He frowned and looked away. "Reinhardt did, and look where that got him. Him and all of those loyal to him." Not knowing how to respond to that, I didn't bother; the bitterness in his voice said it all. I wondered if he would speak at all after that—if our lesson was over before it had begun—but he seemed to calm himself before changing the subject. "You said the day I met you that you got the amulet from Kingston," he said, side-eyeing me. "I want to know how you managed to take from him something that powerful."

"You don't believe me," I said, anger flushing my cheeks.

"It's not a matter of belief, Piper. It's a matter of understanding. And I don't understand how you were able to do what you say you did."

"That's because you're a lone wolf, so to speak. I work with a pack."

"Did they help you?" he asked, taking my comment a bit too literally. In hindsight, maybe it wasn't the best analogy ever.

"No. They were trapped behind a burning wall of magic that Kingston had erected. By the time I got the amulet, it was just Kingston and me—and Grizz, of course. His distraction was what gave me my chance. The second I had the amulet in my hand, I smashed it on a rock. After that, all hell broke loose. The magic wall fell, and the warlocks were up to their eyeballs in pissed-off werewolves."

"Not an enviable position," Drake said, pinning serious eyes on me.

"No. Between them and me, the whole thing only lasted a minute."

He took a step closer to me.

"What did you do?" His voice was low and dark and filled with anticipation.

"Like I said before, I buried Kingston and the others somewhere near the Earth's core."

"I thought you were bluffing."

I shook my head.

"I don't bluff about dead warlocks."

"Tell me the last thing he said."

There was a need in Drake's eyes that I couldn't understand but felt obliged to erase. Maybe he needed closure about Reinhardt's death. Maybe he needed to know that he was avenged. Or maybe he had his own beef with Kingston that the knowledge about his death would help satisfy. I didn't know, and I sure as hell wasn't about to ask.

"I had him suspended above a gaping hole in the ground. His feet were scrambling, like he could somehow reach the edge of it. Then he turned and looked at me and said 'you can't do this to me'."

"And?"

"I told him 'I just did', and then cut the magical ties that held him and watched the Earth swallow him whole."

Silence.

"I would have enjoyed seeing that."

For a brief second, I thought there had been a hint of pride in his voice. Like my mentor had finally seen me as an equal. Then he turned his focus back to the horizon and the moment disappeared as if it'd never happened.

"Your turn," I said, drawing his attention back to me.

"My turn to do what, exactly?"

"To answer one of my questions."

He looked at me, his brow furrowed with uncertainty.

"One. One question only. You need to be training, not talking, especially given the recent turn of events."

I considered his counteroffer and nodded in agreement.

"You know that I am part warlock." I hesitated and looked up at his face. I would have sworn his skin had turned pale. "Do you know who my father is?"

Drake's eyes went wide.

There was no taking back my question at that point. There was only holding my breath and praying for the truth to be revealed. Good or bad, I would finally have an answer.

He took a deep breath before he spoke. The silence between us seemed to drag on for hours, though I was sure it was only seconds. He let out a loud exhale, and my heart quit beating.

"Yes."

Yes...

That word, though it told me nothing, meant everything to me.

"Who?" I asked, excitement raising my voice to a shrill sound. "Who is it? Who's my father?"

"I answered your question—"

"NO!" I shouted, cutting him off. The blue sky mirrored my anger, rumbling loudly, like a storm was rolling in. That was true enough, really. The storm's name was Piper. "Tell me his name."

"Piper," Drake started, sympathy blooming in his gaze. "You don't want to know. Not really."

"Yes, I do. Now tell me his name."

Another loud exhale from Drake, followed by swearing under his breath.

"Reinhardt. Reinhardt was your father."

"Is," I corrected, hopeful that my initial assessment of

Drake had been right and he was just covering for the warlock lord. But the downturn of his expression made that hope disappear in an instant. He wrapped his arm around my shoulders to comfort the blow I feared was coming.

"No, Piper. *Was*. Past tense."

A crack of thunder so loud my eardrums rang boomed around us and the sky opened up, letting loose rain from the cloudless blue above. It pelted my face, hiding the tears that streamed down my cheeks. Camouflaging my pain.

"I only recently came to this realization, which means he never knew about you," Drake said gently. "I know if he had, he would have found you. He'd have done anything he could to keep you safe—moved heaven and earth. He'd have trained you to be what you've become without him." His hand squeezed my shoulder. "He'd have been so proud."

I let loose a sob, bending in on myself as I did. The pain of losing a father I'd never known hurt far more than I could have ever imagined. It hurt even more to know that he had been in the same city with me all that time and no one—neither I, nor anyone close to me—had known it. The fact that Kingston had been the one to kill him only made it worse. I wanted to kill him all over again.

But slower.

"I know what you're thinking right now," Drake said, still holding me up.

"Do you?" My reply was harsh and sardonic and every bit as biting as I'd meant it to be. "Do you really?"

I looked up at him to find pain in his eyes.

"More than you could possibly know."

I stood up to face him, the rain still pouring down around us. His light grey hair had been darkened by the storm, and it hung limp in his face, nearly covering his eyes.

"Answer me one last question then, if you understand me so well. Who is my mother?"

His shrewd eyes narrowed.

"Someone I never knew."

My heart sank further.

Drake was kind enough to leave me alone to process his answer, not pushing me to start our lesson. He was more compassionate than I would have thought him capable the day I met him. Maybe he finally cared a bit about me.

Regardless, the truth he'd just shared was tearing me up inside. I needed something else to think about: something to distract me from his revelation. That method seemed to work well enough for Kat. It was worth a shot.

"So," I started, wiping my eyes and nose on the sleeve of my shirt. "Any suggestions on how to handle this coven queen you think is up to no good? Any magic hacks you can suggest?"

He turned to pin cold, dead eyes on me.

"If she tries to fuck with you in any way—anything at all—burn her to ash."

Point taken.

"Okay," I replied, nodding a bit too frantically. "I can do that."

The weathered bridge groaned under the weight of the grizzly bear attempting to walk out and join us. With every step he took, I prayed the chubby bugger wouldn't break the damn thing and send us all to the bottom of the gorge. Yes, it was a way out of the impending meeting, but not one I found acceptable.

I heard a loud crack as the bridge shook, and I screamed, grabbing hold of the railing as tight as I could. By the time I calmed myself, I felt the nudge of a wet muzzle against my arm. It brought my attention back to Grizz, who was standing beside me, sadness in his eyes. At first I wondered why, then the reason plowed into me. Once again I'd put myself in a position where he couldn't help me. Helpless as always. How painful it must be for him to be tethered to a magical being that he couldn't actually follow. One that wouldn't allow him to do the job he was called to do. My heart ached knowing that, once again, I'd have to leave him behind—possibly for good, if everything went to shit.

He'd never know what had happened, either.

"I'm so sorry, buddy." I scratched behind his ears, loving him up a bit before I dropped the bomb he seemed to be anticipating already. "You can't come tonight."

He grumbled at me, leaning his head against my arm. But his eyes were all for Drake. I couldn't see what they were saying, but judging by the warlock's reaction to them, his message had been received.

"Or maybe he can," Drake said to no one in particular. He took a step or two back from us, assessing something in the bear that I didn't understand. As if responding to a command, Grizz stood on his hind legs and let loose a growl that shook the trees. "Yes… I think that's a perfect idea."

"What is?" I asked. Silence was all I received in response. While I stood there trying to figure out if Drake was losing it or if he suddenly spoke grizzly, the bear walked toward him and bowed his head as if waiting to be knighted.

Little did I know how close that analogy would really come to the truth.

"You are more worthy of this than any of your kind," Drake said, resting his hand on the bear's head. It was then that I felt magic coursing through the ground at my feet, the swell of it crashing into Grizz. He snapped up to standing, his fuzzy body looking as if it were being yanked in every direction at once. I reached for him, but one quick snap from Drake stopped me cold.

"NO!" he shouted, pinning hardened eyes on me. "You must trust us. Trust the magic."

With his head extended at an angle I didn't think possible, Grizz shot me a look that begged me to stay. Even as tears streamed down my face, the bear forced a strange smile at me, his best attempt to cheer me up. But how could I? I thought he was dying—sacrificing himself for me in some bizarre attempt to keep the queen of the fey from collecting me.

How wrong I was about that.

Instead of a lifeless ball of fur at my feet, I got something wildly different.

Drake chanted something in a tongue I didn't comprehend, and I looked on as Grizz's fur shed from his body in tufts. I balled my hands at my sides in an attempt to stop myself from reaching for him. Drake's words echoed in my mind. Trust the magic...

So I did.

I stood by and watched as the hairless grizzly began to morph—painfully—into something else entirely. Something tall and strong and incredibly human. And naked. Very, very naked.

I tried to look away, but my eyes were transfixed on the man that stood where the bear once had. With his back to me, he looked back over his shoulder. I gasped when I saw his eyes—eyes I recognized as Grizz's. They were just as warm and brown as they'd been when they'd belonged to the grizzly.

"Oh my God..."

"He is of no use to you in bear form here in the city, a point you seem all too aware of. I decided to remedy that problem. Besides, I will feel much better with him escorting you tonight in my absence. So much better."

"Is he... can he..."

"He is still very much the bear you know and love. He's just packaged a little differently." Drake looked at Grizz, admiring his work. And really, he should have. It was impressive. Grizz stood taller than either Knox or Merc, and he was huge. His stubbled face and disheveled brown hair suited him well. He looked like a rugged outdoorsy type, and while that might make him stand out a bit in NYC, he was at least human in appearance, which was a big plus. "He has the ability to change back into bear form while on the property," Drake added. "Something tells me he probably prefers it."

Grizz grunted in agreement.

I couldn't move, my feet seeming to have grown roots that tethered me in place. Shocked was an understatement to say the least. My mind still couldn't quite grasp what I was seeing, and Grizz—still very naked in front of me—seemed to be annoyed by that. He turned to face me, standing defiantly as if daring me to take him in and get over it. In fairness, he'd always been nude in bear form. He didn't seem to get why his change made any difference.

"I'm sorry, Grizz. I'm just... it's just a lot to take in." He looked down at his man bits and shrugged. He didn't seem very impressed by them at all. "Not that! I mean you... as a human."

His shoulders softened a bit, his sympathy for my plight showing through, and he walked over to me, closing the distance between us in three easy strides. Before I realized what he was doing, he wrapped his arms around me and crushed me against his strong body. I could barely breathe and had to tap him until he realized that was my emergency release cue. After I stopped coughing from lack of air, I looked up at him and smiled.

"Looks like you get to come this time after all." He returned the gesture, and I laughed at how awkward it looked on him. "Let's go find you some clothes."

He took my hand in his and started off toward the mansion. I looked back at Drake, who stood smiling at the sight of the man-bear and me. He seemed satisfied that I would be well looked after at our meeting with the witches.

He looked at me like I no longer needed him.

❧

OUR ENTRANCE into the mansion went about as well as I could have expected.

We'd only made it halfway up the stairs when Knox and the boys appeared on the landing, staring down at us. And they didn't look especially friendly. Grizz took it upon himself to growl at them and their wall of hostility.

That growl damn near started a brawl.

Knox, flanked by Foust and Brunton, started down the stairs toward us, with Jagger close behind them. I jumped in front of Grizz and threw my arms up in a defensive posture to thwart them, if only for a second—just enough time to explain.

"Knox! Don't! It's just—"

"Holy shit!" Knox replied, coming to an abrupt halt only a couple stairs above us. Given the wide eyes on the rest of the wolves, they'd either put two and two together, or they'd scented who Grizz was. Either way, they looked shocked as hell.

"Yeah. I know," I said, looking up over my shoulder at Grizz. "So that happened."

"How?" Knox asked, closing the distance between us with considerably slower steps. Grizz had stopped growling, but he still didn't look super happy that the boys were about to come after him. So much for him being part of the pack.

"Drake. He decided I needed—" I cut myself off, realizing that the full truth wasn't going to fly with the alpha—that Drake thought I needed someone without a sketchy past at my side that night. I had to tread lightly on the issue. Very, very lightly. "He decided it was about time that Grizz be able to go with me when we left the mansion. He said he's my familiar—my guardian."

Knox turned his focus to me, eyes narrowed, like he was trying to pry my half-truth open to see what lay behind it. When he didn't find anything, his face relaxed a bit.

"Sorry, big guy," he said to Grizz, giving him one of those weird shoulder slap things that men always do. "I didn't realize it was you." Grizz let out a halfhearted grunt in response. "Don't hold it against me, okay? You can't really blame me. You'd have done the same if you'd seen some strange naked guy strolling in here with Piper."

"That's really the fucking bear," Brunton said, the words escaping his mouth before he could corral them. "What a mindfuck."

"Wait," Jagger said. His brow was furrowed as he tried to work through whatever had him puzzled. "If he's your guardian or whatever, has he always been able to do this? Like he's a werebear or something?"

"No. As Drake put it, this is his man suit, nothing more. He's still the bear and he can change back while on the property. But outside the glamour of the estate, this is the Grizz we need to come to know."

"He's huge," Foust added. I couldn't help but laugh, thinking it sounded like something Jagger would have said.

My eyes fell south for a split second before snapping back up to Grizz's face. Again that strange smile stretched across it.

"Yeah," I muttered under my breath. "He really is." The four of them, in eerie unison, all looked down at what I'd just taken in, then turned to me. "Anyway, he needs clothes. Like right now. Anybody got something he can borrow?"

"He's built like an oak tree, Piper," Foust said. "Pretty sure you need to check with Merc on that one. He might have something that would work. *Might*."

"Good idea," I said, heading up the stairs before coming to a grinding halt. Grizz was far from a fan of Merc, and I didn't think Merc would be super excited to have a naked Grizz paraded into his room so I could pick out clothes for my guardian. Merc was patient with me, but not that patient. "Can one of you go ask him for some pants? We need pants. Now. Preferably loose ones..."

I heard Grizz let loose something that sounded like a cough and a sneeze combined behind me. I looked back to find him still smiling at me.

"Was that a laugh?" I asked him. The look I received in response was not an appreciative one. It read, "what the fuck did you think it was?" Point made, Grizz. Point made. "You can feel free to change back into my furry little buddy any time now. I think I like you more that way."

I heard him snort behind me before the sound of his massive footsteps followed me up the stairs.

"Merc is going to shit a brick," Jagger said, laughing nervously.

"Nah," Knox replied with more confidence than I would have expected. "Grizz knows where he stands, don't you, Grizz?"

The man-bear stopped beside Knox, flashing him a look

that screamed "I stand wherever the fuck she stands," then kept walking.

"Looks like the bear might be a problem after all," Brunton said.

I picked up my pace, wanting to escape the tension so badly I'd have jumped out of my skin if I could have. I rounded the corner, Grizz right on my heels, and headed to my room. But not before I heard Knox's response echo up the stairs after us.

"Not if he knows what's good for him."

Before Grizz could wheel around and go after him, I reached back and grabbed his massive hand to haul him down the hallway to my room. I dragged him through the doorway and slammed the door behind us.

"Have you forgotten that Knox kept you protected when he didn't have to?" The man-bear honest to God rolled his eyes at me. "Oh no you don't! You don't get to roll those eyes at me, mister. Like it or not, you know I'm right. The wolves have been good to you. They accepted you into the pack, for fuck's sake. You do not get to try to pull rank on them the second you turn into..." I flailed my arm at him, trying to indicate his human form "... whatever all this is. You need to play nice with them. They want what's best for me, just like you do. Don't get all petty just because you think you can finally kick Knox's ass, which I'm not convinced is actually true, by the way."

The sound of knuckles cracking was not exactly the response I was looking for.

"Grizz," I said, sounding every bit as exhausted as I felt. I walked over to him, took his hands gently in mine, and looked up into his eyes. "If you're my guardian—if you're here to stand by my side—then you can't be fighting with everyone in the house. They're not the threat." He stared at me like he wasn't so convinced of that. "You're just going to have to trust me about that, okay?" With a put-upon sigh, he nodded. Then he wrapped me up in his massive arms and gave me a squeeze—one that didn't threaten to crush my lungs this time. "Thanks, buddy. Now I'm going to go hunt down some clothes for you. I need you to stay here while I do that. And no arguing!"

He let me go and stared down at me, willing me to see the futility in my command.

"Listen, you don't like Merc at the best of times. I'm pretty sure that you won't be on your best behavior if we go to his room now and bum some clothes off him." In a surprising show, he slapped his hand over his heart. "Wait... is that you swearing you won't?" He nodded. I stared back at him with a healthy dose of skepticism in my expression. "If you cause any problems—any at all—I'll make Drake take away your man suit, and you'll be relegated to the mansion all over again. Got it?" Another nod.

With an exhale that had my lips flapping, I started toward the bedroom door. Along the way I snatched a stray towel off the floor and wrapped it around Grizz's waist. The gesture earned me another cough/sneeze/laugh sound in return.

"Yeah, well, you'll thank me for that later. Males and their dicks... it's like a never-ending contest with you guys."

Satisfied that he looked much more decent, I made my way into the hallway, headed for Merc's room. The one we'd once shared, if only for a little while. I hoped he'd take the news of Grizz's change well.

I hoped he wouldn't see a threat where there was none.

25

Merc was nowhere to be found, so I snatched some pants and a shirt and left his room. I heard Grizz's stomach growl, so we made our way down to the kitchen where we found Kat. She was perched on the island, drinking a beer and reading a magazine.

That quickly stopped when she took one look at us.

"Well well well," Kat drawled from her perch on the kitchen counter. "What do we have here?" She hopped down and started toward us, smiling like a Cheshire cat. Then she stopped short, dropping the bottle of beer in her hand. It shattered into tiny pieces all over the marble floor. "No fucking way..."

"Yes fucking way."

"But... he's massive." She walked up to him and grabbed his arm, squeezing it as she shook her head. "Like a tank..."

"I know, Kat. I've been through this more times than I care to recount."

"So Knox—"

"Already seen him."

"And Merc—"

"Not in his room when we went to get clothes." I shot her a pointed look. "And his arm isn't the only thing that's massive…"

Her smile widened.

"Atta boy, Grizz. Show these guys who the real boss is." She held out her fist toward him and he tapped it with his. "He's caught on fast, huh?"

"You have no idea," I grumbled. "And he apparently needs to be fed, so…"

"Ah," she said, nodding in recognition. "I can handle that. Leave the big guy to me." She walked over to the fridge and started rustling through its contents. She emerged with an armful of produce that I didn't even know we had. Apparently I hadn't been eating much as of late. "Who knew a vegetarian could get so big?" she said to herself, arranging the food on the counter.

"Hey, what time is the meeting?"

"Not sure. Check with Jase." She looked up at Grizz and put two and two together. "Is that why he's all decked out in his new skin? To come tonight?"

"Yeah, Drake thought it would be best. That guy really doesn't trust the coven queen."

"Because he's a twitchy motherfucker, but I like that about him. His cynicism."

"He has it in spades, that's for damn sure."

"That he does. But for the major pain in the ass that he is, he's been good to you, Piper. And I wouldn't be quick to dismiss any warning he gives you. Twitchy motherfuckers survive for a reason."

"Yes, yes… I hear you. Now you babysit the man-bear while I go find out what the plan is for tonight. I kinda missed that part."

"Yeah, ya did," she replied, poking her tongue into her cheek. "How did your little meeting with Knox go, anyway?"

"Not like that, I can tell you that much."

She scoffed.

"Too bad. Sounds like a missed opportunity if you ask me. Especially if everything blows up in our faces tonight. You might regret not having one final romp with him." Grizz growled at her sentiment, and she patted his forearm to calm him. "I'm just messing around, big guy. No need to get all roid-ragey about it. Piper will be fine. We all will."

He seemed satisfied with her answer and went back to eating. Kat flashed me a look that said, "holy shit, is he ever sensitive." I gave her my "you have no idea" glare in return, then walked out of the kitchen in search of Merc. He needed to learn about Grizz's change from me, and I needed answers from him before we left to meet with the witches.

I needed to know the odds on everything going wrong.

26

I searched everywhere I could think of in the mansion, but Merc was still nowhere to be found. Neither was Jase. Or Dean. The sibling trio was completely MIA, which made me nervous. It was still daylight outside, so they had to be somewhere inside. The fact that I couldn't find them was totally unnerving.

I killed the little free time I had before we needed to leave searching for them and trying to find Grizz something more suitable to wear to the club. Sweat pants weren't going to cut it at all. Not by a long shot.

Finding him something club-worthy took way longer than it should have. I got a shit-ton of strange looks from the other enforcers, whom I convinced to donate to the cause. I didn't bother explaining myself, and thankfully they didn't ask. But when they showed up to head to the club, they got their answer in the form of a strange being wearing their borrowed threads.

I simply shrugged and walked out the door.

We all piled into various vehicles and drove off toward the club, convoy-style. Sandwiched between Grizz and

Brunton, I tried to calm myself and pray for the best: that both sides wanted the same thing. A truce.

I kept that thought in mind as we pulled up in front of the building and climbed out.

Because it was standard operating hours at the club, humans were everywhere. That was what ensured it was neutral ground. No matter what, nobody ever broke the 'never in front of humans' rule. At least nobody had until the wolves attacked the witches the night before.

That said, I still wasn't convinced that the witches had been fully innocent in that altercation. I didn't trust them, period. Though they may not attack us directly, I wouldn't have put it past them to magically wire our cars to explode when we left, or something like that. Something that would look accidental to human eyes.

Merc, Jase, and Dean were waiting for us outside when we arrived, and as much as I wanted to ask them where they'd been, I knew it wasn't the time. One stern look from Merc told me that it wouldn't be a short explanation, so I shelved that concern for the moment to focus on what needed to be done that night. Get in, come to terms, and get out—alive.

The brothers led the way in, having been the ones to set up the whole thing. Knox followed behind them. I could see his golden hair above the crowd as they made their way upstairs to the VIP area. To an outsider, it would look like there was a large private party going on. Had they any clue what was really going down, they'd run from the building screaming bloody murder.

Grizz walked so close to me that I nearly fell forward. I knew he was on high alert, but damn—could a girl get a little space? I elbowed him in the gut, and he seemed to get the point. He gave me a whole extra foot of breathing room after that.

We took the stairs up to VIP, and by the time we crested the final step, I could see the witches all spread out, creating a semicircle of sorts, focusing on the brothers, Knox, and a few others in the center of it. I was instantly put on the defensive. I didn't like the setup one bit.

Jase appeared to be addressing one of the witches—one I recognized from my teen years. Not my favorite person. I managed to make my way over to where they stood so I could better hear over the music.

Some of us didn't have superhuman hearing.

"Shall we see if we can come to terms?" the dark-haired witch asked. She was average in looks, but her confidence outshined that fact. She looked like she could snap you in half with just a thought. The desire to shrink under the weight of her stare was hard to stave off.

"I don't think this needs to be complicated," Jase replied. "We came to your aid. You owe us something in return. To show a little good faith."

At that, she laughed.

"And what, pray tell, do you think that is, enforcer?"

"You want peace between our kinds? Prove it." Her eyes flashed with anger before she schooled them to neutrality. "Agree to our terms and you shall have it."

"You would make us cower to your commands?"

"If you want peace and a chance to end this war before it wipes us all out, then yes."

"It won't." There was such confidence in her reply that it made me wonder if she knew something we didn't.

"Maybe it will. Maybe it won't. But I don't feel like finding out, do you?" He took a step closer to her, assessing her as he did. "You've been alive for only decades, while I have seen centuries come and go. Which of us do you think is better equipped to survive this war if it comes to that? Me or you?"

Her bravado wavered at that comment, and I knew Jase had her. Like it or not, she was going to agree to his terms.

"Say what you have to say, vampire."

He took another step closer to her.

"You will cease to use magic of any sort against my kind. You will refrain from attacking any of the other breeds. You will use magic for defense only. Any infractions and the punishment is death. Quick and painless, but death all the same."

She didn't answer, looking past Jase to Knox, who weathered her stare like it was nothing.

"You would bring wolves to this meeting? After what happened yesterday?"

"Different pack. Different rules," Knox said, sounding bored. Knowing him, he probably was. He'd admitted more than once to loving danger. If he kept it up, he was headed for a whole lot of it.

"Perhaps," the witch replied, returning her gaze to Jase. "He has sided with you? You two have a truce?" Holy shit was that a loaded question.

"He has, and we do."

"Funny," she said, stepping around Jase to walk toward Knox. "I do not recognize him."

"Can't know everyone," Knox replied.

"But I can," a voice called from deep within the witches. A stunning middle-aged woman stepped forward, pulling a hood back from her face. Her sharp features were intimidating, and I tried to remember if I'd ever seen her before, but I came up with nothing. It made me wonder if she'd maybe pulled a Drake on me and erased any memory of the encounter I felt certain we must have had. Everything in my body said I knew her. "I will vouch for the wolf and his pack."

Though her words were a relief, there was an undercurrent of hostility in her voice when she spoke them. Judging by how tense Knox became, he heard it too. And he was surprised. Another bad sign.

"Coven Queen," Jase said, nodding his head in respect. "Do you agree to the terms?"

She glanced at him, then focused her intention on Knox as she approached him. My desire to get between them was hard to rein in. Something in her eye—the way she looked at him—had me on edge.

"It's been a while," she said to Knox, looking him up and down. "You look well."

"As do you."

Silence.

"Don't you want to ask what I've been up to?" she asked him, cocking her head to the side.

"Seems like you've been busy."

"And you? Have you been busy?" She cast a catty look my way. "It looks like you have. Tell me, who is the girl?"

"Nobody important." He said those words like he believed them, and even though I knew he was deflecting her attention away from me, it still hurt to hear them.

"Ah," she sighed. "You forget how well I know you. You almost had me for a moment, but you gave yourself away when your left ear moved. It always does that when you're lying. It's always been your tell."

"Are you agreeing to the terms or not?"

"We will need something in return," she replied, her eyes sliding over to me and back again. "A show of good faith, as the enforcer called it. Insurance that you won't turn on us the moment you see fit."

While Knox's eyes blazed amber, Merc stepped to the witch, taking her arm in his hand.

"You need nothing to ensure that," he said. I knew what he was doing, and I prayed that his recklessness wouldn't out his abilities. If he had any intention of keeping them secret, he wasn't acting like it.

The coven queen looked up at him and smiled.

"No," she said, gazing up at him lovingly. "Perhaps I don't."

"I'll ask you once more only," Jase said. "Do we have an agreement?"

"We will not attack your kind. We will refrain from attacking any of the other breeds. We will use our magic for defense only."

"Or the punishment is death," he added for effect.

"Or the punishment is death." She looked over at Jase and nodded. "To this, we agree."

"Good," Dean said, looking a bit on edge. "Now let's get the fuck out of here."

We all turned to leave, and I let out a sigh of relief. Though tense at times, the meeting had gone off without a hitch. That was all I could have asked for.

Or so I thought.

Then I realized that one of the witches had Grizz encased in an orb of pink light. The set of his features told me all I needed to know. She was electrocuting him slowly.

"NO!" I screamed, lunging for him.

"What is the meaning of this?" Merc growled.

The coven queen just smiled at him again. The menace in it was plain.

"He is not a breed of supernatural," she replied. "And neither is she."

Her slender, elegant finger pointed at me accusingly.

"Let him go," I said, stalking toward her.

She cocked her head to the side, clearly amused.

"Make me, you *mutt.*" Suddenly her 'neither is she' comment made more sense. She knew I wasn't purebred—that I came from mixed parentage.

Before I could ponder that any longer, Knox's harsh tone pulled me back to the present and the problem at hand.

"This is over," Knox snarled, storming over to Grizz. He tried to snatch him out of his pink trap and received a jolt of electricity for his efforts.

"Let. Him. Go." I didn't speak those words to the coven queen that time. Instead, I spoke to the magic pulsing through the room. Like an obedient dog, it released the bear and sat the fuck down. The pink orb disappeared, and Grizz fell forward to his knees. I scrambled toward him, wrapping my arms around him. "Are you okay, buddy?"

Before I got an answer, all hell broke loose.

❧

THE WHOLE THING had been an ambush: a cleverly woven ambush. I knew a thing or two about those.

In the blink of an eye things went from mundane to shit-show. Fire and bodies and blood rained down in the club on all that were there. Some of the humans lay strewn about the floor, the rest screaming and running for the exits, stampeding over the wounded like they were already lost. For a moment the shock of it all paralyzed me.

Then a scream from Kat woke me to reality. I could help

them all if I pulled my shit together. I could save the innocents.

"Protect the humans!" I shouted over the din of blades and explosions and cries for help. I felt my magic course through the room, collecting around me, but it wasn't enough. Encased in concrete and far from the elements, I couldn't summon enough to provide shelter for those that needed it. Fear still polluted my mind.

Become the force of nature you are...

Drake's words rang through my mind and I clung to them, hoping it would be enough to pull forth the amount of power I needed. Rooting my feet to the floor, I closed my eyes and inhaled deeply, pulling magic from deep within the Earth's core, dredging it up through me. "Protect them!" I screamed, my voice loud and harsh—a thing of fury. A roar of wind tore through the building, lifting the humans (both alive and questionably so) and carrying them to the upper VIP area. The swirling winds encased them, creating a shield from everything going on around them. They were safe there, providing the building didn't burn to the ground with them in it.

I wasn't sure my magic had accounted for that.

With the cannon fodder out of the way, my mind focused hard to keep that magic in place, I turned my attention back to the battle at hand. Swarms of witches and shifters I didn't know squared off against Knox's pack and Merc's enforcers. In such tight quarters it was almost impossible to see which side had the upper hand. We were outnumbered and had been taken by surprise. Not the best start to a showdown.

A fireball whizzed past my head, and I turned to see a witch I recognized smiling back at me, her eyes full of malice. She charged toward me, chanting something along the way, but she didn't make it far. Grizz intercepted her, picking her up above his head and slamming her down over his bent knee. The sound her back made when it broke echoed through the room in a way it shouldn't have over the melee taking place. He tossed her body aside like she was nothing and looked at me, his normally warm brown eyes cold and dead.

It scared the shit out of me.

"Get the coven queen!" Kat shouted in my ear, startling me. "If we can take her down, the rest will fall easily."

I nodded, scouring the crowd to see if I could determine her location. Then I realized there might be a much simpler way to find her.

"Show me where she's hiding..."

At the far end of the room a light blue halo glowed above the head of the stunning female, who stood alone, not fighting. Of course the bitch wasn't lifting a finger. The top of the food chain so rarely did.

"There," I said. "With the light above her."

"Great. I'll be right back." Kat moved to go after her, but I caught her arm.

"No. She's mine."

As if the coven queen had heard me, she pinned vibrant green eyes on me and smiled. Then I went flying through the air until my back struck the wall, and I slid down it. Wheezing hard, trying to get my wind back, I stood up to find her before me.

"I've come for you," she said, eyeing me strangely—like a curious bird. "She said you wouldn't come willingly, that you would not be so easy to collect, but I think she has overestimated your abilities." She looked up to where I'd harbored the humans and laughed. "Petty magic won't keep you safe where you're going."

She grabbed me by the collar and hauled me the rest of the way up. As she muttered indecipherable words under her breath, a vortex started to open beside us. What had just been an exposed brick wall was suddenly a window to Faerie.

"Your sacrifice is going to be so worthwhile," she said. I had no idea what she was talking about, but I didn't have time to sort it out. Just as she was about to force me through the divide, I found my breath. I blurted out the first thing I could think of and prayed it would work.

I didn't have time for a do-over.

"Away!" I managed to bark out. The coven queen and her makeshift portal flew across the room just as I had only moments earlier. I smiled at the justice in that.

But that smile was soon wiped from my face.

I watched the fey queen appear in the still-open portal, glaring back at me. I'd thwarted her ambush, and she was none too happy about it. With everyone else engrossed in the fight, they didn't see what happened next. It occurred so fast that there wouldn't have been time to react anyway. With one swipe of her arm, the fey queen ripped the rug out from under me—from under the pack too.

"No!" I screamed, but it was too late. I watched as a flash of red hair was swallowed up by the portal, Jagger's wide eyes full of panic as he realized where he was going. I screamed again. This time it shattered glass and tumbled walls and halted everything going on before me. Everyone in that building stared at me, their eyes suddenly too large for their faces. Whatever they saw looking back at them frightened them.

Good, I thought. Be afraid. There would be no hiding from my wrath if anything happened to Jagger—if the queen's mischief harmed a single hair on his freckled head.

I stood before the masses, breathing hard, the tang of blood thick on my tongue. At first I couldn't figure out why. Then I felt liquid running down my face and wiped it on my sleeve. It came away drenched in blood.

"Piper," Merc called to me, his voice calm and sure. "Piper, listen to me." He stepped through the crowd that stood frozen in place until he was before me. His large hand cupped my face, and my body relaxed instantly. "Piper, come back to me. Tell me what has happened."

With fear creeping back in, I looked over at Knox. He too seemed unable to move, but his eyes were all over me and full of pain. I wondered if he already knew what I was about to say. If he could feel it.

"It's Jagger—the fey queen took him." I gently pulled Merc's hand from my face and started toward Knox. "I tried to stop her, but it was too late. He was already through the veil." Knox didn't move, but there was a sheen to his eyes that hadn't been there a second before, and the sight of it damn near broke my heart. "It's my fault."

When he didn't immediately argue with me, my heart sank into my stomach. Then I saw him straining against an unseen captor and realized why he hadn't. Whatever meltdown I'd just had had shut them all down entirely. His body was not his own.

"Free those that are mine," I said. Everyone on my side of the battle started to stir.

"It's not your fault, Piper," Knox said, wrapping his arms around me. Then he let loose a howl that shook me to my core. Losing Jagger wasn't an option for him either.

"We have to go after him."

"No!" Merc shouted, storming toward us. "That might have been her plan all along. We can't be certain. And we don't have the element of surprise this time. Even if we went, she would be waiting for us. It would be a slaughter."

Though Knox looked as if he wanted to argue, he didn't. Even when clouded by anger and the need to retrieve what had been taken from him, he saw the truth in Merc's words.

"Then what do we do?" I asked, irritation starting to take over my tone. "Because I will not leave him there alone."

Laughter from the back of the room drew my attention. I didn't have to think hard about whom it could have come from. She was the only one there with enough power to override mine long enough to let loose that sound.

I stormed through the mob until I found her, still slumped against the wall.

"You got something to say, then say it."

Her mouth twisted to an ugly smile, marring her otherwise beautiful face.

"She knew what you were planning," she said, her voice strained. "Seems she truly does have eyes *everywhere*." The way the coven queen spoke about the fey queen's spies gave me chills. "I think she wanted to motivate you a bit."

"Who is the spy?" I asked, grabbing her by the collar of her bloodied shirt.

The coven queen shrugged.

"That's not for me to know. All I knew was that I was to take the redheaded wolf by whatever means necessary. You as well, if I could."

"And if you failed?"

"Then someone else would have stepped in and done it for me."

"Why?" I asked, hauling her to her feet. "Why take him?"

"I cannot say, though I imagine she took him for leverage."

"How could she possibly have known that she'd need leverage?"

The coven queen shot me a patronizing look.

"Because, as I just said, she has spies everywhere, foolish girl. There are so many that would turn on you to gain the fey queen's favor. Or to be out of her debt."

"I'm only going to ask this one more time. Who is the spy?"

"I don't—"

"WHO?" I screamed, pushing her up against the wall by her throat. "You will tell me a name."

"I cannot tell you what I do not know."

"Piper," Merc cautioned. He must have seen the aura of blue flame around my hands. He knew what that would mean for the coven queen.

"She's going to tell me what I want to know or she's going to die. Her choice."

There was a notable lack of argument from Knox on the matter.

"I can't tell you that, but I *can* tell you that she was adamant that it was him that I take."

A flash of cold shot through me, and my flames faltered. An echo of the conversation I'd had with Jagger in my room flashed through my mind. How his past had caught up with him in New York. How he'd never wanted to return here for that very reason. He'd argued and argued with us when we were leaving Alaska. Knox had told him it would be okay. I'd told him I would keep him safe.

I'd promised him as much.

The pain of realizing how badly I'd failed him impaled me, and I let go of the coven queen, staggering back a step into Merc. I had no doubt that Jagger's fear of returning and his encounter with Mack factored into this mess. I just didn't know how.

"Was Mack the real reason Jagger left the city, Knox?" My voice was low and strangled when I spoke, and I was glad the alpha couldn't see my face. My shame was written all over it.

"Piper—"

"Was he? I need to know."

"He left because he needed sanctuary, just like all the others."

"But from what exactly?"

Silence.

"Not a what, but a who."

My head spun around on my shoulders to look at him, standing just off to my side. I could see how badly he wanted to keep the truth from me, and that he wouldn't because I needed to hear it. Even if it cut like a knife.

But I figured it out before he had the chance.

"The fey queen." Not a question: a morbid realization, one with consequences I wasn't ready to contemplate. We'd just delivered Jagger to his worst-case scenario. His worst fear had come true.

"We couldn't have anticipated this," he started, taking my hand.

"That's why you didn't bring him to Faerie to help save Merc." He nodded. "What will she do to him?"

His face devolved into a murderous mask of vengeance and hatred.

"If she is smart, nothing."

"But the queen of the fey is not always smart," Merc added, yanking my heart down into my stomach yet again. "You know this." The two men glared at each other for a moment, and I wondered if a second battle was about to go down that night. I hoped to hear the word *lie* from Knox, but all he gave in response was his silence. Acknowledgment of what Merc had said and what I feared. That no matter what we did—whether we attacked the queen or not—we might never recover Jagger.

Alive or dead.

27

We'd barely made it into the foyer when my cell started buzzing. I picked it up and hit talk without looking at the number. I already knew who it was.

"Piper." Drake's voice held concern, as if he already knew that some major shit had gone down. Like he knew the meeting had turned into a bloodbath.

"I can't right now," I replied, stealing away to the kitchen for privacy. "Something's happened."

"Tell me."

Not a request.

"There was an ambush; the fey queen took one of Knox's wolves. We're scrambling to figure out what to do."

"Meet me outside," he said, voice stern.

"I told you, I can't—"

"Meet me outside." His tone was notably sharper that time, letting me know that, whether or not I thought following his instructions was optional, it wasn't. Then the line went dead.

"Shit," I muttered under my breath before racing toward

the front door. Grizz intercepted me in the hallway, still in human form. Not wanting a silent argument, I let him follow me outside while the others discussed our options for rescuing Jagger. I could tell by the quiet in the room that there still wasn't a viable plan.

I burst outside, the cool night air blasting my face. The bite of it felt good: like the slap I needed to pull myself together. Drake had said I couldn't let fear rule me. That it would be my downfall. And he was right.

As I strode across the yard, Grizz right behind me, I realized what I needed to do. What had needed to happen all along. If the queen planned to use Jagger as leverage, then she'd be returning to barter him for someone else.

I would be the someone else.

The coven queen had said the fey weren't after me, but I couldn't help but wonder whether, if the fey queen knew the truth, she'd rethink that. Whether she'd see me as more valuable than the others.

Maybe I'd make her see.

With my newfound resolve to throw myself into Faerie to save Jagger, I broke through the forest's edge to find Drake skulking about behind a huge oak tree. He turned to look at me, eyes full of suspicion.

"Who did she take?" he asked, cutting right to the point.

"Jagger. The redheaded wolf." My reply was met with silence. "He won't last long there, Drake. Jagger's special—he's sensitive and loving. She'll eat him alive."

"Literally," he replied, doing little to quell my concerns. "What is the plan?"

"We're trying to figure that out, but we're getting nowhere with it. Knox and Merc agree that we can't go there because they'll be expecting us."

"Glad they managed to put that much together."

"There has to be another way to access Faerie—one where they wouldn't be waiting on the other side of the portal for us."

His expression darkened, even though the moonlight lit his features. He was all angles and harsh lines and the image of determination.

"Even if there was, Piper, what would you do when you got there? You don't have the luxury of knowing where he's being kept, and I can assure you that the queen won't have her new pet far from her. She's probably entertaining him right now." The way he said 'entertaining' made a shiver crawl up my spine.

"I know she took him to make sure she gets what she wants when she comes tomorrow, but the thought of leaving him there that long—it's making me sick."

"Time moves more strangely in the queen's realm," he pointed out. "For his sake, I hope it's moving more slowly at the moment." That remote possibility did little to calm my nerves.

Grizz put his hand on my shoulder, and I reached across my chest to rest mine atop his.

"I know, buddy. We're going to get him."

Drake's eyes narrowed.

"We? We who?"

I narrowed my eyes right back at him.

"I am. I'm the reason Jagger is there. I didn't save him when I should have. I promised to keep him safe when he came back to New York, and I failed him. That's on me, and I have to live with it, but I'll be damned if I'm going to stand around and do nothing."

"Like get yourself killed?"

Grizz growled at his reply.

"No. Like get him back."

"Do you think that's even possible at this point? That he's even alive—"

"He'd goddamn better be," I snarled, lunging at Drake. "Because if he's not, I'll flay that fucking bitch while she still breathes."

Drake's eyes went wide at the sight of me—all feral and full of rage.

"You're bleeding," he said softly. "You need to calm yourself, Piper." He put his hand on my shoulder and took a deep breath, centering himself with the intent to help me do the same. Surprisingly, it worked. Not in the way it did with Merc, but a different way altogether. Perhaps it was the warlock in both of us. Like recognizing like.

He offered me a rag from his pocket, and I wiped my nose with it. When it came away dry, I looked at him strangely.

"Your eyes, Piper. Your eyes are bleeding."

Holy. Shit.

I dabbed at the corners of them, and sure enough, blood coated the fabric.

"What the—"

"Don't get upset. That's surely not going to help matters." He looked at the rag and sniffed it, then tossed it aside. "You're letting your emotions run you instead of you running them. Rage and anger fuel your magic, but not if you don't remember to focus and harness them. When they run you, there is no control. That is the danger for you, Piper. And it's the reason that you cannot face the fey queen. She's had centuries to master her gift. You've had days."

"I appreciate your concern, but if you want to help me, you'll tell me how I can get to the queen," I said, ignoring his attempt to scare me—even if it did work a little.

"You don't," he bit out, turning to walk away from me.

"You know, don't you?" No answer. "Tell me," I said, pulling out of Grizz's grip to chase after the warlock with the answers. "Tell me!" The trees shook with the echo of my command. Drake halted and turned to look over his shoulder at me. I didn't know if my attempt to use magic to drag the answers from him was working or not, but I figured I'd try to capitalize on the moment and call forth everything I could from the earth at my feet. Then I spoke, a bellow filled with a millennium's worth of dormant magic flying past my lips, scaring me shitless. "Tell. Me!"

Droplets of blood fell at my feet.

Drake struggled against my demand, bracing himself against the trunk of a nearby tree. His breath came in ragged gasps as he attempted to withhold what I wanted to know. I wondered if his resistance would tear him in half.

Then I wondered if I cared...

"No," he said, his voice strained as he struggled against the magic. He reached into his coat and clasped something in his hand. He seemed to stand a little straighter with it in his palm.

"You will tell me what I want to know."

He straightened to his full height, towering tall like the trees in the distance.

"No! You cannot go!" He flung his hand to the side, and a bolt of lightning crashed down from a clear blue night sky and struck a nearby tree, felling it at my feet. "I forbid it. It is a fool's errand. Anyone with a brain in her head could see what the queen is doing."

"Doesn't matter. I'm going," I said again, stepping over the divide he'd just laid between us. "I'm going because Jagger is mine and she cannot have him. She cannot hurt anyone else I love."

"She will," he said through clenched teeth. "She will

bring you to your knees with pain the likes of which you cannot imagine. She will torture you with possibilities and collar you with threats. You will be her lapdog of your own volition. And by the time she is done with you, there will be nothing left of this fearsome being standing before me."

His words broke through the curtain of rage I felt and reached my heart. It was then that I understood why Drake was fighting so hard to not tell me what I wanted to know. Beneath the anger and bravado, there was fear in his eyes. Fear for me. He'd seen the future I would have as the queen's captive, and he did not wish that for me.

I reached my hand out to his face and cupped his cheek.

"I will be all right," I said, forcing the sadness I felt from my voice. "She will not win. Have more faith in me than that."

I moved to pull my hand away and he caught it, pressing it harder against him.

"It is not my lack of faith that is the problem, Piper." He closed his eyes tight and took a deep breath, centering himself before he let my hand go. "And I will not let you go there alone. If you insist on doing what you claim you must, I'm going with you."

"Drake, this isn't—"

"Do not argue with me!" he shouted, his eyes snapping open to stare at me. I could have sworn that, if I looked hard enough, I could see the flicker of blue flames in their depths. "I will go because it is what needs to be done and that is it."

"What will the queen do to you if we're caught?" I whispered.

"That, I choose not to think about."

We stood there for a moment, each looking at the other, wondering what fate awaited us in Faerie and what madness of the queen's making would greet us. Then I shook my head, clearing it. I needed to remember why it had to be me; that I was the only one who had a chance to stand against the queen and save Jagger. I was so much more capable of doing what needed to be done than anyone around me realized.

Even Drake.

"Will you tell me how to get there?" I asked, my voice softer this time.

"When I come for you, we will go. Together. Those are my terms." I nodded in agreement. "Good. Now... I should go. I have things to prepare. And I suggest you go and enjoy whatever time you have here with those you love." His expression turned sour. "I cannot guarantee when or if you will see them again."

He said nothing more before walking away. In true Drake fashion, he disappeared a moment later, leaving me with my heavy thoughts, a painful truth, and the realization that my plan might not work out quite like I wanted it to.

We might get Jagger back, but at what cost?

28

"Piper," Merc called, walking down the hall toward me. I'd just gotten in from my tense meeting with Drake. Judging by the look on Merc's face, I was in for another one. "I need to speak with you." He looked down at Grizz, who stood at my side in bear form. "Alone."

Not surprisingly, the grizzly growled at him.

"The bear stays, Merc. It's just easier that way."

He looked irritated but didn't argue. Instead, he took me by my hand and led me into his room, the bear tight on our heels. He'd barely wedged his massive furry frame through the door before Merc closed it on him. Then he led me into his en suite and turned on the shower: all three heads. He closed the bathroom door, too. Whatever he had to tell me, he sure as hell didn't want someone eavesdropping on us.

"Merc, you're freaking me out a bit. What's going on? Is it about Jagger? Do you know how we can get him back?"

His lips pressed to a thin line.

"I do not. I wish that were the news I have to bring you, Piper. Unfortunately this is far more ominous."

Great.

"Ominous how? About what?" His lack of immediate response made me more nervous than I already was. Then a rational thought fought its way to the front of my racing mind. "Is this about where you were before we went to the club? Before the meeting with the witches?"

He nodded once.

"Jase, Dean, and I found ourselves the guests of the king."

"And 'guests' is a euphemism, I take it."

"Most definitely." His dark eyes narrowed as he thought about whatever dark secret he was about to throw my way. All I could think about was how badly I didn't want to know. Not with the Jagger mess already on our plate.

"But when did you go over there? It was the middle of the day when I was trying to find you."

"We were detained the night before. We went over not long before sunrise, thinking he needed to discuss a last-minute issue about the war with us. Unfortunately, it became something else entirely."

I swallowed hard.

"Is it about what I did at the party?"

"Partly. That's the least disturbing news I have for you." He stepped closer and took my hands in his. "I told you the other night that I needed to confirm my suspicions about something before I told you. That I didn't want to say anything until I was certain."

"Yes..."

"My concerns have been substantiated, as have yours. The king did know of Kingston's attacks on you. He was, in fact, behind them. Everything that you suspected about the king and the warlock is true. All of it."

Holy. Shit.

"He tried to kill me..."

"His reason at first was to try to force your powers to come. When they didn't, he assumed that you were not who he'd hoped you were."

"So I was disposable?"

"Yes."

"But now he thinks I really was born of that fey child because of what I did to Sylvia? Is that why he dragged you three there? To grill you about me? About Alaska?" He nodded. "Motherfucker..."

"I have done what I can to subdue him, Piper, but I fear it might not be enough."

"Subdue him? You need to subdue me right about now!" I ripped my hands out of his and stormed toward the vanity, swiping a glass vase off the surface. The sound of it shattering into a million pieces was far less satisfying than I'd hoped. "That conniving asshole! He used me. He made my life hell in the hope that I could be made a weapon for him to control." I whipped around and stared down Merc. "Did you tell him what he brought you back to tell him? Did you tell him I'm the child?"

Merc exhaled hard.

"I told him what he wanted to hear. That you were everything he'd hoped for and more, but that you were compromised. That you would never be on his side because you knew too much. Had put too many pieces of the puzzle together."

"And?"

"He didn't look concerned about that at all. That is why I'm here. I fear he has a card up his sleeve—one that I could not see no matter how hard I tried to search his mind. No matter how hard I tried to compel him. Something about him has changed. I cannot put my finger on it, but it cannot be a good sign. Jase and Dean felt it too."

My breath was coming hard and ragged, and I clutched the edge of the marble vanity like a life depended on it. Because it did, really. I knew exactly where I'd go the second I released it, and I knew nothing good could come of that. Still, the urge was almost impossible to tamp down.

"Merc," I said calmly through clenched teeth. "Tell me where you were for those eighty years. Where you were held. Where you would still be now if it weren't for me."

"Piper, that—"

"I need to know. I need to know what he did."

I heard him moving behind me. He stopped only feet away and inhaled deeply before starting.

"I was entrusted to a neutral party. I stayed there—a prisoner—until the vampire king bartered for my release. I do not know the details of either, but I know that I am glad to be gone."

"Who was the neutral party?" I asked, turning to look at him.

"The fey king."

"Is he as bad as his wife?" I asked, my blood starting to boil.

He shook his head no.

"He's far worse."

My vision turned red. I couldn't see or think or feel anything but blood and murder and rage. As if he knew I was on the brink, Merc wrapped his arms around me and pulled me back to him, grounding me in a way I didn't want to be. I wanted my blinding hatred. I needed it for what I was about to do.

Knowing this, I broke from his embrace and headed for the bathroom door where Grizz stood, waiting for me. When I reached for the knob, Merc clamped his hand down on mine. Grizz snapped at him, biting his wrist and growling at the vampire to stand down. Merc's eyes were narrow slits with beads of black in the center. He looked ready to tear the grizzly from stem to stern.

"No!" I screamed, and flung my wrist toward him. Merc flew back against the far wall, held there by whatever magic I had just thrown his way. "I'm sorry" was the last thing I said to him before I ran out of his room, then the front door. I saw Knox and some of the others in the rearview mirror as I floored it out of the driveway. Kat flipped me off, clearly unhappy that I was abandoning her, not allowing her to come on whatever harebrained mission I was on. But I needed her to stay. I had to do this one on my own.

The only witness I could afford was the naked one in the back seat, throwing on whatever clothes he could find there. For once he was the only one I needed to come with me, a fact he seemed pleased with as he smiled at me in the rearview. Grizz and I were going to go pay a little visit to the vampire king.

And it was far from a social call.

29

He had the nerve to look unfazed when I stormed into his office. Having blown my way into his home, I'd expected more of a reaction, but he probably knew that and didn't give me one because of it. Instead, his eyes drifted up to me and then back down to the paper he held in his hands. A silent dismissal. Little did he know, I had no intention of being sent away like a child—a nuisance. I was there to have a little chat with the vampire king.

And he was damn well going to listen.

"Why did you do it?" I asked, stepping farther into the room.

"I haven't the time to answer your poorly directed questions at the moment, Piper. Unless you're more clueless than even I thought, you know there is a war going on in this city."

"One you no doubt had a hand in."

That comment didn't go over well. He placed the paper down on his desk and pinned murderous eyes on me. My instinct was to run, but I held fast against his glare. I wouldn't be scared off.

"Explain yourself well while you have the chance, girl, because it will be the last one you're given."

I let my eyes drift away from the predator ready to fly over the top of his desk and strangle me and stared at the wood fire burning to my right. The flames flickered and danced and sparked, spitting embers and ash that fell slowly to the floor like grey snow.

When I looked back, the vampire king was only inches away, his wrath wound tightly around him like a second skin. His hand shot forth to grab me, but it met fire instead. Fire that came when I called to it.

That murderous expression bled to one of fear and regret.

"You know what I am, don't you?"

His features tensed.

"What do you want, Fire Bender?"

I leaned forward, an evil smile overtaking my countenance; one that mimicked the same expression I'd seen him wear more times than I could remember. He'd caused me so much pain—pain I was still trying to dig my way out from underneath. It wasn't the time to answer his question. No—it was time to warn him of my intentions.

"To bring you to your knees."

With a gust of wind and swirling fire, I picked him up off the floor. His screams—loud and tormented at first—were eventually swallowed by the twister's howls and the crackle of flame. I laughed aloud, the sound of it slightly unhinged even to my own ears. I was drunk with power and bloodlust and the desire to destroy things in a way that should have scared me, but it didn't. Instead, I reveled in it. Gone was the weak little Piper who needed the protection of others. Dead was the girl who had been used and cast aside. That shell of a Magical being had been shed, leaving behind a force of nature in her wake.

And her fury would know no mercy.

Burn, I thought, my delight at the sight of the king engulfed in flames plain in the smile I wore. Every time that thought ran through my mind, the fire grew brighter. Hotter. A raging glow of blue death set to take the king.

I could feel Grizz behind me, standing guard while I worked. He made no move to interfere, but why would he? I think he liked watching the one who'd caused me so much pain burn to death as much as I did.

Unlike Sylvia's, the king's screams were loud and clear and rang out through his den and far beyond. Yet nobody came to his aid. It seemed too simple—too undignified for a king to die in such a way—without anyone to fight for him. Such was the price of ruling the way he had.

Then I heard rapid footfalls echoing through the hall outside and wondered if I'd been wrong; if he did indeed have a cavalry coming to save him. A figure loomed in the doorway, blocking out the light from beyond the room. Grizz growled but didn't move, which meant there was no threat to me, but he didn't like who'd come.

Merc.

"Piper," he said, his voice calm and low. "You cannot do this."

"I can," I said simply. "And I will. You need to leave. Now." Grizz added another growl to punctuate my statement.

"You don't know what you're doing," Merc said, continuing into the room. I turned to see him staring at me with concern in his eyes.

"He deserves this."

"He does. And he will pay for his crimes against us both, I will make sure of it. But not like this."

"How, then?" I asked, stepping toward him. "How will he pay if not with death?"

"I don't know, but we will figure it out together." There was desperation in his tone that I couldn't understand. Couldn't puzzle out.

"You're afraid..."

Silence.

"Yes."

"For me?"

"For us both."

"This will not fall on your shoulders," I argued, annoyance in my tone. I turned back to watch the king slowly burn.

"But it will, Piper. In a way you couldn't have foreseen." When I didn't reply, he continued. "Who do you think will become king once he is dead?"

The blue flames consuming the king flickered and waned. Clarity cut through my fog of vengeance like a knife, showing me the potential consequences of my actions. Ones, like Merc had stated, I had not entertained.

"You," I said softly, turning back to face him. "You will become king..."

A conversation I'd had with Jase a very long time ago slammed into the front of my mind. When I'd asked him about the king's wife—if he'd ever had a mate—Jase had made a sad face and put his arm around my shoulder. I remembered thinking his reaction strange at first, until he'd explained the severity of the situation. Being the vampire king came at a heavy price; one that few would ever pay. As with most things in the supernatural world, power came at a cost, and the position of king of the vampires was no exception. It was a prison sentence of sorts: an eternity of solitude. The king was bonded to his charges.

He could not have a mate.

With that cold, hard truth chilling me to the bone, I looked at Merc. I realized why I'd seen fear in his eyes. He wasn't afraid of becoming king. He was afraid of losing me in the process. This was the only out I would ever be afforded—the only way to undo what had been done between us. He feared I would jump at the chance to sever the ties that bound us.

He feared I'd choose my freedom over him.

"Please do not do this," he said, stepping closer to me. "I can see it in your eyes—that you know what his death would mean for us."

"It would sever our bond."

He hesitated for a moment before taking one final step toward me, closing the distance between us.

"Is that what you want? To be free of me?" I stared at him silently, stunned by his question. "If it is, then let him burn. Exact your vengeance."

"No," I said, turning to where the king still blazed. The fire died out immediately, and he collapsed to the floor in front of his desk. He was burnt to a crisp, but still alive. "I want him to die—but not at that cost." I pulled my eyes away from the charred mass on the floor to look at Merc. His masked expression withheld what he was feeling, but I knew the hope in his heart had only deepened. "So... now what? We can't leave him here like this, but we can't let him go either. He's our enemy."

"And we will treat him as such." Merc walked over and scooped up the king in his arms. "I will see you back at the mansion." He shot Grizz a look that said 'be sure you get her there safely', and Grizz returned it with 'you did just see her nearly kill the king, right?' Merc gave the man-bear a nod, then disappeared from sight, ghosting off with the king in tow.

To where, I could only imagine.

30

I didn't see Merc when I got home. I didn't know where he'd gone with the king, and I had zero intention of asking when I saw him. I knew I wouldn't be able to contain myself—that I might finish what I'd started, or accidentally torture him until the outcome was the same. The death of the king. Knowing what that would mean for Merc and me, it was best that I was kept out of the loop in all matters regarding the whereabouts of the king.

It was safest for all of us.

Grizz (the furry version) followed me around to the backyard where we sat in silence, enjoying the way the nearly full moon seemed to hang lower in the sky than usual. Its eerie silver glow cast my skin in a ghostly hue, and I kept staring at how it made my hands look deathly pale. I ran my fingers mindlessly through Grizz's fur, enjoying how it calmed me. Enjoying the quiet sounds of the night.

"Am I interrupting something?" Knox called out as he walked up behind us.

"Nope. Just lovin' on my bear. And who could blame me?" I asked before smooshing Grizz's face between my hands. "Look at this face... he's just sooooo adorable." Grizz shook himself loose from my grip and looked at me as though I'd temporarily taken leave of my senses. Knox, however, found the whole thing rather amusing. "Well you are, you know?" I said, looking at Grizz.

He dropped his head in response, shaking it as though he were a disappointed parent whose child had done the wrong thing for the fourth time that day. Utterly exasperated, the grizzly lumbered off into the woods, leaving Knox and me alone.

"Sensitive little furball, isn't he?" he asked, sitting down behind me in the grass.

I immediately felt the tension in the air grow.

The moon looked a little fuller in that moment.

"Yeah. He's still trying to figure out where he fits in around here."

"That makes two of us," Knox replied, letting his legs stretch out. They fanned out on either side of my hips, enclosing me without touching me. Though the gesture was intimate, it didn't disguise the bite of his comment. The sudden realization that Knox was hurting on more levels than I could fathom hurt my heart.

"I'm sorry," I said softly.

"You don't need to be sorry."

"My indecision is hurting you, Knox," I said, looking over my shoulder at him. "I can be sorry for that."

"It's not your indecision, Piper. I understand that fully. I knew what I was signing up for when I chose to follow you to the city."

"But...?"

"But what I didn't know—what I couldn't have known—was how crazy being around you and not being able to touch you would make me. How hard it would be to see you near him. How insane it would make me every time he looks at you the way a man completely devoted to a woman looks at her."

My chest seized up with every word he spoke. Hurting Knox hurt me, and I felt it in a visceral way that I could never quite feel with Merc. It made it hard to breathe, and I wondered if that's how Knox felt every time he saw Merc and me around each other. What torture that would be.

I heard the grass rustle beside me as Knox went to move away. I put my hands on his thighs to stop him. His body went dead still under my touch.

"How do I make it better?" I asked, my voice low. "It can't stay this way."

He leaned forward, his breath heavy on my ear.

"I can't tell you what I want to tell you because if I do, I'm an asshole who doesn't understand your predicament, Piper. But if I were that asshole, I'd tell you to pick me like I've chosen you. I'd tell you to leave this city with me and start a new life." He took a deep breath while I sat stock-still like a rabbit in a thicket with a predator on the prowl. "I'd tell you to lie down right now and let me show you what I'm feeling because I'm less about words and more about action." My breath caught in my throat. "But I'm not an asshole, so I can't say those things, Piper. I'll never say them unless I think you're ready to hear them. And I know you're not. I can feel it."

He pulled away from me, the crunch of grass under his hands as he rested back on them cutting through the air like a knife.

"I don't know what to say..."

"You don't have to say anything. I just wanted you to understand. I didn't say that to make you feel worse.

Besides," he said, pausing for a moment. "We have other issues to deal with at the moment."

For a second I couldn't seem to remember exactly what that problem was. Then his name slapped my mind, and I broke out in a cold sweat.

"Knox... what happens if we can't get Jagger back?"

"We will."

I shook my head. The movement knocked my hair loose, the long tendrils falling against my back. Knox's fingers immediately found their way into the curtain of black.

"I'm glad you're so confident about that. I wish I were."

When he didn't respond right away, I craned my head back to look at him. His piercing blue eyes reflected the bright light of the moon at me.

"We will find a way to bring him home, Piper. There is no other option."

I nodded, feeling no more certain that we would succeed than I had before he'd replied. As if he could feel my anxiety, he wrapped his arms around me and pulled me back into his chest, letting the steady rise and fall of it lull me just enough for the tension I held to leave my shoulders. Breathing was so much easier when he held me.

He made it hard to ever want to leave his arms.

"Knox?"

"Yeah?"

"Can I ask you something? Something about your past in the city?"

The rhythmic beat of his heart sped up.

"What do you want to know?"

"Drake said something to me. Something about how the heads of all the breeds had a certain amount of unscrupulousness—that they had to in order to lead."

Silence.

"Where's the question, Piper?"

"The question is, why did he lump you in with them? I mean, I get that you're an alpha, but you're hardly the only one in the city. There are tons of packs here; it's not like the other breeds where there's just one leader. So why did he imply that you might share qualities with the vampire king and the coven queen?"

He let out a long breath before letting go of me. He was on his feet before I even felt his absence, headed for the tree line, preparing to disappear into the woods without a response. "Knox!" I called, running after him. "I'm sorry! I didn't mean to offend you."

"You didn't," he said, plowing through the brush. "I just don't know how to explain this in a way that won't give up more than I'm ready to give up. That's all."

When I finally caught up to him, I grabbed his arm to force him to stop. I was breathing hard, having sprinted to catch him. The moonlight cut a path through the canopy, highlighting his rugged features. He was so good-looking—all hard angles with a square jaw—but there was so much pain in his eyes when he looked at me. So much hiding behind them. I could feel that he wanted to tell me—to let the truth out, if for no other reason than to no longer have to hold it in—but for reasons all his own, he just couldn't seem to.

"I said this to Jagger, and I'll say it to you too: there's nothing you could have done that would make me feel any differently about you than I do now."

His shoulders sagged a bit.

"I wish that were true."

"It is true. I don't know why I know that, but I just do, Knox. I mean, Jesus... I forgave Merc, and he tried to kill me. I think I'm rather adept at letting things go."

"Merc's actions weren't his choice. Mine were."

I reached out and took his hand in mine. Standing there in the woods, with the moon smiling down on us, I felt our connection so deeply that my breath caught in my throat.

"No matter what you did, it can't change how this feels." I placed his hand on my chest over my heart and closed my eyes, soaking up the energy I felt coursing through him from the Earth to me.

"It's bigger than us, Piper," he said, his voice heavy with some unknown burden. One he seemed bent on sharing with me. I opened my eyes to see hope in his. "There is a reason why we're drawn to each other. It's more than just your call to the natural world."

"What? What is it? Does it have anything to do with what Drake said to me?"

He looked away from me, walking over to brace his arms against a massive oak tree.

"Yes and no." He looked back at me over his shoulder. "Do you know how the werewolves came to be, Piper?" I shook my head. In truth, I'd never really thought about how they'd originated. I only knew how they could infect others. But I was about to get a hard and fast lesson about it, whether I wanted it or not. "We were created to be loyal guardians of the one who made us." When he turned to look at me, there was pain in his eyes that I couldn't comprehend, but I hated seeing there. I wanted to push it away more than I wanted answers.

"Knox—"

"No, Piper. You need to hear this. At least let me tell you this much—it might come in handy one day." With a sober expression, he continued. "Our creator was evil and cruel, and the wolves eventually found a way out from under his reign. A place to start over. A place to be free."

A cold sensation snaked its way down my spine, freezing everything it passed—including my heart. I feared what he was about to tell me. I feared even more what it could mean.

"Who created you?" I asked, my words barely a whisper.

He pinned his tortured eyes on me, begging me to see what I could not know.

"The fey king."

"The fey king?" To say I was surprised would have been an understatement. I had been certain he was going to tell me that the fey queen had made him, and because of that, he could not stand against her, or something along those lines. That he had been her pet on the other side of the veil. But he hadn't. Instead, he'd thrown a new player into the game—one I hadn't even known was on the roster. "I don't understand."

"The king and queen reign over separate parts of Faerie. Their union is on paper alone at this point. It has been for longer than even I can remember. Faerie evolved as their hatred of one another grew deeper, eventually fracturing the realm into two kingdoms."

"He created your kind to serve him? To protect him from the queen?"

Knox nodded, taking a step toward me.

"We were only beasts then—Magical ones. When we escaped to this world, we became the hybrid beings you know as werewolves. Our human form is our curse, not the other way around."

"Why are you telling me this?" I asked, my mind still reeling from his revelation.

"Because," he said, closing the distance between us. "I wanted you to know the truth—as much of it as I can offer. It helps explain why the queen knows me so well. Why I know my way around Faerie. And why my return there again would risk so much. I am the king's to command—all werewolves are, regardless of whether or not they are one of his originals or if they were created on Earth. None of us can afford to fall into his hands—"

"You won't," I told him, throwing my arms around his waist as though I alone could keep him from being taken by the queen of the fey. As though I alone could outsmart and defeat her.

"I need you to understand what I'm saying, Piper." He pushed me away so that he could lean down and stare at me, his blue eyes boring holes in my own. "If he is present, I *must* do his bidding."

Reality crashed into me. Hard.

"Like if he decided to come after me for some reason—to harm me."

His lips pressed into a thin line.

"I wouldn't be able to refuse his order."

Shit.

"So we just have to keep you all away from the king then, right? I mean, it's not like we were all planning a big field trip back to Faerie. And as far as I know, he has no interest in me."

"True, but I don't know what would happen if he ever came here. I have not met him on this side of the veil before."

"There's no reason for him to come," I argued, capturing his face in my hands. "Unless he wants a piece of what's going down in the city. And, if he does, we have a pretty badass lineup to meet him if he does."

He choked on a laugh.

"Except he would have command over half of them—"

"*Possibly* have command over half of them," I said, correcting his pessimistic observation.

"True." A flash of amusement broke through his tight expression. "But if he did, it wouldn't be safe for you to be around me."

My heart sank at the thought of him leaving. It was selfish—possibly even deadly—but I didn't want him to go. Not even if the consequences could be dire if he remained. And judging by the tormented look on Knox's face, he felt the same way.

I guess he really did love danger.

"Do you want to go?" I asked, fearing his answer.

His pained expression fell to one of shock, then determination. Actually he almost looked angry, but not at me. It was as if the thought of abandoning me infuriated him.

"When I'm around you, I feel like a bit of the magic that created my kind awakens. Like you are a piece of me. I cannot walk away from that. Not now. Not ever."

I could feel a shift in the air around us, the warm breeze wrapping the two of us in a bubble of wind. The more it blew in its twisting circle, the closer it drove Knox and me together. My connection to the elements and their desires for me were far from subtle.

So was the heat in Knox's eyes as he stared down at me.

His heart was pumping wildly in his chest as it met mine, the beat of it resonating deep inside of me. Within seconds mine synchronized with his life force, the two of us becoming one frequency. One elemental pulse.

"Piper." My name was a plea, his control fading with every moment.

I knew what he wanted—what he needed—because it was as if our bodies were no longer our own. Whatever we'd tapped into allowed me to feel his desires as if they were mine. And I could only assume he could do the same.

I could no longer hide from him.

"Knox—"

His name had barely escaped my lips before his crashed down upon mine, creating a fiery inferno of need that I didn't bother trying to fight. My rational mind was nowhere to be found. I was too consumed by the feel of him and the magic and the connection that coursed through us both.

The rough scrape of bark on my back forced me to come up for air for a moment, but Knox was having none of that. Pressing against me harder still, he took my face in his hand and forced me to look at him as his other hand made its way up my leg, climbing higher and higher until he reached his target. Again I sucked in a breath of air that filled my lungs with a heady sensation that flooded my body.

"You are a part of me," he said. His penetrating blue eyes locked on mine as he pushed my underwear aside and slipped himself inside of me. "And I am a part of you."

The trees groaned as I unleashed a cry that echoed through the forest. I felt so full of Knox and the magic we shared between us that I feared my body would explode into a million pieces. But he held me together, either by his will or his rough hands on my hips as he drove himself into me. Bright, golden wolf eyes stared at me, demanding I look at them as we explored just how deep our connection could go—how far we could push that magic before we were both lost to it forever.

And when we came, the Earth quaked with relief.

31

I was barely decent by the time Grizz came barreling through the forest to see if I was okay. He took one look at Knox and sniffed the air. Then he let loose a growl, his lips curling back to show his teeth.

"And here I thought we had this all sorted out last time," Knox said, taking a step toward Grizz. "Looks like we need a refresher."

"Oh no you don't," I said, grabbing the alpha by the arm to draw him back. It was too near the full moon for his own good. Like Brunton had once said, fucking and fighting were the only two outlets for a wolf around that time. I thought Knox would have just had enough of the former to not need the latter, but it seemed as though I was wrong. "I'm taking the bear inside. You go take a run—or get furry and kill something—whatever you need to do to blow off some more testosterone. You're on overload at the moment."

Knox looked down at me, his eyes full of mischief.

"Can't imagine why."

He winked at me before taking off at a dead sprint through the trees.

I breathed a sigh of relief at his disappearance.

"You two have seriously got to get your shit together, Grizz." The bear stared at me, unblinking. Apparently he didn't share my opinion. "Ugh, fine. Can we just go in now, please?"

He didn't argue with me. Instead, he turned and started off toward the mansion, making sure I wasn't lagging behind. I don't know if he thought Knox was going to tackle me and drag me off to have sex again, but it didn't seem like he wanted to chance it. It made me wonder if the bear had full moon issues too.

He was testier than usual.

We were near the edge of the trees when Grizz went still. I followed suit, wondering why he'd stopped but knowing full well he had his reasons. For a moment I stood there, not breathing. I tried to see what he was looking at through the tangle of tree limbs obscuring my view, but it was hopeless. To gain a better view, I carefully made my way up to his side and crouched down.

Through a tiny window in the branches, I saw dark figures encircling the mansion. They moved with a stealth and grace that I'd seen before—in Faerie. Apparently the queen had come for us.

I reached to my back pocket for my phone, but it wasn't there. It must have fallen out somewhere in the woods—probably where Knox and I had had sex—and I had no way of alerting those inside that they were about to be infiltrated. The mansion's defenses were top notch, but the fact that the fey had just wandered onto the property without sounding any alarms or tripping any wards made me nervous. That shouldn't have happened.

"Grizz," I whispered. He leaned his head toward me but

never took his eyes off the army of fey amassing on the property. "You have to go find Knox. Now."

He shook his head no.

"Buddy, I know you don't want to leave me, but you have to. We need Knox, and we need him now." The bear glanced down at me. He looked torn, the pain in his brown eyes telling me as much. "I'll be okay. I'll wait for you here."

He let out a light snort, then rubbed his face against mine before quietly making his way back into the woods.

Still crouched away, hidden from sight, I watched the fey encircle the mansion and tried to figure out their next move. They were just standing there, perfectly still, like little toy soldiers awaiting a command. It was eerie and terrifying and almost impossible to watch. My skin itched with the urge to do something.

Then they forced my hand.

Suddenly, they all lifted their right hands toward the building, their arms parallel to the ground. With a rumble that shook the ground at my feet, the mansion started to move. They were uprooting it, their arms rising as the building separated from the foundation.

I watched in horror as the twenty-thousand-square-foot home floated along the ground toward a bright light near the funeral pyre. Though I couldn't see what it was, I had a pretty damn good idea. And if I was right, making our decision about who would go to Faerie was about to get a lot simpler.

Because the whole damn mansion was going there.

Panic rose up in my throat with every inch the building traveled. I looked over my shoulder and tried to call for Knox and Grizz as quietly as I could, but nobody replied. Flashbacks of Kingston's attack on the lodge in Alaska ripped through my mind. If the fey trapped my friends as the warlock had then, only I could stop them. It wasn't that I was afraid to stand against the fey; I'd done it before and succeeded. What scared me was the possibility that I wouldn't stop. That I still didn't have enough control over my power to rein it in when I needed to.

But the risk was worth it if it would keep everyone out of the queen's reach.

With my mind made up, I stepped out of the woods and strode across the open lawn toward the army of fey surrounding the floating mansion. Whether it was because of their concentration on their task or my stealth, none of them even turned to see the threat that approached them. Maybe they were just arrogant pricks. Regardless, they were about to find out that it wasn't safe to turn your back on me.

"Make them stop," I whispered to the night air. Right on cue the wind that loved to come to my aid gusted toward the massive building, blowing it back toward the foundation it'd been torn from. Only then did the fey bother to look around for the one who'd dared disrupt their task. I was a little offended that they looked more annoyed than concerned. "Put it back where it belongs."

Seconds later the mansion fused to the foundation like nothing had ever happened.

Then the shit hit the fan.

Werewolves (both man and beast) and enforcers spilled from the front door, ready to tear apart whatever had attacked them. The fey stood there, unfazed by their approach, and drew their weapons. I ran toward the fight, blue light glowing from my hands. I focused on the battle magic Drake had tried to hammer into my head, tried to find the balance between anger and calm that would help me control my weapons and use them wisely. It was a hard line to walk as I watched those I cared about dodging blades and arrows, but I had to find it for them.

We had to take them down.

Just before I could join the melee, I was sacked by Knox. The two of us rolled across the grass until we came to a stop only feet away from the bright light that had tried to swallow the mansion whole. Though it was no longer glowing, I could see it plain as day. The portal to Faerie was wide open, the queen staring out at me.

And the bitch smiled.

"There you are, Piper," she said, her voice somehow cutting through the din around us. "I see I now have your attention." She looked at Knox, who hovered over me like I was his to protect. Her smile widened at the sight. "Trevor. So glad you could join us as well. Tell me, where is the vampire?" I looked back at where the battle was waging and tried to find Merc, but I couldn't. There were too many bodies. "Oh yes. How silly of me," she said, sounding like she'd forgotten her manners.

She then made the strangest high-pitched sound that reminded me of a recording of a dolphin underwater. The fey all turned to her in unison and walked toward the portal, filing through it as though they hadn't just been embroiled in a fight. As though they were just out for a walk. No big deal at all.

"Better?" she asked, feigning friendliness. "Now where is Mercenary?" Seconds later he was at my side. I stood between the two males and stared at the queen, scared of what she was going to do next. She was unpredictable at best; at worst, she was a motherfucking psycho. "Excellent! Now that you're all here, we can talk. In light of recent events and my newest acquisition here in Faerie, I'm assuming you're ready to surrender someone to me," she said, pulling Jagger into view. I gasped when I saw him. He was chained and bound and bruised from one end to the other. Drake's words about how the queen liked to play with her toys echoed in my mind. Terror shot through me before I centered myself and let the rage I felt at the sight of my friend's injuries wash over me.

The bitch was going to pay for that one.

"Jagger," Knox called out. Though he withheld the concern I knew he felt from his voice, his body was rigid, ready for a fight that he wouldn't get to have. We both knew damn well that the queen wouldn't be setting foot on our side of the portal. And to go to her would be a suicide mission.

"I'm good, Knox," the ginger replied. But he sounded anything but. His voice was weak and distant and not his own.

Merc put his hand on my back to anchor me. He knew how much I cared for the wolves, especially Jagger. He knew I blamed myself for his abduction.

"Now that we have that settled." The queen yanked on the chain encircling Jagger's neck and brought him to his knees at her feet. Knox let loose a growl that he'd somehow managed to withhold before, and the rest of the pack followed suit. I could see Brunton out of the corner of my eye, edging closer to the portal. For a second I feared he'd jump in after his friend and wind up in the same scenario. Apparently Kat thought the same and came out of nowhere to stop him.

The look he gave her could have melted steel.

"Have you made your decision?" the queen asked, unfazed by the mounting tension on our side of the veil. "Do you know who will be coming to stay with me?"

Merc and Knox stepped forward at the same time. The

two looked at one another, surprise and respect in their eyes, before they turned them back to the queen. In perfect unison, they both replied, "I will."

The elation on the queen's face made me ill.

"Excellent!" she cried, clapping her hands with delight. Jagger's chains rattled as she did, and my anger rose with every clink and clank. I wanted to wrap them around her throat and pull as hard as I could until the air left her body —or her head left her shoulders. Either was perfectly acceptable. "But wait," she said, her expression twisting with confusion. "Who is this new male that stands to flank you, Piper? Is there no end to your harem of bodyguards?"

Man-Grizz stepped in front of me, silent as always. The queen seemed irritated by his lack of response. She hauled Jagger closer to the portal, her dark eyes shooting daggers at my guardian. In true Grizz fashion, he gave zero fucks about her attempt to intimidate him. He looked back at me as if to ask how to proceed. If he should go in place of the other two.

It was then that I truly realized that all three of them would walk into whatever hell she had planned; each with their own reasons, but they all had one thing in common. They'd do it for me.

"No, buddy. You can't go," I said. I stepped around him, stopping to pull him down so I could plant a kiss on his cheek, then kept going until I stood between Merc and Knox, slipping my hands into theirs. I instantly felt the rush of magic from Knox and the cancellation effect Merc had on it. I knew what I had to do.

What needed to be done to save Jagger.

"I'm sorry," I said to Merc, squeezing his hand. "I love you."

Before he knew what hit him, a surge of magic slammed

into his body, sending him flying back into the crowd of wolves and vampires behind us. I threw up a wall of fire around them, cutting them off from Knox and me. From behind it I could hear the roar of a pissed-off bear, letting me know just how much he liked being left behind again. But I couldn't let him go where I was about to go.

I couldn't let anyone.

I knew I was near the point of no return—the point where my magic would consume me whole. Where before I wouldn't have cared, Drake's training now had me aware of the danger I was courting. Having gained all the amplification I needed from Knox, I stared up into his stormy blue eyes and smiled.

"This is for Jagger," I said, and he smiled down at me. "I love you too, Knox. Never forget that."

His eyes flashed gold before he too went flying backward through the wall of fire.

And then there was one.

"I'm afraid you're stuck with me, Queenie," I said, stepping closer to the portal. "But I'm not going anywhere until you return Jagger."

"Return him?" she asked, her voice tinkling like bells—like the whole fucking scenario was amusing to her.

"You will give him to me, and then I'll go with you. Deal?"

Her serpent's smile widened.

"Most definitely. Though I will be sad to let this one go. I've enjoyed his company."

I cringed at her words.

"Just shut up and give him to me. Now."

Her smile fell.

"Enjoy yourself while you still can, Piper. I'm afraid

you'll find I don't tolerate your tone very well once you arrive."

I didn't bother responding, mainly because I didn't want to drag out our conversation any longer than necessary. Fear was starting to creep back in, and I needed my anger if I were to stand any chance at all of surviving the queen.

For a fleeting moment while she walked Jagger toward the portal, I wondered if I could somehow grab him and run. Somehow outsmart her. Though it seemed a good plan for the short run, I knew how it would end. She wouldn't stop until she got what she wanted; until she'd hurt everyone I cared about. She was immortal. She had nothing but time on her hands. She'd make me pay in ways that I couldn't comprehend.

Drake had told me that too.

Seeing the queen's face right in front of me pulled me from that train of thought, and I stared back at her. Only inches appeared to separate us, but we were literally worlds apart. If I didn't get Jagger now, I knew there wouldn't be a second chance. She'd make sure of that.

I smiled at my friend rather than look at the queen. He forced one in return, but it was alien. It held none of the warmth that it normally did.

"Heal him first," I demanded, shifting my gaze to the queen. "Heal him or there is no deal."

"My my... aren't we the clever girl," she said, her eyes drifting up and down my body to better take me in. "You clearly have a little fey in you." She squinted as though she were trying to see something she'd missed before. Then that fucking smile returned. "I wonder whose you are..."

"Fix. Him."

She sighed, feigning annoyance.

"Fine." With a flick of her wrist, Jagger's wounds—both

visible and not—seemed to disappear. The terror in his eyes was plain as he stared at me. Then he shook his head no. One simple slice of the air with his head. One clear warning.

"There. All done. Now, if you would." She gestured for me to come through the portal.

"Very cute," I replied, my tone sharp. "First send him through. That was the deal. You give him to me, then I go with you."

"Right." The word escaped her lips like a purr. "That was the agreement."

She reached over and magically unlocked the chains, freeing Jagger. The fear in his eyes remained, and I wondered what he knew that had him so scared. Had the queen told him what she'd do to whichever of us came for him? What she had in store?

Unfortunately it didn't really matter. The deal was about to be done either way.

"Run along little pup," she said, smacking him on the ass for good measure. He stood there for a second, hesitating. "I said go." The command in her voice was plain. She was tiring of the game.

"Piper—"

"Silence!" she shouted, and Jagger went rigid. "You will walk out of that portal right now or you will never leave at all. Understand?"

He nodded.

"It'll be okay, Jags."

The look he gave me told me that couldn't have been further from the truth.

With careful steps he walked toward the portal, pressing his hand against the invisible barrier. I reached mine out toward him, our palms meeting as he emerged from Faerie.

With him still half in and half out, I took a step back to give him space.

That was where I went wrong.

The second he was all the way through, the queen's slender hand shot out of the portal to grab me, but Jagger intercepted it. It seemed like he'd planned to pull her through to our side, but that didn't happen. I heard him shout the words "I'm sorry" to me, then, in the blink of an eye, he was sucked into the portal.

Right before it disappeared.

"Jagger!" I screamed. In my emotional breakdown, as the grief at knowing Jagger would be lost to us forever set in, the wall of fire behind me must have fallen. I soon found myself surrounded by bodies and questions, none of which I could make out. But I knew Knox when found me. With one touch from him, I found my rage yet again.

I blocked out everything around me until all I could hear was the pounding of blood in my ears and the thumping of the broken heart in my chest. I focused on the pull of Faerie—the familiarity of the magic that I'd experienced there. The magic that had felt like it was mine to call. I let it pull me toward it, guiding me to the spot where Jagger had just stood. I reached my hand out and held it against the open air as if there was something pressing back against me.

Then I channeled my guilt and my anger into that spot and called forth my power.

I could feel the air changing in front of me, felt the rush of magic pushing back against my invasion. But I was stronger than it was. Anger was such powerful fuel. Clutching the air like a handle, I yanked it down, ripping a gaping hole in the ether before me. I could hear the collective gasp of those looking on.

Nobody, including me, would have thought it possible.

"Come and face me!" I screamed into the portal. I didn't know if the queen would hear me, but I imagined it wouldn't take long for her to learn of what I'd done. That I'd just torn a hole in the fabric of her twisted realm.

Moments later a livid queen of the fey stood before me.

Jagger, however, was nowhere to be seen.

"I will enjoy torturing you, Piper."

"You'll enjoy fuck all if you don't give me Jagger."

"I kept up my end of the bargain."

"*Liar*," I roared in a way that would have made Knox proud.

"I said I would give him to you. I didn't say I wouldn't take him back. Now, this time, we do it my way. You come to me. Then I let him go—for good this time."

"The fey are tricky, Piper," Merc whispered in my ear. "They cannot be trusted."

"Don't even think of pulling another stunt like the one you just did," Knox rumbled in the other ear. "I'll tear Faerie apart looking for you if you do."

"She won't be going anywhere," a male voice called out from behind us. We all turned to find Drake cutting through the crowd like a shark through minnows, his face twisted with a snarl. The glow of ice blue magic swirled all around him. "Give us the wolf, *Larken*."

Drake's demand—and his use of what must have been the fey queen's real name—seemed to amuse her.

"Silly warlock. Last I heard your leader was dead. Do you think that leaves you in charge?"

He pulled the amulet from his coat and held it out before her.

"This says I am."

She leaned closer to the veil, taking in what he showed her, then laughed.

"It seems to have been damaged since it switched hands."

Drake shrugged.

"And yet it works just fine." I tried not to show my surprise at Drake's bluff. Whatever he thought he had up his sleeve would come crashing down if the queen called him on it. From what little I knew about her, that seemed a likely outcome. "Care to come over and find out?"

Her smile devolved to a snarl.

"Here or there, I would tear you apart."

Drake shrugged.

"Maybe. But I don't think you'd last long against the rest of them. Especially not Piper."

"You seem to know a lot about her," she said, her eyes still scrutinizing us. "I wonder why that is?"

"Because I've been training her. She is something to see."

"Then she should not be afraid to come over and show me."

While the two of them blustered, I tried silently to call Jagger forward, to locate him on the other side of the veil. I trusted that my connection to the pack would help me, so I channeled that feeling—homing in on it and nothing else—until I felt a heartbeat somewhere far in the distance. In another world. I locked onto it and drew it toward me. My magic's call met resistance at first, but the second I clasped hands with Knox, it bulled its way past it.

Over the queen's shoulder I could see a flash of red heading toward the portal. He was followed by a slew of the queen's sentinels, but for whatever reason, they couldn't subdue him. Jagger was protected by an invisible barrier that halted their attempts to slay him.

Thank God for that.

The queen seemed to pick up on what I was doing and turned to see the werewolf trucking it toward the thin, invisible separation between our realm and hers. I heard her mutter something under her breath as he neared. Her hand went up, and I immediately felt as though someone were standing on my chest. Her magic battled mine in Faerie, and it felt like hers was winning.

But judging by the strain in her neck, it wasn't by much.

Knox squeezed my hand, forcing whatever he could into me, but it just wasn't enough. Jagger was frozen, an invisible noose around his neck hauling him up into the air—exactly how I'd killed the queen's sentinels during our rescue mission. Fear spiked through me, and I watched as he shot up higher still, a silent scream escaping his lips. I started to succumb to the panic I felt as I watched my friend being strangled to death at the cruel hands of the queen, but Drake put an end to that.

"Focus!" he shouted at me, slamming the broken amulet into my chest. "Focus or he is gone forever!"

A blinding flash of blue light shot out in every direction around his hand, and my anger surged to the surface. It made me wild and feral, and I turned all of that on the queen.

"STOP!" I screamed. My voice was not my own, but something from a nightmare realized. The queen herself turned her head to look at me. The whites of her eyes told me all I needed to know. Whatever she saw scared her. "Give him to me."

Though the queen never moved, it didn't matter. My magic

was no longer speaking to her; it was speaking to the realm she commanded. The world beyond the portal started to distort and twist like a funhouse mirror, and the barrier itself started to ripple, taking on a three-dimensional texture. Fingerlike projections reached toward me, and I stood fast against their approach. At first I thought the queen was trying to abduct me. Then I looked beyond the distortion to where the queen and Jagger were. He drifted toward the veil, unopposed by the queen and her men. As if she couldn't stop him if she wanted to.

He was so close that I could have grabbed him, but I didn't dare. With my chest burning under the blaze of the amulet and my hand nearly crushed by Knox's grip, I shouted out one last warning to the queen.

"Do not come for what is mine again!"

Her eyes went wider as Faerie spat Jagger out to where we awaited him. Knox let go of me to catch his charge, but Drake held fast, securing the amulet against my chest. His grey eyes were heavy on my face, but mine were all for the queen. As the portal withered up and disappeared, I stared her down until she was gone.

There was a moment of silence among us all when it was all over. Some were shocked. Others in awe. I, however, was relieved and exhausted and thankful that I hadn't just been swallowed up by the power that had coursed through me. Drake caught me as my knees gave out from under me. Merc and Grizz were at my side in a flash, each fussing over me in his own way. Jase and Dean hovered above them, concern in their eyes. Grizz growled at Merc when he pulled me to his chest, and the vampire growled back. Clearly, even in moments of life or death, they weren't ready to get along.

Dean laughed at their display, earning him a punch in the arm from Jase.

Knox pulled Jagger into his arms and held him tight

before patting his back, signaling the young wolf to release him. It was a solid twenty seconds before he did, though. Then Jagger turned his eager embrace on me, pushing his way past Grizz to pull me from Merc's hold. The redheaded wolf scooped me up in his arms and squeezed me so tight I thought I might explode.

"I tried to tell you not to do it," he said, his voice strained with emotion.

"I know you did. I just didn't feel much like listening. It's not really my style anymore."

He pulled away to look at me, searching my face to make sure I was okay. Then his body folded in on itself, his shoulders sagging. For the second time since I'd met Jagger, he could not meet my gaze.

"This is all my fault," he said softly, pulling away from me even further. He managed to stand up and turn to face Knox, but everything about his body language reeked of guilt and submission. "Knox. I have to tell you something."

Without skipping a beat, Knox said aloud what Jagger was just about to admit.

"You're the spy." There was no judgment in Knox's tone, no anger behind his words. Jagger looked up at him, his mouth agape with shock. He was too stunned to even confirm what Knox had already put together. "I knew the second you were taken that night, Jags. It made too much sense. Your encounter with Mack. The coven queen's tale of a spy in our midst—possibly in our own house. Combined with your history, I knew it had to be you."

"But you're not angry. Why aren't you angry?" he asked. "You should be furious."

"I should be murderous," Knox corrected, taking a step closer to his wolf. "But I made you come back here. I didn't hear you out when you pled your case to stay in Alaska. And

I didn't forbid you to leave the house alone. This is as much my fault as it is yours."

"I didn't realize what she was going to do, Knox." Jagger choked on the words as they left his mouth, and I got to my feet, unable to watch him hurting from afar. I closed the distance between us and wove my arms around his waist, squeezing him until my arms ached and burned. Then I squeezed a little more.

"Jagger, it's okay."

"When Mack called me—after I saw him that day—he said I needed to tell him some things, or he'd let the queen know where I was. That he'd turn me in to her." He turned sad eyes down at me. "I guess he followed me after all, Piper. Guess I wasn't as elusive as I thought I was."

"Looks like he told her anyway," I replied.

He nodded.

"When we met with the witches, I knew something was going to go wrong in the end. I could smell Mack somewhere in the club. Right after that everything went to shit and I was taken."

"To tie up loose ends," Knox said with a growl.

"When you were standing in the portal—when you were about to come back through—you shook your head at me. You were trying to warn me about something." He went pale right before my eyes.

"I was trying to stop you."

"Why?"

"Because you're the prize she's wanted all along, Piper. It was never about them." He looked at Merc and Knox, then back at me. "It was always about you."

I took a deep breath and tried to calm my racing heart.

"Well I think she might be thinking twice about that

after tonight." I forced a smile up at him, and a little color seemed to return to his cheeks.

"Yeah, maybe."

He turned to look back at where the portal had been, and I noticed the bruising on his neck from where the queen's magic had choked him. I laid my hand on his throat and said the words I had once before.

"Help me heal him."

With a flash of white-blue light, the werewolf was as good as new. His childlike grin returned, and he hugged me again. This time there was a playfulness to it that made me smile.

Jagger was back.

"So... am I still in the pack?" he asked.

Knox nodded in return.

"But you're going to be doing every shit chore I can think of for the next year or two, and I don't want to hear a word of complaint. Understand?"

"Totally. No bitching about scrubbing the toilet after Brunton's used it." That seemed to garner laughter from the group. "I don't want to be an asshole or anything right now, but is it cool if we get something to eat? I'm really hungry..."

I heard the pack laugh even harder, which was exactly what we all needed. The air around us immediately shifted, the weight of the queen's terror lifted for what I hoped would be forever. But I wasn't naïve enough to believe that.

"Piper..." Drake's voice was distant when he spoke my name. I looked up to find him staring down at the amulet, eyes wide with shock.

"What?" I asked, running over to him. "What is it? What's wrong?" I came to a screeching halt in front of him, and he held out the amulet to me. I gasped the second I saw it. Where there had once been a fractured stone was a flawless one. "Oh my God."

"You fixed it." There was awe and pride in his voice as he said it.

"You said I was a force of nature," I replied with a shrug, hoping to make him laugh too—not that I was sure he had it in him. I received a smile in return and accepted that as the closest thing to a laugh as I might ever see out of my mentor. "So, about that getting something to eat..."

"Dibs on the leftover chicken," Kat said from behind me. I turned to see her take off toward the house, Foust and Brunton hot on her heels. The rest of the group looked around for a moment before following suit—a mass exodus of werewolves and vampires—leaving only Knox, Merc, Drake, and Grizz standing around me.

"You know the queen will not let this go," Drake said, his tone cautionary.

"I know."

"You were amazing, Piper," Knox said, pure awe in his voice.

I winked at him.

"I had a little help."

"You will always have that," Merc added. "From me, at least."

Knox, taking that as a challenge, was quick to agree.

"And me."

Drake gently took the amulet from my hand and placed it around his neck.

"And me as well."

A growl from behind me drew my attention.

"I'm not forgetting you, buddy. How could I? You and I are like PB&J. Okay on their own, but so much better together."

His severe expression softened a bit, letting me know my answer had been satisfactory—at least for the time being.

"We should head back," Merc suggested. "I still feel as though we are not alone here."

Knox scented the air and growled.

"Low fey," he said.

"The queen's spies."

Knox nodded in agreement.

"Take her inside," Drake said, heading off in the opposite direction. "I will ward the property against them. Erase any trace of the fey energy that was here."

Before I could thank him, Drake disappeared into the woods.

Knox walked to my side, drawing my attention. I smiled up at him and pulled him down so I could kiss his cheek.

"I meant what I said tonight."

His face brightened with the mischievous smile he'd worn the day I met him.

"Truth."

"You'd better go get some food before the others eat it all."

He cast a dubious glance at Merc, then turned toward the mansion. Without a word, he took off after the others. Grizz followed him, probably as worried about the culinary situation as Knox was. Maybe more so.

"How about you? Do you need a snack too?" I asked Merc, who looked slightly amused at something—something I didn't understand.

"Perhaps later. First I want to show you something. Something I have not had a chance to." His arm wrapped around my body, pulling me against his. For a second I could feel the weight of his stare on my face. Then we disappeared into thin air.

32

Word of our battle with the fey queen spread through the supernatural community, putting a temporary halt to the war. It seemed that nobody was too keen to face the unknown Magical who'd stolen a piece of Faerie from right under the queen's nose. The respite was welcome after all we'd just faced, but the calm between storms allowed another problem to come to light; one that I had all but forgotten about because it wasn't life or death.

But when I walked in on Kat packing her bags, it damn sure felt like it was.

I knocked on her door before sticking my head into her room. On the bed that she and Jensen had once shared were multiple boxes and bags filled to bursting. My heart sank at the sight of them.

I knew exactly what they meant.

"You're really going to leave." The sadness I felt was impossible to hide.

She looked over her shoulder at me and gave me a weak smile.

"You knew I would have to eventually, Piper. You and I have always known how this would end."

"But—" I blurted out the word, then cut myself off. I had no argument to provide, though I wanted to. Kat was right. I had always known how it would end.

She put the clothes she had in her hands down on the bed and walked up to me, resting her hands on my shoulders.

"It's not goodbye, Piper. I'll be around. At the club..."

"That's not the same."

"No, it isn't. But it's what we've got. And I want to leave before that shit king orders me to go. I want to leave with my head high, not like some outcast."

A light bulb went off in my head.

"Hold that thought," I said before darting out of the room. I ran into Grizz in his furry form on the way and nearly flipped over the top of him. Once I'd stabilized myself, I told him what was going on. "I need you to guard Kat's room until I get back, okay?" He eyed me strangely. "We can't let her go."

The grizzly nodded, and I took off down the hall, shouting for Merc and Knox. Seconds later Merc appeared out of thin air in front of me, with Knox not far behind, flying up the stairs, taking five at a time.

"What's wrong?" he asked as he crested the final step with Brunton, Foust, and Jagger behind him.

I looked at him and then Merc.

"It's Kat—she's packing to leave. I can't convince her to stay. But I think you two can."

Merc looked at me, his dark eyes searching mine for what I wanted.

"You want me to tell her about the king."

"Yes."

"What about that prick?" Knox asked, stepping up to flank Merc.

"He is missing," was my mate's only response. I prayed that Knox wouldn't ask me for any details. I knew I couldn't lie my way out of this one. Especially not since Merc had taken me to see the bastard right after our battle with the fey queen.

"That puts you in charge temporarily, right?" I asked, hoping he'd see where I was going with my question.

"It does."

Without further explanation, Merc started off toward Kat's room. The rest of us followed, Knox asking me questions along the way. When we reached her room, Grizz stepped aside to let us in just as Kat zipped her final bag closed.

She turned to look at the group standing just inside her doorway and frowned.

"I don't do goodbyes, if that's what you assholes are expecting."

"No," Merc said, his tone full of authority. "I'm here to tell you that you can stay."

She quirked a brow at him.

"You running this show now?"

"The king is missing. In light of that, yes. I am."

Kat's mouth fell open. Then she snapped it shut.

"He'll be back, and then we'll be in this same situation all over again. There's no point in putting this off."

"My offer still stands," Knox said, stepping toward her. "You're the perfect candidate to be part of my pack. You're an orphaned outcast. You'll be in great company." Kat's eyes searched the wall of wolves behind Knox, staring each one of them down before returning her gaze to their alpha. "What do you think, Foust? Should she stay and join us?"

"I think she should," his second replied.

"Jagger?"

"Definitely stay." He added a wink for good measure.

"What about you, Brunton?" The hint of hesitation in Knox's voice when he asked the prickly werewolf that question was duly noted. "What do you think she should do?"

I dared to glance over at Brunton, whose typical angry expression remained intact as he looked at Kat. She mirrored his glare with a scary amount of accuracy. My eyes darted back and forth between them as the tension in the room grew. Then I saw the tiniest upward turn at the corner of Brunton's mouth.

"I think she should do whatever the fuck she wants."

I let out the breath I was holding. Knox, Foust, and Jagger seemed to do the same before the alpha looked back to Kat for her answer.

"What do you say?"

Kat laughed and shook her head.

"What am I supposed to say to a bunch of men begging me to stay in the mansion?" She returned Jagger's wink, and the ginger turned as red as his hair. "If the crazy vampire says I can stay, and you wolves are so desperate for my company..." She shrugged, making a show of her feigned indifference. But I saw right through it. She was relieved beyond belief. "I guess I can stay for a bit longer. Until the king returns." She walked past Merc, giving him a nod, and continued on to Knox. "That said, I don't think I'm ready to join your merry band of rejects just yet." She looked over at Brunton and smiled wickedly. "I don't do so well with authority—I like doing whatever the fuck I want way too much for that."

"So you're staying?" I asked, unable to contain my excitement.

"I can't disappoint the boys," she said with a smile. "I don't think they'd survive it."

"Yay!" I launched myself at her, wrapping my arms around her neck and squeezing her tight.

"Okay, okay. Time to let go." When I didn't, she turned to the boys for aid. "A little help here, guys. I've got a stage-five clinger on my hands."

"You love me and you know it," I argued.

Her arms snaked around my back and squeezed me back.

"I really do." Her words were barely a whisper. "Now get the fuck off me."

The boys broke out laughing as I let go and pulled away from her. The sound of it warmed me in the dark place, calming a piece of me that hadn't settled since our encounter with the queen. It was then that I realized that life was all about balance. Good and evil. Right and wrong. Rage and love. Without the depth of love I felt from those around me, I would never be capable of the blinding rage necessary to take down the fey queen.

That bitch had a reckoning headed her way.

And its name was Piper.

EPILOGUE

Kat's decision to stay did come with a couple of requirements, the first of which was that she and Knox switched rooms. She wanted to start over on her own terms in the mansion—not as Jensen's mate—and I couldn't blame her for that. Knox didn't argue, primarily because her room was way bigger, and with him sharing the space with Jagger, Foust, and Brunton, it was really a no-brainer.

She also made them do all the moving while she sat outside on the patio with Grizz, sipping a beer.

My guardian seemed to find a balance between spending time as a human and as his grizzly self. He remained in my room with me, forever at my side. That was fine with me. He was a welcome distraction from the clusterfuck that was my love life.

In fact, I could have done with a few more of those.

Jagger seemed to bounce back from his ordeal without issue, but there were quiet moments when he thought no one was looking that I could see that guilt and something else still haunted him. There was an emptiness in his eyes that I knew well; the kind of emptiness that only being a victim of someone else's cruel schemes could cause. I tried to find a time to bring it up with Knox, but I could never find one. Not a good one, anyway.

I wondered if Knox already knew—already saw what I did.

Drake continued to train me, playing with new ways to combine my fey magic with my warlock abilities. He brought the amulet every time. There was something lighter about him when we spent time together. Something warmer in his eyes. I thought maybe it was just that training me had become more enjoyable to him, but I doubted that was it. Because beneath it all, I still felt like he was hiding something from me.

Something all the men in my life seemed to have a knack for.

Knox still hadn't come fully clean about his past, and Merc wouldn't tell me his plans for the king. For all their differences, Knox and Merc seemed to share the same views on keeping secrets, a practice I was hell bent on shutting down. If we were going to have to stand against the fey queen together, then I needed to know everything I could about both of them so there would be no surprises. No way for her to create doubt and distrust among us.

No way for her to hurt the ones I loved.

Next in Series

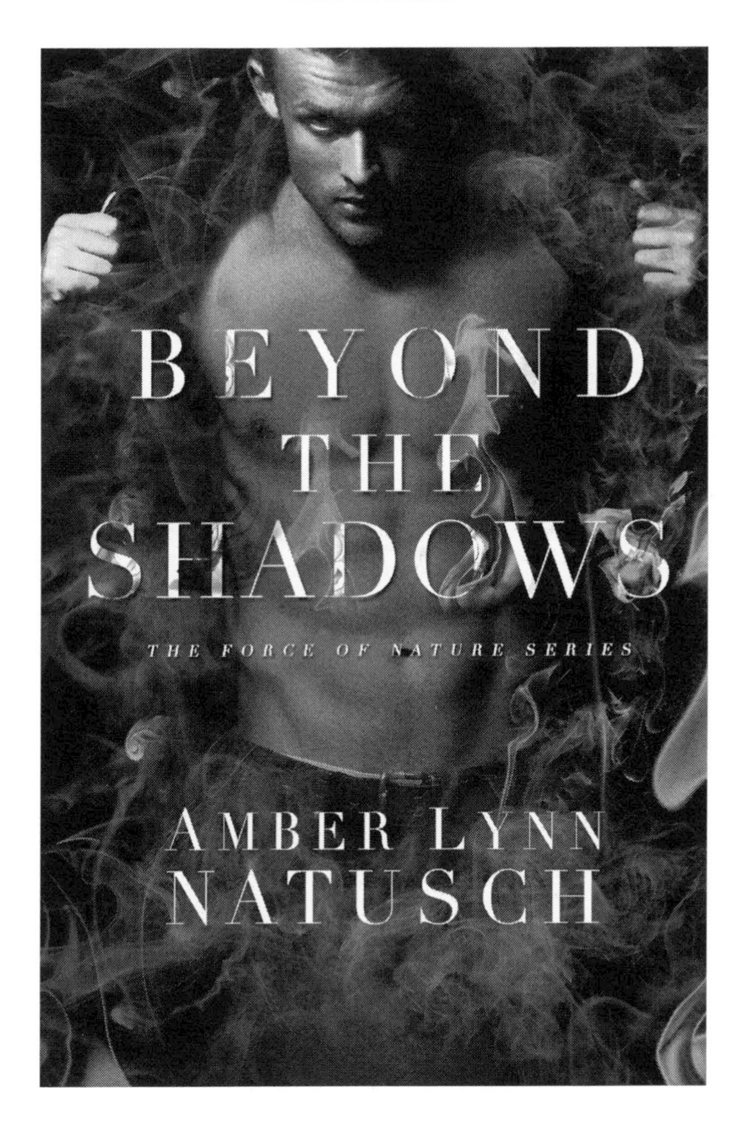

ABOUT THE AUTHOR

Amber Lynn Natusch is the author of the bestselling *Caged*. She was born and raised in Winnipeg, and speaks sarcasm fluently because of her Canadian roots. She loves to dance and sing in her kitchen—much to the detriment of those near her—but spends most of her time running a practice with her husband, raising two small children, and attempting to write when she can lock herself in the bathroom for ten minutes of peace and quiet. She has many hidden talents, most of which should not be mentioned but include putting her foot in her mouth, acting inappropriately when nervous, swearing like a sailor when provoked, and not listening when she should. She's obsessed with home renovation shows, should never be caffeinated, and loves snow. Amber has a deep-seated fear of clowns and deep water...especially clowns swimming in deep water.

Made in the USA
Monee, IL
03 September 2019